MW01235810

THE TAVERNER'S SON

THE TAVERNER'S SON

LESLIE PARK LYNN

CLEAR ROAD PUBLISHING, INC.

The Taverner's Son is a work of fiction. The names of characters, events, and incidents are the products of the author's imagination and are fictitious. Any resemblance to actual persons, living or dead, or actual events is purely coincidental. Certain businesses, long-standing institutions, agencies, public offices, cities, towns, and states are mentioned, but the characters involved are wholly imaginary.

Published 2023 by

Clear Road Publishing, Inc.

Branford, FL 32008

United States of America,

First Edition

Library of Congress Control Number: 2023915274

ISBN Paperback: 979-8-9889306-0-0

ISBN Hardcover: 979-8-9889306-1-7

For Luke, because you always believed in me.

PART ONE

10 SEPTEMBER 2022

CHAPTER ONE

T he ringing of his cell phone jarred him out of his deep sleep. The after-party had kept him out late, and he'd only been in bed for a few hours. He struggled to pull himself awake as he reached for his cell phone on the nightstand. He instinctively knew the call was not good news.

"Hello?" he said in a sleepy voice.

"Mr. Kendrick?" the voice asked. "Is this Will Kendrick?"

"Yes," he answered.

"Mr. Kendrick, I'm sorry to call you so early. My name is Connor West. I'm an attorney, your father's attorney, exactly. I, uh, am sorry to tell you that your father has passed away."

Will was silent for a few moments as he absorbed the news. He had not expected this and hadn't even thought about his father in a while.

"Okay," he said, not knowing what else to say. He glanced at his watch and saw that it was six a.m. West Coast time. Because of the early hour and the unexpectedness of the call, he was speechless.

"Mr. Kendrick," the lawyer said, "I realize my call has been a bit of a shock, and I've woken you up. I'm sorry. If you would like to call me back later, when you've had a chance to collect yourself, we can talk then."

"Okay, I can reach you at this number?" he asked, glancing at the caller ID.

"Yes," the lawyer said, "anytime."

"Okay, I'll call you later today. Thank you for letting me know."

He disconnected and lay there for a while, letting the news settle in. Though he had not spoken to his father in some time, he could not escape the finality of the situation. It was as if their relationship had been in suspended animation and now had fast-forwarded to the end. As indifferent as he'd felt in the past few years, he was suddenly sad.

Swinging his long legs off the bed, he set his feet firmly on the smooth marble of his bedroom floor. He sat momentarily, contemplating his slight headache from the wine and lack of sleep. As he ran his fingers through his sandy-colored hair, he pulled his tall frame off the bed and headed to the kitchen to make coffee. He knew there wouldn't be any good sleep in the foreseeable future.

He tried to think through the implications of the news. Certainly, it meant he would return to Florida for the funeral soon. Though they hadn't been close, he held no contempt for his father. They had just never seen eye to eye. The man who had called said he was his father's lawyer. He hoped that meant his father had put his affairs in order before he died. He didn't want to deal with that.

As he sat sipping his coffee on his terrace overlooking the hills, he tried to remember the last time he'd spoken to his father. He couldn't, and the realization deepened his sadness. He had known in his gut he would have regrets when his father passed, but he hadn't expected them to set in so soon. Time had just passed too fast, and he had let things get away from him.

Not sure what to do next, he sat there long after his coffee cup was empty. He would need to make travel arrangements and plan to be away from work for a few days. He couldn't do that until he talked to the attorney again.

"Hello, Mr. West? It's Will Kendrick calling you back."

"Oh, hello," the lawyer said. "I apologize for the early call this morning. I probably should have waited until later, but I promised your father I would notify you right away. Are you doing okay?"

"Yes, I'm okay, and I appreciate you letting me know. I'm sorry if I was groggy. I was out late last night and hadn't been asleep very long. Have any arrangements been made for my father, or is that up to me?"

"No," the lawyer said, "your father made plans in advance. It's all taken care of. It's just a matter of timing now. I know you are in California. Do you know when you'll arrive here?"

"I haven't made any travel arrangements yet, but I could be there in the next twenty-four hours or so."

"Okay, why don't you make your plans and get back to me with the details? Then, I can set things in motion here. Your father insisted on something simple, so it won't be hard to arrange."

After hanging up with the lawyer, he booked his flight and arranged his work schedule. He would worry about where to stay when he got there. That evening, as he left for the airport, shutting the door behind him, he felt on edge. It felt strange to be going back, not knowing what he was heading into.

GETTING to Apalachicola from Los Angeles was difficult, and when he finally landed in Tallahassee after connecting through Atlanta on the red-eye, he was exhausted. He rented a car and headed out. It would only take an hour and a half to get there, but as tired as he was, he dreaded the drive. When he remembered he hadn't arranged a place to stay, he called around but couldn't find anything. He hadn't known an art festival was happening, and tourists had descended upon the place. He called the attorney to see if he could give him any suggestions.

"I'm sorry. Unfortunately, most things around town are booked up. I assumed you would stay at your father's place above the tavern. If that's not suitable, I can inquire around for you, but I'm afraid it might be difficult to find anything."

"Above the tavern?" Will asked. He hadn't realized his father had moved out of the home he'd grown up in and into one of the apartments above the tavern he owned.

"Yes, he's lived there for a few years now. I can give you a key if you want to swing by my office."

"Okay," he said. "I guess I don't have much choice. I'm about an hour out. Will you be in your office then?"

"Yes, Mr. Kendrick, I'll be here."

The drive was easy compared to getting around in LA. Once he rounded the bend across from Alligator Point and started down the scenic coastal highway, he began to remember the simple beauty of the place. The giant pines nestled against the ragged, driftwood beaches were so different from California, and he'd forgotten about them. Somehow, over the last decade, he'd managed to forget a lot.

Across St. George Sound, he could see Dog Island, its beaches white and pristine. The small barrier island was home to only about 100 houses, most of which were vacation homes. He'd always been fascinated by the windswept strip of sand that had no access other than a weekend ferry. The few full-timers lived a simple existence with none of the typical amenities such as restaurants, watering holes, or hotels. As a kid, he'd visited the island by boat and remembered collecting shells and playing on the white sugar sand.

As he passed through the small fishing village of Carrabelle, he noticed a few newer homes along the water, but it was mostly how he remembered it. The road between there and Eastpoint was rough from the asphalt repairs made after the last big hurricane, but it looked no different from his memory of it over a decade ago. What was known as Florida's Forgotten Coast still seemed largely undiscovered.

The causeway into Apalachicola seemed longer than he remembered. It, too, was rough from the beating it had taken from the last big storm, and he had to keep his attention on the road. Dotted along its rocky edges were recreational boats and local fishermen looking to take advantage of the schools of fish congregating there.

Finally, he navigated over the high-curved bridge that deposited him into the heart of Apalachicola. Childhood memories flooded his mind as he turned off Market Street and headed for the lawyer's office. Being there was like stepping back in time. Almost nothing had changed.

The lawyer's office was in a small house that looked old but well-kept. When Will started up the steps, he realized by the plaque on the clapboard that the old structure was historic and remembered there were several hundred around town. Apalachicola was one of America's oldest cities.

"Hello," he said to the young girl at the desk as he stepped inside. The smell of the old house took him back to his childhood home, and a wave of nostalgia washed over him. Living in California, he hadn't experienced that in years.

"Hi!" she said and smiled at him. She was pretty and young with a fresh-faced innocence. It was a welcome change. Women in his circles on the West Coast were a study in plastic surgery.

"I'm Will Kendrick. I'm here to see Connor West."

"Oh, hello, Mr. Kendrick. I think he's expecting you."

She left her desk and disappeared into the back, where Will could hear them talking quietly. After a few minutes, Will saw a tall, dark-haired man come down the hall toward him. He stepped around the reception desk and extended his hand.

"Mr. Kendrick, it's good to meet you. Come on back to my office where we can talk privately."

Will followed him down the hall and felt the old floor creak under his feet. The house was nicely repurposed into an office while preserving its historic charm. He saw a large oak desk with stacks of files and paperwork when they reached the office door. Although Connor West was a small-town lawyer, he seemed to be a busy one.

"How was your trip over from LA?" the lawyer asked as he shuffled through the files.

"It was okay. I was able to get a little sleep on the flight to Atlanta."

The lawyer nodded and, upon finding the file he'd been looking for, opened it and studied it for a moment, rubbing his chin.

"Everything is pretty straightforward," he said. "Your father had me put everything into a trust not too long ago. Everything will pass to you seamlessly, with no need to go through probate."

"Okay, can you define *everything* for me? My father and I have had little contact in the last few years. I have no idea what his assets look like."

"Well, there is the tavern, of course, the business itself, and the building. Your father also owned several pieces of real estate around town. As far as cash and liquid assets, there are some, but not a lot. Other than that, there are just his personal belongings. By the way, his truck is parked behind the tavern. The keys are hanging by the door in his apartment if you want to use it while you're here."

Will nodded and thought for a moment. "Do you think you can help me dispose of some of these assets?" he asked.

The lawyer looked up and held his gaze for a moment. "Are you sure you want to do that, Mr. Kendrick? You would probably benefit more from holding on to them for a while. Things are starting to improve a little with our local economy. The value of our real estate is beginning to look up."

"Living on the West Coast would make it difficult to manage anything here, especially the tavern. Maybe it would make more sense to shut it down and sell the real estate," Will said.

The lawyer sat for a moment and studied the paperwork. "Mr. Kendrick, perhaps it's better to think about things for a while. You've only just arrived, and I know you must be tired. Why don't you get some rest and we can talk again after your father's service? There is no reason to make these decisions now," he said, smiling at him. "And please, call me Connor."

Will smiled back at him. "Thank you, that's probably good advice. And you can call me Will."

There was a momentary pause in their conversation.

"Speaking of the service," Will said, "do we know when that will take place yet?"

"Yes, it will be the day after tomorrow, at ten in the morning, at the gravesite. There will be a repast at the tavern afterward. As I mentioned, your father insisted on simple arrangements. He didn't want to burden you with any of it."

Will felt the sadness wash over him like a wave. He looked down as he tried to get ahold of himself, somewhat embarrassed to become emotional in front of the lawyer. He cleared his throat and nodded, unable to meet the lawyer's gaze.

"It's an emotional time, Will. Why don't you get settled in and call me later? Here are the keys to your father's apartment. Please call if you need anything. If I'm tied up, Jessica, my secretary, can help you. I'm here to help make this as easy as possible."

"I appreciate that," Will said, his voice thick with emotion. "I guess I didn't realize how hard this would be. My father and I hadn't even spoken in years."

"Yes, he told me that. It was one of his few regrets in life. He wanted you to know that."

Will only nodded, afraid his emotions would overtake him again. He reached for the keys and stood to go. Connor walked with him to the small reception area, and the two men shook hands.

"Thanks, Connor. I appreciate everything. I'll be in touch."

BEFORE HEADING to his father's apartment, he drove around a little and thought about getting something to eat. He wasn't ready to be in the presence of his father's things yet, and he hoped taking in the sights and sounds of the little town might help him adjust his emotions.

When he crossed Market Street, he realized that most of downtown was closed off for the festival, and parking was scarce. He found space by the old jail and walked the few blocks to where he might find something to eat. Having not been there in several years, he didn't know what the town now offered in the way of restaurants.

The heart of town was swarming with tourists. While he knew Apalachicola depended on tourism, seeing the hordes of people made his heart sink a little. He decided on a little seafood restaurant for lunch, but there was a wait, so he got a beer from the bar and found a spot to sit on a bench outside.

The weather was cool and breezy, typical for the Florida panhandle in the fall. The area had a distinct change of seasons, and he remembered his melancholy as a boy when the winds would shift around and start to come in from the North. Apalachicola Bay would become rough and inhospitable, and the damp, cold would soak right through to his bones. Starting at a young age, he'd worked with his father on the weekends harvesting oysters during the winter months. He'd dreaded the harsh, wintry days and was sure it was why he'd headed to California for college. Back then, it seemed he couldn't get far enough away from the muddy oyster beds and the smell of the mollusks as they'd loaded them into the boat.

He'd read a bit about the state of the oyster fishery in Apalachicola Bay. Oyster harvesting had stopped about a year or so ago. With a myriad of issues, the fragile ecosystem had been unable to sustain itself, and the state had put a five-year halt on any harvesting. The small coastal enclave, once known as "Oystertown," could no longer depend upon the abundant resources it once had. He could not imagine the effect on the local economy.

When they finally seated him inside, he realized how hungry he was. He hadn't eaten since before he'd gotten on his flight in LA, and then it had only been a quick sandwich. Now that he was perusing the menu, the thought of the fresh seafood made his mouth water.

He checked his messages, and to his surprise, he didn't have many other than a few condolences from close friends and work associates. He guessed word had gotten around about his father's passing, and his phone would be quiet for a few days. That was fine with him. He hadn't had a break from the world in a long time.

After lunch, he took a long walk around town. He realized he was avoiding the inevitable. Sooner or later, he would have to face going to the tavern and his father's apartment. He walked along Water Street, where the shrimp boats sat peacefully in their moorings. They had always been a part of his memories of the place, their distinct profile etched in his mind whenever he thought of his childhood. As he gazed upon them, he realized how lucky he had been to grow up in such a beautiful and unpretentious place. Where he was now was anything but.

CHAPTER TWO

T he old building that housed the tavern was a two-story
structure built before the turn of the last century. Like
so many other buildings around town, its red brick
exterior looked no worse for the wear, even after years of
weathering the harsh, salt air. It was a handsome building, Will
thought as he admired it from across the street. Its stately
facade and gold and black signage gave it a distinctive appear-
ance. He hadn't remembered it that way.

The tavern had been central to his life as a child. Every day
after school, he'd walked there and taken up residence at one of
the small tables in the back to do his homework. In the summer,
he'd have a sandwich and a coke, but if it was cold out, he'd have
a bowl of soup or some chili. The bartender looked after him
when his father wasn't around. Penny was a tough woman,
easily handling the sometimes unruly patrons, but she had a
tender spot in her heart for Will. Sometimes, if the tavern
wasn't busy, she'd sit with him at the table, help him with his
homework, or carry on a conversation. He suspected she felt
sympathy for him after he lost his mother at such a young age.

Will had always been fascinated by her husband, who was a

local fisherman. He was a huge, burly man with almost white hair, bleached by hours spent in the sun on the bay. When Penny was working, he'd come in late in the day and sit at the very end of the bar close to Will's table. He'd give him a hearty slap on the back, then grip Will's shoulder with his big, meaty hand. He always made him feel important, and sometimes, he'd imagine that Penny was his mother and her husband was his dad and wonder what life would be like for him if he weren't living in a house with a solemn old man.

Will's mother died when he was only three years old, and though sometimes he'd have a flash of some memory, when he really tried, he couldn't remember her much. The thing he did remember was his father's depression and withdrawal after she was gone. Because his father was older, Will had no grandparents on his father's side and only a grandmother on his mother's. His grandmother lived up in Wewahitchka, and while it was only about an hour away, she didn't come to Apalachicola often. As he grew older, Will suspected being around him was too painful for her after his mother passed. There must have been too many memories and not enough healing.

He crossed the street and entered the tavern, the memories washing over him in waves. His eyes went immediately to his small table in the back near the end of the bar. It was empty as if it sat waiting for him, and the sight of it made his heart constrict a little. There were quite a few people in the place. Tourists, Will suspected, who were looking for a place to have a beer out of the cold wind of the late afternoon. He wondered if, on a typical Saturday, there would be as many patrons there. He had no idea what kind of business the tavern did these days, but he assumed it was the locals who kept it alive. From what he remembered, his dad struggled to keep the place going, always grumbling about the prices of things and making payroll. If he'd been a betting man, he would have never wagered that the tavern would make it all these years. Somehow, his dad had made it work.

Still reluctant to go up to his father's apartment, he sat at the bar and waited for the busy bartender to notice him. When she finally made eye contact, her eyes went wide with recognition.

"Will?" she said. "Oh my God, it's you! It's me, Jess!"

At first, he didn't recognize her as his eyes moved over her features. Then, as her smile broadened, the pieces fell into place for him, and he remembered.

"Jess?" he said. "Really? I can't believe it. How long has it been?"

"It's been a minute, Will," she said, laughing. Suddenly, her smile faded, and her face clouded over and turned serious. "Oh, Will, I just remembered why you're here. I'm so sorry about your dad. He meant a lot to me, to all of us here. No one can believe he's gone."

Will was taken aback by the emotion in her voice. He hadn't been expecting it.

"Thanks, Jess." It was all he could think of to say. They were quiet for a moment as they looked at each other, her eyes searching his.

"How long will you be in town?" she asked.

"Probably a bit into next week," he said. "I've got a few things to take care of here before I go back."

"Oh," she said. "Where are you these days? Last I heard, you were in California, I think."

"Still there," he said with a smile. "I've been living there since college."

Just then, an impatient patron called out to her.

"Listen," she said, "I'm finishing up here at six. I'd love to catch up. Wanna grab a bite and a drink later?"

"Yes," he said, smiling at her. "I'd like that very much."

"Write your number down, and I'll text you when I get home

and get changed," she said as she slid a cocktail napkin and a pen across the bar toward him.

He jotted his number down, finished his beer, and was headed to the stairs at the back of the tavern when he remembered his car was parked several blocks away with his bag inside. He reversed his course, and when he stepped outside the front of the tavern, he noticed the wind had picked up. He zipped his jacket and started across town towards the old jail.

Jess Wilder was a childhood friend. They had grown up just a street apart and had been in the same grade throughout school. As a young girl, she'd been a tomboy, and they'd shared a lot of adventures and spent many hours talking and scheming in the old tree fort at the back of her property. They had been best friends back then, and it had stayed that way until they got to high school. Then, they seemed to drift apart, and before they knew it, high school was over, and they were headed in different directions. They had never kept in touch.

The memories of his days on Scipio Creek fishing, paddling around in the old John boat, and riding their bikes through the streets of old Apalach had come to him many times through the years and always made him smile. Will had been shy and awkward as a young boy, but Jess had always made him feel like he belonged.

Many nights, he'd had supper at her house. Her mother always seemed to sense when he needed a little tender loving care and would invite him to stay. Afterward, he would trek through the backyard in the dark over to the next street and up three houses to the one he shared with his father. Most nights, his father would be home, but some nights, he'd have to stay late to close up the tavern. Even when his father was there, it was often lonely for Will.

When he swung the gate open and pulled the rental car in behind the tavern, he parked next to his father's old truck. He had to smile at the realization that he could not remember his father ever driving anything else. He guessed the truck was at least 40 years old and was probably in pretty good shape, knowing it had only been driven a few miles a day. With his father living above the tavern for several years, he was sure there were many days it hadn't been driven at all. It looked to be in near-perfect condition. He would check it out tomorrow.

He entered the back of the tavern and started up the old staircase, the worn steps creaking under his weight. There were only two apartments on the second floor, and he realized he hadn't asked the lawyer which one was his father's. At the top of the stairs, he turned left towards the street side and knocked loudly on the door. When no one answered, he tried the key. The lock turned easily, and he swung the door open.

The apartment was neat and clean, and Will was relieved to see that his father seemed to have kept his mental faculties up until he died. There were no odd placements of things or disarray of any kind. The kitchen was tidy, with only a single glass on the drainboard. The living room couch had a carefully folded lap blanket draped over the back and a few pillows neatly arranged. There was an oversized leather chair by the window with a stack of books on the side table next to it, and under the window was a long bookcase full of books that looked to be arranged purposely and lovingly. Everything was neat, clean, and dust-free. His father seemed to have left this world gracefully.

"I put some fresh sheets on the bed in the guest room for you," a voice said from behind him.

Will turned and saw an older woman standing in the doorway. "I'm Loretta Owens. I'm not sure if you remember me, but I've worked for your father for many years and live across the hall there," she said as she pointed over her shoulder. "I helped care for your father these last few months."

Will walked towards her, not sure exactly what to say. "Oh yes, Loretta, of course, I remember."

"He was doing pretty good until a couple of weeks ago," she said as she lowered her head and shook it. "I think he just got tired of fighting it, you know?" She paused for a moment to compose herself. "Anyway, here's his key."

He took the key, turned it over in his hand, then looked up at her.

"Do I owe you anything for all you've done here and for caring for my father? I see the apartment has been well looked after, too. I'm sure that was your doing," he said.

She smiled at him. "No, you don't owe me anything. Your father and I were good friends for a long time. Helping to care for him these last few months was an honor. He was a good man." She paused for a moment, then went on. "He talked about you a lot in the last days, you know, about you as a child. We would sit, and he would tell me stories and tell me about your job in California. He was quite proud of you and had a very good memory right up to the end."

"No one has told me anything about his illness or his death at all," Will said. "Perhaps you could fill me in? I'd like to know."

"Your father died of liver cancer. He was diagnosed about a year and a half ago. He didn't tell anyone for a while and refused any treatment other than some pain pills near the end. He said there was no use putting off what the good Lord had planned for him," she said with a slight chuckle, but Will could see she had tears in her eyes. "He had a peaceful passing, though, here at home where he wanted to be."

"I didn't know he was sick. We hadn't spoken in a while," Will said. "I wish I had known. I would have come to see him."

"He didn't want to burden you. He said that many times. He was a proud man, too, and didn't want you to see him old and frail." She paused for a moment. "Well, I'm going to let you settle in. I know you had a long trip over from California. I'm just across the hall if you need anything." She turned to go.

"Loretta? It doesn't seem enough just to say thank you for all you've done. If there's anything I can do for you, anything at all, please let me know."

She waved over her shoulder, and Will stood there until she stepped inside her apartment and softly closed her door.

He heard the ping of a text message and, when he checked it, saw that it was Jess. She wanted to meet in thirty minutes. He hustled to unpack his clothes and hopped in the shower. He was going to have to hurry if he was going to get there on time.

CHAPTER THREE

The atmosphere in the old hotel bar seemed to conjure up the spirits of the wealthy ship captains that once frequented it. Its huge carved bar, rich woods, and nautical elements were reminiscent of a time of abundance in Apalachicola. Even before the turn of the last century, the coastal town had been one of the most robust seaports in the Gulf of Mexico. Back then, the little enclave enjoyed the wealth created by the trade of cotton, timber, seafood, and, eventually, the railroad's commerce. The historic hotel had been a central point for important people to congregate over the decades, as only those with means could afford its finer amenities.

Jess was seated at the bar with her back to him. Looking at her there, he could see the girl he knew when they were young. Her dark hair, cut shoulder length, and how she held herself struck a chord in him and made him realize parts of her were etched in his memory.

"Hey, there," he said as he slid onto the bar stool beside her. She turned and smiled at him.

"Hey," she said, "I hope you are okay with meeting here. I love this old place, and the food in the restaurant is really good."

"No, this is great, really beautiful," he said as he looked around. "Looks like the place has been renovated since I saw it last."

He returned his gaze to her, and she smiled at him, her elbow resting on the bar and her chin in her hand.

"Things tend to change a bit when you stay away for a decade or so, Will Kendrick," she said, her eyes tinged with amusement.

"I guess you're right about that. I've only been back once since I left for college," he said, "and that's been a while."

She looked at him for a moment as if sizing him up.

"California's that great, huh?" she said with a wry smile.

"It's okay," he said. "I've made a life there, and it's where my work is. You know how it goes. Hard to get away, especially this far away." He ordered a drink, then turned back to her.

"What about you? What have you been up to all these years?"

"Oh, I went off to school in Tallahassee, got my degree in marketing, and worked for a Public Relations firm up in Atlanta for a while. I wasn't fond of the big city, though, and when Mama fell and broke her hip, I came home to help out. I never went back. I've been here in Apalach ever since."

"And what else?" he said as he sipped his drink.

"What do you mean, *what else?*"

"Husband? Kids?" he asked. "Any of those?"

"No husband," she laughed, "but one kid. You?"

"No, life has been too hectic to settle down. I don't know, maybe someday."

"Ha," she said as she laughed, "famous last words."

They were quiet for a minute, sipping their drinks and thinking.

"So what is it that you do out there in the land of fruits and nuts?" she asked.

He laughed. "I'm a screenwriter."

"What?" she said with surprise. "Seriously? Are you rich and famous or something?"

"Most screenwriters don't get famous," he said, with a wry smile, "or rich. It's really not that big of a deal."

She smiled at him. "My Will, humble as always."

They were quiet again. Each caught up in their thoughts. He had a lot he wanted to ask her, especially about her child, but decided to wait. He wanted to enjoy this time with her and not complicate it.

"Are you hungry yet?" he asked. "Do you want to get seated for dinner?"

"Let's have another drink if it's okay with you," she said. "I've been working so much lately that I could use a little time with my vodka."

"Well, that makes two of us," he said. "Despite everything, I haven't felt this relaxed in a long time."

THE HOTEL'S dining room was beautifully renovated while keeping its old, historic feel. The rich color of the rustic heart of pine floors was beautifully offset by its architectural elements of broad beams, elegant moldings, and paneling. The cream-colored botanical wallpaper, table linens, and candlelight created a soothing and relaxed atmosphere. It was wholly old Florida, and Will could not help but admire how the owners had preserved that essence.

When he perused the menu, he was surprised and impressed by the offerings. While the restaurant was decidedly Southern, it had a sophistication one would not expect to see in a small town in Florida.

"What a great menu," Will said, "I'm impressed."

"Didn't know our little ol' Apalach had it in her, did you?" she said with a smile.

"Frankly, no," he said, laughing.

"Our town has become quite the tourist destination. I'm afraid we've been discovered while you were gone."

"Well, as much as I know it's good for the local economy, I'm not sure I like it."

"You and me both," she said, "but it's helping the town. Since the moratorium on oyster fishing, there are a lot more folks depending on tourism."

"Yes, the lawyer said the price of real estate has been picking up. He advised me to hold onto what my dad owned."

"The lawyer?" she asked.

"Yes, Conner West, do you know him?"

"Will, it's Apalach. Everybody knows everybody here," she said as she gazed at the menu.

"He seems like a nice enough guy," Will said. "He's been really helpful with everything."

"He is," she said, still not meeting his gaze. "Are you thinking of selling the properties your dad owned?"

"I don't know. Living so far away might make things hard to manage. I'm thinking about it."

"Including the tavern?" she asked.

"Especially the tavern," he said. "I don't know how I could manage that from California."

She went quiet momentarily, and he noticed her mood shift a little.

"Would you like to have some wine with dinner?" he asked, looking to change the subject. "They have a pretty nice selection."

"Sure," she said.

"Red or white?"

"Whatever you want," she said. "I don't drink much wine."

He called the waiter over and ordered a nice bottle of Merlot. If Jess wasn't much of a wine drinker, he thought it would be more palatable for her than the bold reds he was used

22

to drinking. Once they'd ordered their entrees, Will sat back, perusing her a bit.

"So, how long have you been working at the tavern?" he asked.

"Off and on for a lot of years," she said. "When I came back from Atlanta, I didn't have a job, and your dad needed some help with the evening shift. It suited my schedule," she said as she ran her fingers through her hair, "with helping Mama out and all. A couple of years later, I opened my shop across the street. Your dad owned the building and helped me get started by not charging me any rent for a while. After I got on my feet, I insisted on paying, but he never charged me what he should have. So, over the years, I've helped him out whenever he was short-handed. When he got sick, I started managing it for him. I hired some help at the shop and have managed to hold them both down. As hard as it's been, it still doesn't seem enough to repay him for everything he did for me."

Will could see the tears glistening in her eyes as she talked about his father, and he felt his heart constrict a little.

"I had no idea, Jess. Thank you."

She just nodded and looked down at the table for a moment. They were silent for a few minutes as they sipped their wine.

"Connor said the repast is at the tavern after the service. What can I do to help out with that?" he asked gently, not wanting to stir up any more of her emotions.

"There's not much to do. All the local restaurants are sending in food, and the tavern, of course, can provide the drinks, so really, all I need to do is set up some tables."

"I can help you do that before the service," he said. "I'm staying upstairs, so I'm available at a moment's notice to do anything you need."

"Thanks," she said as she smiled at him. "Are you available tomorrow morning? The tavern doesn't open until after the church hour, so I thought I'd spend a couple of hours there going over some things and getting ready. It might be good for you to learn a little about it, no matter what you plan to do with it."

"Yes," he said, "that would be great, and you're right. I know nothing about the business. What time do you want to meet?"

"Nine o'clock, if that works for you."

"Sounds perfect."

WILL FELT his phone vibrate in his pocket for the third time that evening as he walked back to the tavern in the crisp night air. Excusing himself to answer would have been awkward, so he'd ignored the calls. Besides, he knew who it was.

"Hello," he said as he stepped off the curb and started across the street.

"Hey," she said, "I was starting to worry about you."

"I'm sorry I haven't called you," he said, feeling suddenly tired. "I've been busy since I got here."

"It's okay," she said. "I just wanted to make sure you got there all right and are doing okay. Are you?" she asked.

"I'm okay. It feels a little surreal to be back here. It's been a long time since I've been home."

"I'm sure it does, especially under the circumstances. Are you outside? I can hear the wind blowing."

"Yes," he said. "I ran into an old friend, and we had dinner. I'm walking back now. I'm staying at my dad's place upstairs from his tavern. There's an art festival in town, so no hotel rooms are available."

"Oh, that must be hard. I wish you'd let me come with you. I hate the thought of you dealing with all this alone."

"It's okay," he said. "I'll get through it."

"I can always come out there if you want me to. I have a light schedule this week and next."

"No," he said, "the service is Monday morning. I don't expect to be here much longer after that."

"Okay, but please let me know how things are going or if you change your mind. I miss you already,"

"I miss you too," he said as he disconnected.

He and Kate had been together for the better part of five years. In the beginning, things had been exciting with them. They were young and living in the fast lane in LA. But as time passed and their careers had taken the forefront, they had settled into a comfortable, sometimes mundane, existence.

They were a good fit, though, working in the same business and running in the same circles. It was just easy to let the time go by. They both seemed content with the way things were.

He'd never considered taking things any further with them, and she had never mentioned wanting anything other than the lifestyle they had of living separately. Now, walking through the streets of his hometown, he wondered why that was. They seemed somewhat stuck. Were all of his relationships in suspended animation?

He slipped the key into the apartment lock and entered quietly. He didn't want to disturb Loretta, and it seemed every little noise echoed throughout the high ceilings of the hallway. Once inside, he stopped to look at the closed door to his father's bedroom. He would have to go in there eventually, but he couldn't do it yet. He guessed he was letting the reality of things sink in a little at a time.

CHAPTER FOUR

He could hear Jess in the bar when he started down the stairs a little before nine. The clanging of bottles and the sound of boxes being moved around told him she was probably stocking the bar for the repast. When he reached the bottom, he could see her through the narrow hallway, pulling bottles from a case and setting them carefully on the back bar. He took a moment to look past the girl who had been his childhood friend and instead at the woman she'd become. As he watched her ruminate over the arrangement of the bottles, hands on her hips, and her hair up in a high pony-tail, he thought she looked quite attractive, something he had never considered when they were kids. He'd never thought of her that way in all the years he'd known her.

"Good morning," he said. "Am I late?"

"Oh, hey," she said, glancing at her watch. "No, I just wanted to finish some of this early. The Irish whiskey will be flowing tomorrow, so I want to make sure we have enough stock on the back bar," she said, her voice tinged with humor and sadness.

"How many people do you think will come tomorrow?" he asked.

"Pretty much everyone in town," she said. "Most businesses in town close on Monday anyway, but those that don't will. I would imagine there will be a couple of hundred people here."

"Really?" he said. "I had no idea."

"Your dad was important to a lot of people, Will," she said as she set the last of the whiskey bottles from the case on the back bar. "This old place has seen a lot of wakes, but I doubt any will compare to your father's tomorrow."

Will didn't know what to say. The idea of facing hundreds of people and answering their questions was off-putting to him. What would he say when they asked him where he'd been for the last ten years?

"I'd like to pay for the alcohol for the repast personally and not have the tavern bear the cost of it," he said. "What's the best way for me to do that?"

"Isn't it all coming out of the same pocket now?" she asked as she wiped down the smooth wood on the front rail.

"Technically, yes, but I would like to contribute. It would make me feel better."

"Feel better about what?"

Will was silent for a moment as he thought about her question and how to answer it in a way that made sense.

"I haven't been home in over a decade, Jess," he said. "To say I feel guilty about it is an understatement."

She was quiet for a moment as she went about her work.

"He would have hated that, you know," she said as she climbed up on the step stool to clean the mirror behind the back bar.

"Hated what?" Will said.

"The guilt," she said, "but especially the whininess."

"Whininess?"

"Yes," she said, not looking at him. "You had your reasons. He could live with that. You should be able to."

That set him back a bit. Her honesty and bluntness had been

unexpected, and her insight into his father led him to believe they had talked about things.

"Come help me arrange these tables over here," she said, "then I'll make you some breakfast."

~

"The tavern pretty much holds its own," she said as she shoveled scrambled eggs onto his plate. "There have been months when it's been tight, but it's always worked out. Your dad had great relationships with his vendors. They knew he was good for it, so they cut him a break if a payment was a week or two late."

"So it barely pays its bills?" he said. "Is that what you're telling me?"

"No," she said, "I'm telling you that it can sustain itself. It wouldn't be a financial drag if you decided to keep it. Your dad was very old school and wanted to run it the way he always had, but I have some ideas on how to make it more profitable."

"Is that what you really want to do, Jess? You have your shop to run, and I assume you have a life to lead. Do you really want to be burdened with keeping this place going?" he asked as she sat across from him at the small table in the tavern's kitchen.

"The tavern isn't a burden, Will," she said as she sipped her coffee.

"Well, it sure seemed to be for my father. He was always grumbling about it."

"Your father grumbled about everything. That was his way," she said with a laugh. "But he loved this place."

"I don't know," he said. "I just don't know how I could manage it from California. It seems like it would be a big hassle."

"Look," she said. "You've got a lot ahead of you right now. Let's table this discussion until later. I'll continue to do what I've been doing for the last few months, and you can make those decisions once you've had a chance to think about things."

"Thank you, that's probably smart," he said. "Are you being paid enough to manage this place? Do we need to talk about that?"

"It's enough," she said. He looked at her for a long moment, trying to read her thoughts by the expression on her face. He sensed that it was a subject she didn't want to discuss, so he let it go.

"You know, I don't know much about this place," he said, changing the subject. "I mean, I spent a lot of time here as a kid, but I know almost nothing about its history. Do you?"

"A little," she said. "Your dad owned this place for almost fifty years, so for most people, it's always been Kendrick's, but when your dad bought the building, it had been a general store. He told me he'd always wanted to own a tavern, so when the building came up for sale, he pulled together every nickel he had for a down payment and made a deal with the owner to finance the rest. He was oyster fishing full-time back then, and it was a pretty good living. He spent the next year working on the place every night, renovating the upstairs and building out the bar downstairs. When he finished, he moved upstairs, rented the other apartment, and opened the doors. His blood, sweat, and tears built everything you see here. He met your mother here, you know."

"No, I didn't know that," he said. "He never told me."

"Really?" she asked. "That surprises me. He told me the story at least a dozen times."

"We never talked about my mother. I think that was part of our problem. It was like a forbidden subject. I don't even really know what happened to her," Will said. "Nobody ever told me."

"Oh, Will," she said, holding her hand to her forehead. "All these years, nobody ever told you what happened to your mother? Did you ever ask?"

"Once," he said. "My father made it clear I was never to ask again. I guess I was around six or so."

Looking up at her, he could see tears glistening in her eyes. The look on her face puzzled him. He could not imagine what would make her so emotional. She looked away and changed the subject.

"So anyway," she said as she blinked away the tears. "Your father told me that one day, he looked up, and she was sitting at the end of the bar. He'd never seen her before, but she was the prettiest thing he'd ever seen. She was new to town, had just arrived from Panacea, and was looking for work. He hired her on the spot even though he didn't need her. He just couldn't let her walk away. He was in his mid-forties, and she was not yet thirty. They were married just a few months later and lived above the tavern until she got pregnant with you. Your dad didn't want her going up and down the stairs with you, so he bought the house you grew up in."

"When did my dad move back upstairs? Do you know?"

"About five years ago," she said. "It made things easier for him, I think. As he got older, running the tavern got harder for him. I wanted to take over the day-to-day for him long before he let me. He just didn't want to let go, even at the end. This place was everything to him."

"I wish I'd known some of this. I'd have come home to help him."

"It's a hell of a time to have these regrets, Will, now that you can't do anything about them. And besides, were you ever going to move back here from California? "

"No, but I could have done something."

"What? What could you have done?" she asked, challenging him.

"I don't know," he said, shaking his head, "something."

"Look, Will, your dad didn't die alone or destitute. He had a lot of people around him who cared about him and for him. He loved you, Will, but he also understood you. Now that he's gone, the best you can do is to try to understand him."

Will went quiet for a moment, unsure how to respond to her. She was right, he guessed. He didn't understand his father, and even if he knew he was sick, he was unsure what he could have done. The chasm between them had existed for decades. It would have been unrealistic to think they could have closed it after all this time. Coming home might have just opened up old wounds for them both.

"What else do we need to do to get ready for tomorrow?" he asked, hoping to change the subject.

"Nothing, really," she said as she cleared their plates. "The tavern doesn't open for a couple of hours yet. Let's take a walk and get some fresh air."

~

THE WATERFRONT HAD SEEN a lot of change over the years, especially after the last big storm had rolled through. Many of the old buildings along the water had taken the brunt of the wind and high water and now stood empty, waiting for some industrious buyer to come along and repurpose them.

As they walked along, making small talk and blowing off some of the emotional steam from their earlier conversation, Will let his memories of the old town wash over him. Something about their earlier conversation had loosened the grip of the angst he felt when he remembered his childhood there. He found himself enjoying listening to Jess and her animated stories.

The weather had turned milder, and the wind off the bay had died down. It was pleasantly warm in the sun, and as they walked, Jess pulled off her jacket and tied it around her waist. Even though the leaves were changing in Apalach and the old town hinted at the oncoming winter, it was a beautiful day.

With no particular destination in mind, they walked for the better part of an hour and ended up in front of her shop across from the tavern.

"Do you want to see it?" she asked as she pushed the door open

"Yes, I'd love to," he said.

He stepped in behind her and smiled at the woman behind the counter.

"This is Tammy," Jess said. "She runs the shop for me on the weekends. This is Will Kendrick, Grant Kendrick's son."

"Oh, hello," the woman said, "and my condolences to you. We will sure miss your father. He was a big part of our community here."

"Thank you," Will said, not knowing what else to say.

As Jess and the woman began discussing business matters, Will took the opportunity to browse a little. The shop was beautiful. The colors of nearly everything in it reflected those of the ocean waters. There were jewelry pieces with charms of mermaids, starfish, and dolphins and exquisite hand-cut stationery depicting sea shells. On one wall, there was a collection of fragrant soaps and lotions, and another corner displayed fine linens and accessories. Everything there was decidedly coastal and beautifully merchandised. Whoever did Jess's buying knew what they were doing. He guessed the store was a favorite among the tourists.

He picked up a few things for Kate and took them to the counter, where Jess was winding down her conversation and looking through the receipts from the previous day.

"Are these for anyone special?" Tammy asked. "Would you like me to gift-wrap them?"

"No," he said, "just a few things for the girls in my office. They're holding down the fort for me while I'm gone."

She smiled as she wrapped the items in tissue paper and placed them carefully into a nicely imprinted shopping bag.

Everything about the shop was top-notch, and he felt proud of Jess as he watched her perusing the receipts, hand on her chin. As he waited for her to finish up, he wondered why he had lied about the gifts and who they were for. He'd done it on instinct, and it bothered him. He guessed he just didn't want that part of his life out there for discussion, especially with Jess, who seemed to have an uncanny ability to see right through him.

"I'm impressed," he said as they exited the shop and stepped off the curb. "Your shop is beautiful and well done."

"Thanks, Will," she said. "That means a lot. It wasn't easy in the beginning. I didn't have much money to invest in it. I sold my car to buy inventory, and your dad helped with the free rent. I did all the painting and built the displays myself. I got it open on a shoestring, but it's on solid ground now."

"You have some really nice things in there. Your store rivals some of the nicer ones I've seen on the West Coast," he said. "Who does your buying for you?"

"I do all my own buying. I have a good group of vendors who make it easy for me," she said.

"Wow, now I'm really impressed. It's not easy to put together such a well-thought-out collection of merchandise."

"Well, I know we aren't as sophisticated as California, " she said with a laugh, "but we aren't all country bumpkins down here either, Will."

"No, I didn't mean it that way at all," he said. "I just didn't know that was one of your talents. Some people make whole careers out of doing that."

"Well, even if I could afford to hire a buyer, I wouldn't. It's the part of the business I like best, that and the merchandising," she said as she unlocked the door to the tavern.

"Well, you're good at it, and I'm not just trying to flatter you."

She smiled at him and held his gaze for a moment. "Are you working the bar with me today, Will Kendrick?"

"Do you want me to?" he asked.

"I can always use an extra hand behind the bar," she said, "and you'll learn a lot about how the place runs. It should be a busy day. With the nice weather and the festival still going on, Apalach will be swamped."

~

WILL HAD NEVER WORKED behind the bar of his father's tavern. By the time he was old enough, he had gone to college. As a kid, he bussed tables for his dad or ran food out, but that was the extent of his experience. As the tavern filled up in the early afternoon, Will could not believe the pace of the place.

He also realized that Loretta ran the kitchen singlehandedly, with a helper who ran the food and fetched what she needed. The kitchen still ran on a written ticket system and, by some miracle, as smooth as glass. The bar had been upgraded with a simple point-of-sale system, but according to Jess, that had been relatively recent. It hadn't been necessary when it had been just locals, but with the influx of tourists, it was now a must-have.

By two p.m., the bar was at least two deep, and all the tables were full. Will wasn't much of a help to Jess, who was buzzing around the bar at an admirable pace. He could draft beer and pour shots, but that was the extent of his bartending capabilities, so he mostly collected and washed empty glasses, bussed tables, and tried to stay out of her way. It wasn't until late in the afternoon that the crowd thinned out. With the festival ending and the weekend coming to a close, the tourists were headed out, and the locals were getting ready for the week ahead. It would be a light crowd of regulars that night.

At six p.m., when the evening help arrived, Jess grabbed Will by the sleeve.

"Come on," she said. "It's my turn to buy dinner."

CHAPTER FIVE

Will fastened the cuffs on his dress shirt and carefully knotted his tie. When he checked his watch, it was eight-forty-five. He and Jess had planned to meet at nine downstairs for coffee before heading to the cemetery. They would have to drive. It was too far to walk.

He gazed out the window at the bright blue skies and was thankful the weather was fair on the day people would pay their respects to his father. It could have been overcast and blustery or rainy. The weather was always unpredictable that time of year in the panhandle.

On the street below, he saw little activity. He still found it remarkable that Apalachicola had changed so little in the last ten years. It was a town ripe for development, yet it was essentially the same as when he was a kid.

He grabbed his jacket and headed out, locking the door behind him. When he reached the bottom of the stairs, he could smell the aroma of brewed coffee and could see Jess sitting at the bar with a cup and a small plate.

"There's coffee in the kitchen, and I set out a light breakfast," she said. "I think you should eat a little something before we leave."

He poured himself a cup of coffee, grabbed a piece of toast, and sat beside her. They were quiet for a moment.

"You okay?" she said softly.

"I suppose," he said. "It feels very surreal."

"I know," she said. "Just take it in a minute at a time. You'll get through it."

"Are you all set here?" he asked. "Is there anything you need me to do here before we head out?"

"No," she said. "Everything is ready. Please don't worry about the repast. I'll handle everything today. There are plenty of people to pitch in and help if I need it."

He was quiet, not knowing what to say. He wanted to protest but didn't have the emotional energy for it. She was right. He needed to pace himself. He was already feeling a bit over-whelmed.

When it was time to go, she stood and cleared their plates and cups and took one last walk around the tavern, straightening chairs and tabletop items as she went. Sometime during the early morning, she had covered the tables they set up for food with linens and set out plates and silverware. There was a nice arrangement of flowers in the center, and Will thought that was probably her doing. She stood there for a minute surveying everything, then turned to him.

"We better get going," she said. "My car is right out front,"

"I can drive us," he said.

"No, it's easier if I drive. It's not far away. Come on," she said, "we don't want to be late."

THE AIR WAS crisp and cool, and the wind was calm as they stood graveside listening to the preacher recite the service. Will could not help but let the tears come. As much as he wanted to remain stoic and unemotional, the dam of emotions had broken, and there was no way to stop it. When he saw his mother's headstone, he realized he was alone in the world now, with his parents gone and no siblings. He hadn't realized that the mere presence of his father on this earth had been a comfort.

Jess looped her arm through his and squeezed it, and he realized how having her to lean on had helped him. He couldn't imagine what it would have been like to go through all of it without her.

The service concluded ten minutes after it began, for which Will was grateful. Connor had been right. His father had clearly wanted to keep things simple. He tossed one of the roses he had been given onto his father's casket and stood graveside as people, most of whom he didn't know, passed by to do the same and offer their condolences. When almost everyone was headed to their cars, he turned to Jess.

"Do we have time for a short walk before heading back?" he asked.

"Yes," she said as she glanced at her watch. "The repast won't start until eleven."

Will stood for a moment more, then placed his hand on his father's casket, taking in the finality of things. He walked to his mother's gravesite, placed another rose, and realized he had never seen where she was buried. At least not that he could remember.

They walked around the cemetery for a bit, not talking, just taking in the quietness and the beautiful weather. He needed this moment of peace to collect himself.

"I'm not sure what to expect at the repast," he said.

"What do you mean?"

"Funerals in California are very sterile. It seems like this will be different."

"Will, the funeral is over. Now comes the celebration of his life. There's going to be lots of storytelling and whiskey drinking. There won't be anything sterile about it," she laughed.

"Do I need to be prepared to do anything? Like, say a few words or something?"

"No," she said with a chuckle. "There will be plenty of that going on. Look, no one's going to judge you or ask you any hard questions. They are just coming to honor your father in the way he wanted them to. This is a time to blow off a little steam, and a repast does that in a celebratory way. Just relax and try to enjoy the moment. As hard as that seems, it's what he wanted."

Will nodded and turned to her. "Jess, thanks so much for helping me through this. This would have been so much harder without you."

Jess smiled at him and squeezed his hand. "Let's go," she said, "everyone will be at the tavern in half an hour."

They drove back slowly. He could tell Jess was trying to give him a little extra time. He slipped upstairs for a minute to remove his tie, leave his jacket, and pull himself together. The service at the cemetery had been harder than he had imagined, and he needed a few minutes alone.

JESS WAS behind the bar pouring the draft beer and handing them over to the outstretched hands from a row back. He could see the shot glasses lined up on the bar rail. As she had predicted, the Irish whiskey was already flowing.

She smiled at him when she caught his eye and motioned him over. When he reached the end of the bar, she poured a full two fingers of whiskey into a highball glass and shoved it in his hand.

"Drink this," she said with a laugh. "You need to catch up to the crowd."

He took the glass from her and took a sip. He tried hard not to wince as the liquor burned going down. He wasn't much of a drinker, much less a whiskey drinker. When he looked at her again, she winked at him.

"It gets easier," she said, her eyes full of mischief, "I promise."

He worked his way through the crowd down the length of the bar and was surprised by the number of people who greeted him by name. They all had nice things to say about his father, yet he felt eager to move on from the conversations. They made him uncomfortable. He was expecting personal questions and wasn't prepared to answer them. Surprisingly, they hadn't come.

When he reached the other end, he found an out-of-the-way place to stand near the corner on the bar rail. He watched as Jess effortlessly managed the crush of the demands behind the bar. He could tell she was a natural back there.

There was a lull as it was announced that the food was served, and everyone converged on the tables near the front. He felt a heavy hand on his shoulder and turned to see who it was. It was a man he didn't recognize.

"Are you doing okay, son?" the man asked.

"Yes, I am," Will said. "I'm sorry, I don't think we've been introduced."

The man chuckled and stuck his hand out. "It's been a long time, Will. I haven't seen you since you were a teenager. I'm Sawyer Hayes."

Will struggled to place him, and the man could see the confusion in his eyes. "My wife Penny was a bartender here when you were a kid."

"Oh, yes!" Will said, "I remember you now. I'm sorry I didn't recognize you. It's been a few years,"

"It sure has. I hear you are out in California now. Doing something with the movies?" he asked.

"Yes," he said with a chuckle, "something like that. How is Penny?"

"Well, she's doing okay, and she's eager to see you. As much as she wanted to be here today, she had one of her treatments on Friday, and she just wasn't up to it," he said as his face clouded over a bit.

"Treatments?" Will asked.

"Yes, she was diagnosed with breast cancer this past summer, but the doctor says she'll be all right. Just needs to get through this time. Stop by and see her while you're in town if you can. It would sure perk her up."

"I will, for sure," Will said. "Does Jess have your address?"

"She does, and we aren't far," Sawyer said. "I appreciate it, Will, and it's been good to see you."

The two men shook hands, and Will watched him work his way through the crowd and say his goodbyes. He looked more closely at the people there and wondered how many of them he had once known but didn't recognize.

It was then that Will noticed Connor West approach Jess at the end of the bar, put his hand on her waist, and whisper in her ear. She smiled up at him, and he leaned in to kiss her. Will felt a streak of emotion run through him, but he didn't know quite what it was. Seeing the intimacy between them wasn't something he expected. When she turned, she caught him looking at her, and their eyes locked. A thousand things seemed to pass between them then, and neither could tear their eyes away. Finally, someone bumped into her and distracted her, and the moment was lost.

"Come on," she said laughing, "you can do it."

With her arm around his waist, she guided him up the stairs. He stumbled a little, and she caught him. When they got to the door, she took his keys, opened it, and led him back to the bedroom, where he collapsed on the bed. She got a glass of water and some aspirin and put them on the nightstand.

"Get some sleep and call me later," she said as she turned to go.

"Jess?" he called.

"Yes," she answered.

"Thank you. Thank you for everything."

"You're welcome, Will Kendrick," she said, smiling back at him.

He closed his eyes, and she quietly left him. She could already hear him snoring when she got to the door.

Downstairs, she began cleaning up. The repast had been a rowdy one, as she had predicted. Once the whiskey got flowing, so did the toasts and the stories. Poor Will had gotten a whiskey pushed into his hand at every turn, and she was surprised he even made it to the end. He would wake up with one hell of a hangover later, and she didn't envy him.

She straightened the chairs, put the glasses on a tray, set them on the bar, and then carried the leftover food to the kitchen. Someone had cleared the plates and silverware and was already running a batch through the dishwasher. She started to load a rack when she heard a voice behind her.

"Don't worry about those, Jess. I'll finish them up," Loretta said as she hustled back into the kitchen.

"It's okay, I'll do it," she said.

"No," Loretta said, "you've done enough for today. You get off your feet. I'll finish here."

"Okay," she said, "but please don't tire yourself out. I'll be in early tomorrow, and I can finish things up then if I need to."

She *was* tired both physically and emotionally. Saying goodbye to Grant Kendrick had taken more out of her than she realized. It was the end of an era for her, one that she knew she could never revisit. He'd been like a father to her, her own having walked out on them when she was sixteen. She never knew why, but she suspected a couple of things. He must have moved on to a whole new life because he'd never come back. As it was, she hadn't seen him in more than fifteen years. She had stopped counting a while ago.

When she had come home from Atlanta to help her mother recover, she had felt a little lost. Apalachicola was not the same for her, and it took some time to feel comfortable again. Almost no one she'd grown up with lived in town anymore. Everyone had moved on.

It crushed her when she and Will had grown apart during high school. She had felt she was his girl for as long as she could remember. Watching him date other girls had been excruciating, and when he left for college without so much as a goodbye, she began to suspect that what was between them was probably nothing more than a childhood friendship. When he never came home, it all but confirmed it for her.

If she were honest with herself, returning to Apalachicola had been as much about him as anything else. Her mother needed her, but she didn't have to stay. She always felt if she were there, at least there was a chance they could reconnect. As the years went by, hanging on to any hope became harder and harder. She knew sooner or later he would marry, ending any chance for them.

She kept tabs on him by Googling him now and then. She'd played dumb at the restaurant when she'd asked him what he did for a living. Will was indeed famous, having worked on some of the most influential films of the last decade. There were many pictures of him, and it used to tug at her heart to see he had only grown more handsome as he matured. The skinny, tow-headed, blue-eyed boy had grown tall, filled out, and could easily pass for one of the celebrities he wrote for.

She'd been tempted to contact him often, especially when his father got sick, but Grant wouldn't let her. She thought he should know, but his father said his dying was no reason to try to heal wounds that time hadn't. Will coming home wouldn't change anything.

Now he was there, and she wasn't sure what to do about it. She knew he would be going back to California soon. Then what? Was she going to spend the rest of her days waiting for him to come back again? Certainly, he had a life he loved there and, most likely, a significant other. She'd often seen the same beautiful blonde in pictures with him. There was no reason for him to stay in Apalachicola.

But something had passed between them that afternoon at the repast. She just didn't know what it was. Was it curiosity about her and Connor? Possibly, but it seemed to be more than that. Maybe she should be honest with him, but what could she say that wouldn't sound ridiculous? His life was in California, and hers was there. It was unlikely there was anything she could say that would change that.

She poured herself a beer and sat down at the bar. Her eyes had begun to wander around the tavern, sizing up what needed to be done before opening the next day when she heard a cell phone buzzing. She found it on one of the chairs, recognized it as Will's, and smiled, thinking about his condition earlier. He'd needed the release, and she was glad he'd gotten it. She glanced at the phone and saw he'd missed several calls. Whoever had been calling was in for a wait.

CHAPTER SIX

J ess was taking inventory in the bar the next morning when she heard footsteps on the stairs. She figured it was Loretta but was surprised to see Will freshly showered and well-dressed, clearly headed out for the day.

"Well, you're looking very put together this morning, Will Kendrick," she said, tucking her pencil behind her ear. "I have to say I'm surprised. You don't look much worse for the wear."

"Don't let outward appearances fool you," he said with a slight smile. "I feel absolutely wretched. Is there coffee made?"

"Yes," she said, "in the kitchen. Did you take your aspirin?"

"I did, but that was several hours ago. I should probably take some more if I'm going to get through this meeting."

"Meeting?" she asked.

"Yes, Connor and I are meeting to discuss my Dad's estate this morning and what I should do with the assets."

"Oh," she said, "I thought you were going think about that for a while. So you've made some decisions then?"

"Yes," he said but added nothing more.

She wanted to ask him about it, especially the tavern, but it felt wrong to pry, so she stayed quiet.

"Can I make you some breakfast before you go?"

"No thanks," he said. "I think I'd be better off operating on an empty stomach. I want to take you to dinner tonight, though, if you're free."

"Yes, I'm free. I'll finish here around six, and then I'll need to run home to change."

"Okay," he said. "Let's plan on seven then if that works. I've somehow lost my phone. Is there anywhere nearby I could get one today?"

"Oh, it's here. I found it last night while I was cleaning up. It's been ringing off the hook. Who's Kate?" she asked.

He didn't answer as he scrolled through the missed calls and messages. When he finally looked up, she tried to explain herself.

"I'm sorry, I wasn't trying to pry," she said. "It was just ringing so much I started to get worried there was an emergency or something."

"No worries, no emergency. Thanks for grabbing it for me. It would have been a hassle to replace it," he said, glancing at his watch. "I better get going. Meet at the hotel at seven?"

"Yes, " she said, "that sounds good."

She watched him go and chided herself for asking him about the woman. It was a stupid thing to do, and the fact that he hadn't answered her made it worse. Now, she was sure he was involved with someone in California.

Why he'd asked her to dinner, she didn't know. They had been spending a lot of time together, and she felt close to him, but there was so much she didn't know about his life now.

But he didn't know much about hers either. She and Connor had been off and on for several years. Jess knew he was very much in love with her; he'd told her so. But as hard as she tried, she couldn't commit to him. On more than one occasion, he'd made it clear that he wanted to marry her and had tried to put a ring on her finger twice. But she had never been able to say yes.

He didn't know the reason for her reluctance. He probably thought she was hard-headed and willful, but she knew the real reason.

She figured Connor would give up sooner or later, but he hadn't. She couldn't complain about him, though. Connor was sweet and attentive and always treated her well, and he would give her a nice life. Maybe with the recent turn of events with Will, she would reconsider.

It was too much to think about, and she had much to do before opening the tavern. She decided to put it out of her mind and wait to see how things unfolded. Besides, agonizing over it wasn't going to change a thing.

"I'd like you to draw a partnership agreement for Jess and me with regard to the tavern," Will said. "If I'm going to keep it, she's going to need to run it. I don't think I'd be comfortable with anyone else. I haven't seen the books yet, but I'm sure whatever she's being paid isn't enough. She felt she owed my father for helping her over the years, but what she did for him these last few months was above and beyond."

"Okay, I can do that. What are you thinking?" Connor asked. "Something like a managing partner arrangement?"

"Yes, exactly," he said. "I want her to have some equity in the business and a share of the profit. And I want to pay her a fair salary for managing the place."

"What kind of a share do you think you want to give her? Twenty to twenty-five percent? Something in that range?"

"Let's make her a forty-nine percent partner," Will said. "That way, I can give her as much as possible while maintaining the controlling interest."

"Are you sure, Will? That's very generous of you, and it's quite a bit higher than what would be considered the norm."

"She deserves it, and I think my dad would want it that way," he said. "I need to know that when I'm in California, I have someone as invested in the business as I am. I'm sure she already does a great job, but I know she has some ideas to make it more profitable. I want her to feel good about investing her time and ideas into the business."

"What about the building? Do we include that, or are we keeping that separate?" Connor asked.

"Let's keep it separate for now. If, for some reason, this arrangement didn't work out, having the building involved would make things much more complicated. Please design a good exit clause for her, too. If she ever wanted to terminate the agreement, make it easy for her and financially fair. The last thing I would ever want to do is make life hard on her."

"Okay, easy enough. Have you talked to her about any of this yet?"

"No, I wanted to talk to you first, but I'm going to have the conversation with her tonight over dinner. She's been lobbying hard for me to keep it, and I know she wants to keep managing it. This is the only way it will work for me. If she agrees, I'd like you to walk her through the details."

"I can do that," Connor said as he rubbed his chin, thinking about things.

"By the way," Will said, "how long have you two been together? I didn't realize you were involved until I saw you together yesterday at the tavern. I hope doing this won't make you uncomfortable."

Connor looked up from his legal pad. "We've been together off and on for a while. I'd marry her if she'd have me," he said with a wry smile, "but the girl can't seem to make up her mind. Lord knows I've tried to convince her."

The two men looked at each other, and a long moment passed between them

"But, anyway, no, it won't make me uncomfortable. I'll send

you a draft of the agreement in short order. I know you probably need to get back to California soon."

"Actually, I made arrangements to stay a bit longer. I want to get all these details settled before I head back."

"Okay, good," Connor said, "and the other real estate? Are you going to sit pat with those?"

"Yes, for now, though I do want to get them appraised. Can you recommend someone? I want to make sure they are properly insured."

"Yes, I can," he said, reaching into his top drawer. "Here's his card. He does a good job, and I trust him. He'll get that done for you with no problems."

"That's great, thank you. When should we plan to meet again?"

"Just give me a day or so to get a draft to you, then we can iron out the details."

WILL DROVE along the coastal highway westbound towards Port St. Joe. He needed fresh air, sunshine, and a little time away from the tavern to think about things. Little had changed along the highway that he could see other than the abandoned oyster houses that dotted the road—the fallout from the collapse of the oyster industry there.

He could also see the lingering damage from the last storm. The big category five hurricane had roared ashore to the west of Port St. Joe and nearly completely destroyed the town of Mexico Beach. In the few days before, the forecast had it headed at Apalachicola, and Will shuddered to think of the historic old city bearing the brunt of such a powerful storm. He was sure the historic buildings and homes would not have survived.

When he passed the turnoff to Cape San Blas, and the road joined the coastline again, he saw the long curve of the bay lined with the white of the sugar sand. In the distance, he could see the old lighthouse, relocated off the cape in recent years to the safe harbor of Port St. Joe. The day was clear, and it stood tall and majestic against the persistent winds of the Gulf. It was a picturesque scene, with the bright sun highlighting the turquoise water. He had not remembered it being so beautiful.

The little town was bustling and had evidently become an inviting destination in the years since he'd been there. He found a restaurant where he could sit outside, take in the beauty of the bay, and think. He needed a change of scenery from the last few days.

As much as he tried, he couldn't get the image of Jess with Connor out of his mind. It bothered him, and the discomfort he felt was disconcerting. The last few days with her had been easy and comfortable, and he had difficulty keeping his mind from wandering to the possibilities. Talking to Kate earlier had made the differences between the two women glaring. He'd spent fifteen minutes explaining himself and what he'd been doing for the last twenty-four hours, even though that had included burying his father. He hadn't realized how uptight the dynamic between them made him. It had taken a virtual tectonic shift in his life to see it.

Even if he could see his way clear to initiating something with Jess, the implications of it were complicated. They lived on opposite coasts and were both involved with other people. He had no idea how they could ever make that work. Maybe it was just better to leave it alone.

He realized that might be hard to do if they became partners in the tavern. Even though he would return to California soon, they would communicate regularly. Could he maintain enough emotional distance to make the arrangement work? He just didn't know.

Still, he wanted to go through with the partnership. She deserved it, and without her, the tavern wouldn't survive.

Though he had initially wanted to close it and sell the building, now, after everything he'd experienced over the last few days, he wanted to preserve it. Knowing it had meant so much to his father, he felt he owed it to him, but it was more than that. The tavern was central to the community there and had a distinct history. He couldn't just shut it down.

He finished his lunch and headed back towards Apalachicola. The bay was a beautiful shade of blue, an almost identical color to the clear sky. Now and then, there would be a break in the trees, and he could see beautiful, pristine St. Vincent's Island in the distance. He suddenly had an overwhelming sense of belonging, something he hadn't felt in over a decade. As much as he didn't want to admit it, he was home.

CHAPTER SEVEN

T he bar at the restaurant was crowded when he got there. Surprising for a Tuesday, he thought. Jess was right. Apalach had indeed become a desirable destination. He could tell this was not a crowd entirely of locals.

He found a seat at the bar while he waited for her. He was a little early, having wrapped up the day's business sooner than expected. On Connor's recommendation, he'd hired the appraiser and taken some time to visit the properties his dad left to him. All in all, he owned six buildings in town, including the one that housed the tavern. All were occupied by rent-paying tenants, adding up to a respectable monthly income. Two, including the one that housed Jess's shop, had a second story with apartments or vacation rentals. Perhaps he had been too quick to judge his dad's business acumen.

Jess was running late. The liquor delivery had been delayed, and the bar needed to be restocked after the repast. It was something she always did herself. The liquor inventory, she told him, represented thousands of dollars of tavern-owned assets. It was too important to leave it to anyone else.

Will saw her through the window, crossing the street in

front of the hotel. She was hurrying, he could tell, and as he watched her, he was struck again by her natural beauty. Her dark hair blowing across her face shielded her large dark blue eyes. They still held a child-like innocence, but she had grown into a stunningly beautiful woman. Though still petite and slender, she was far from the tomboy he had known when they were kids. He didn't understand why he hadn't noticed her blossoming when they were teens.

"Sorry I'm so late," she said as she joined him at the bar. "That took longer than I thought it would."

She was out of breath from her brisk walk and ran her fingers through her hair, trying to straighten her windblown locks.

"It's okay," he said, "I've been running all day. It was nice to sit for a bit."

"What did you do today? I haven't seen you since this morning?"

"After I met with Connor, I rode to Port St. Joe for lunch, then met with an appraiser he recommended," he said. "I've decided to hang on to the buildings for a while."

"How did your meeting with Connor go?" she asked. "Did you get everything worked out?"

"Yes," he said, "I think I did. We can talk about it over dinner."

"Partners?" she asked. "I'm not sure I understand why. You don't need to do that, Will. I'm happy to manage it for you,"

"I know you are, Jess, and I appreciate that, but you deserve this, and I think it is what Dad would want. Besides, If I'm going to be in California, I think this is the best way to handle things. I don't think the tavern would have a chance of making it without you in charge, and if you are going to put your heart and soul into it, which I know you will, I want it to be worth your while."

"I don't know, Will. It seems complicated. Why don't you just let me manage it for a while? You can think about things, and we can talk more about it later. I don't want you to make a decision you might regret," she said.

"No," he said. "I've thought about it, and this is the only way it will work for me. Connor is drawing the agreement and will go over all the details with you."

"This seems very generous, Will, maybe too generous," she said.

"It's actually quite selfish of me. If I make you a partner, you'll work that much harder to make sure the tavern turns a good profit and is well run. You're the only one I would ever trust enough to offer this to. Please tell me you'll do it, Jess. I can't go back to California until I know I have you," he said.

She looked at him for a moment, a sweet, sentimental smile on her face. "You have me, Will. You've always had me."

The two looked at each other for a long moment, each searching for answers to the unspoken questions between them. It was Will who looked away first. The moment's intimacy was too raw for him, and he wasn't sure what to say next.

"So you'll do it, then?" he asked softly.

"Yes," she said. "If it's what you really want, then yes."

THE MORNING SKY was lit up in a brilliant array of red, its reflection off the bay a firestorm of colors. But by the grey clouds in the distance, low on the horizon, Will knew the weather was about to change in Apalachicola. He watched as the fishermen returned from their night out on the Gulf, their crews standing at the ready to dock the boats. Their eyes were also trained on the ominous sky, and he knew they were thinking the same thing.

Now that Jess had agreed to the partnership and he had the rest of his affairs in order, he didn't need to stay. He could easily return to California and get back to his life there. He had tossed and turned all night thinking about things and had finally given up the idea of sleep a couple of hours ago. Eager to get out of the apartment, he had come down to the waterfront to watch the sunrise. He felt entirely unsettled.

Coming home to Apalach had tilted his axis. Thoughts and beliefs he'd held for years had started shifting, and his perspective on things had changed. He guessed it was easy to form an entirely new reality in a place as far away and different as California and forget the one you came from. But now, as good as his life was there, it somehow felt hollow.

He hadn't been entirely honest with Kate when he told her he needed to stay a few days longer, that it would take a little more time to settle his father's affairs. The current film project he was working on was wrapping up, and he'd told his agent to put his availability on hold. He wasn't sure why he was doing all of it. He just knew he needed to.

The last few days with Jess and their dinner the evening before were gnawing at him. She was unavailable by most standards, yet he couldn't get her off his mind. Getting involved with her would potentially send a wrecking ball through his life as he knew it, and possibly hers too, yet he felt powerless to stop it. Somehow, his sensibilities had taken a back seat to her gravitational pull.

He also hadn't been completely honest with anyone about his reasons for making Jess a partner. Not with her, not with Connor, and certainly not with himself. He realized he wanted the connection. He wanted a reason to talk to her often and to make trips back to Apalachicola. If she were just his manager, she could leave him anytime. If she were his partner, he would have an opportunity to persuade her to stay.

After she agreed, he'd ordered champagne to celebrate. It had made her relaxed and giddy, and he enjoyed seeing a slightly less serious side of her. She became animated as she recalled stories from their childhood, ones he barely remembered, and he delighted in her sense of humor. Now, the memory of her face highlighted in the candlelight did something to his insides. Something was happening between them for sure.

"You look like you could use a friend, son," a voice behind him said.

Will turned to see Sawyer Hayes standing behind him.

"Is it that obvious?" Will said with a chuckle. He watched over his shoulder as Sawyer came around the bench and sat down beside him.

The men didn't say anything for a while, the two of them watching the changing sky and the gulls catching the winds over Big Towhead Island.

"You know, son, it's not always easy to go back and rethink the past. Sometimes, you're forced to admit things to yourself that are hard. But you're always better for it."

Will nodded. "You're right about that. Coming home has been hard," he said, then paused momentarily, "but enlightening."

"Will, your father wasn't easy to grow up with. He would be the first to admit that. In fact, he did in a conversation I had with him not long before he died. He knew he'd driven you away."

Will thought about that for a moment. "I guess I could never figure out why he didn't seem to like me," he said, finally realizing for the first time that was the heart of the matter. "I do know he loved me, but…."

"Grief affects everyone differently, Will. After your mother passed, it took a long time for him to see clearly again. By the time he could, you were already gone to college. I think he wanted to fix things between you, but time got away from him."

"So much wasted time," Will said, his voice full of emotion.

"Well, that's true, but no amount of regret is going to fix that now. Better to try to understand the situation for what it was and work through the hurts."

"I know you're right. Jess said the same thing."

Sawyer nodded. "They were pretty close, you know. He took her under his wing when she came back home, and she became like a daughter to him. I think he wanted to give to her everything he couldn't give to you."

"Well, I guess I should be happy about that. If he couldn't have a relationship with me, at least he had her, and I know she was good to him."

"You know Jess's dad left when she was sixteen. The family was pretty quiet about it, and not many knew, but those girls were devastated. I think your dad helped to fill that void for her."

"I didn't know that. She never told me. We were always close as kids, but we sort of went our own way when we got to high school. That must have been hard for her."

They were quiet again as they thought about things. Finally, Sawyer got up and put a hand on Will's shoulder.

"You should come out on the water with me sometime, Will. There's something special about the bay and the salt air that will clear your mind and help you sort out your thoughts."

Will nodded and watched as Sawyer, hands jammed into his jacket pockets, strolled down the waterfront toward the docks, seemingly in no hurry. At that moment, he reminded him of his father with his hair that had gone gray and a full beard covering his face. That made them look similar in his mind's eye, but it was more than that. He just couldn't put a finger on what it was.

"FORTY-NINE PERCENT?" she said as she waived the papers at him. "Have you lost your mind, Will Kendrick?"

He laughed. "What were you expecting?"

"I don't know, but it wasn't half the business. I can't accept this, Will. It's too much!"

"No, it's not. You get to do all the work, and I get to sit back and collect my half of the profits? I'm not even sure it's enough," he said, amused at her dramatics.

"Will, this is your inheritance, your father's legacy. You can't just give half of it away," she said, her hand on her forehead as she paced in front of him.

"The hell I can't. It's either this or I shut it down and sell the real estate, Jess. I can't go back to California unless you're on board, and I'm not leaving the tavern in anyone else's hands."

She looked at him, clearly flustered, then turned her back on him. He was bluffing. He'd figure out something if she wouldn't accept his offer, but he wasn't letting on.

"It just seems wrong, Will. I don't deserve this. It's too much," she said, lowering her voice to a near whisper. He could hear the tears coming and felt terrible for provoking her that way, but he needed her to agree. The tavern was closed, so there was no one to witness the scene between them. It had been a light evening with the stormy weather, and they had closed early. As the silence opened up between them, he was keenly aware of the sound of the pounding rain.

"It's not wrong," he said as he got up and crossed the room to her. He gently took her by the shoulders and turned her around to face him. His heart clenched a little as he saw the tears sliding down her cheeks as she quickly tried to wipe them away.

"Listen, Jess. I feel in my heart this is the right thing to do. I think it's what my father would have wanted. Please don't say you don't deserve it. You absolutely do."

She put her head down, and he pulled her to him, slowly wrapping his arms around her. She let the tears come in earnest then, and he held her, knowing it was the culmination of all the emotions from the last few days. Her petite frame felt fragile in his arms, her head pressed against the hollow of his chest. He realized then they had a connection that superseded time and distance, and he knew, without a doubt, that a part of him belonged there.

CHAPTER EIGHT

I t was rainy when he got out of bed early the following day. The weather that had rolled in the evening before lingered, and as he peered out over the wet streets below, he felt a bit haunted by the scene between him and Jess the evening before. Holding her while she cried had broken open something he'd been holding back. Now, he felt powerless to put the proverbial genie back in the bottle.

He spent most of the morning reviewing the tavern's books. He wanted to understand its financial picture and assemble a list of questions. Once he felt he had a good handle on things, he would meet with Jess to talk them through.

He had invested in several businesses on the West Coast over the years and had always been careful to do his due diligence. He'd seen too many of his colleagues, eager to invest their money, go headlong into deals that were sure losers. He'd always taken a hands-on approach. While never involved in the day-to-day management, he'd kept his eye on the books.

Fascinated with the restaurant and bar business, he'd helped finance several startups over the years. He'd seen enough to recognize a solid business and was glad to learn the tavern operated pretty well. Even so, Jess was right. It had a lot of potential, especially with the robust tourism Apalachicola was now enjoying.

By the afternoon, he'd closed the files and, feeling satisfied he understood the operation well, had moved on to some other work. His stomach grumbled, so he headed downstairs to grab a bite in the tavern. When he reached the bottom of the stairs, he saw a young boy sitting at one of the small tables with his head bent over his schoolwork. The boy seemed not to notice him, so he didn't disturb him and instead poked his head into the kitchen to see if Loretta was around. Someone must have been in the backroom because he could hear them, but they were out of sight. Rather than interrupt whatever they were doing, he decided to wait and sat down at the bar. When he did, the boy looked up and smiled at him.

"Hi," Will said.

"Hello," the boy said, then bent his head and started back on his work.

Intrigued, Will tried again. "I'm Will Kendrick, what's your name?"

The boy looked up at him and smiled again.

"I'm Kip Wilder," he said but offered nothing more.

Will was perplexed for a moment but then realized who the boy was. When he took a good look at him, it was obvious. His dark hair swept over his forehead, framing his dark blue eyes, and his delicate features were dead giveaways, but it was his straightforward demeanor that jogged the memories of the little girl he used to know. This was Jess's boy.

"Where's your mom?" Will asked.

The boy pointed over his shoulder toward the kitchen and returned to his schoolwork. The sight of him sitting there, as Will had done so many times as a kid, tugged at him. It was like watching history in real time.

He heard some rattling and saw Jess carrying out bar supplies.

"Hey," she said. "What have you been up to? I haven't seen you all day."

"I've just been going over the financials for the tavern," he said. "Maybe if you have some time later, we could talk?"

"Sure," she said. "I'll be free after six."

She turned toward the boy and called to him.

"Kip, honey, Nana will be here in five minutes to get you. Get your things packed up."

The boy nodded and began to put his things away. When finished, he got up, slung his backpack over his shoulder, and walked toward them.

"Will, this is my son, Kip," she said, taking the boy by the shoulders.

"Oh, we've met," Will said, offering the boy a handshake. The boy gave him a nod and grasped his hand, and Will was impressed by his eye contact and the firmness of his handshake.

Just then, the tavern's front door cracked open, and Will heard a woman's voice call to the boy. He quickly kissed his mother goodbye and ran, slipping outside with a wave.

They stared at the closed door momentarily, then turned to each other. Will smiled at her.

"Seems like a great kid," he said.

She smiled. "He's a handful, but you're right. He is a great kid."

"Looks to be about eight?" Will asked as he tried to do the math in his head.

"Just turned seven," she said. "He's tall for his age. His dad was tall."

"Oh," Will said. "Is his dad around?" He realized it was a direct question but wanted to get to the heart of things. He wanted to know if she had any other entanglements.

"No, he was a little in the beginning, but I haven't heard from him in a few years. Kip doesn't know him."

"That must be tough for you both," he said. "Does he ever ask about him?"

"He does now and then," she said. "But I've always been honest with him. His dad isn't such a great guy."

Will wanted to ask more questions but didn't want to pry.

"Well, I admire you, Jess. It can't be easy raising a kid on your own, especially while running two businesses," he said with a smile.

"Thanks," she said, but he could tell her mood had shifted.

"I didn't realize all these evening meetings were keeping you from him. If you have a few minutes, we can go over a couple of things now," he said.

"Okay, give me ten minutes to finish up a few things, and we can grab a table and something to eat."

Will went upstairs to grab his notes and sat for a few minutes thinking. Meeting the boy had cast a different light on things. Seeing Jess as a mother opened up a different dimension to her and one he was eager to see more of. Growing up without a mother and a distant father left him with a lack of understanding about such relationships. At that moment, he realized that was probably why he had not yet married. He couldn't picture himself as a father, having no idea what a functional relationship looked like. And he couldn't even begin to imagine Kate as a mother. She had never expressed any desire to have children and seemed to avoid them altogether whenever they were around.

Still, it was another reason for him to hesitate when it came to getting involved with her. Not that he objected to her having a kid. He didn't at all. It just made things more complicated. And, he wondered what role Connor played. That was a situation he had yet to think through.

Yet she seemed to be leaning in, and so much of him wanted

to explore the possibilities there. He found himself thinking about her nearly all the time, and the thought of returning to California was becoming increasingly difficult. Though he knew he would eventually have to go, he kept finding reasons to put it off. In all practicality, he should have left already. The situation seemed impossible, though. She certainly would never leave Apalachicola, and he couldn't stay forever. Maybe it was just better to leave it be.

JESS LET her mind wander as she made dinner for Kip and her mother. She had been waiting for the right time to introduce Will to her son and had been glad when it happened naturally. She didn't want it to seem forced.

When she'd first told Will about him, he hadn't had much of a reaction and hadn't asked her about him since. She wasn't sure what that meant. Things had been busy the last few days, and she knew he'd had a lot on his mind. Now that they had met, she was curious to see how things would unfold.

When she'd found out she was pregnant, she'd been terrified. Kip's father wasn't someone she would have picked to father her child. She'd known early on in their relationship that he wasn't someone she could ever settle down with. He was a bit wild and a lot reckless and drank too much, but she'd been bored with her life, and he'd been an exciting distraction. Now, with a child on the way, she was afraid of the idea of forever being tied to him. At first, he'd seemed somewhat intrigued at the thought of becoming a father, and she thought for a short time he might come around. But in the end, he only saw it as a burden, and she was glad when he'd finally moved away from Apalachicola.

It was during that time that she and Grant Kendrick had grown close. He looked after her and was constantly worried she was working too hard. She often wondered if her being pregnant reminded him of his wife and if he felt maybe helping her was a second chance to right the wrongs of his earlier years. She didn't know, but she was grateful to have him in her life. Having a father's guidance was something she needed.

When Kip was born, he'd taken an immediate interest in the boy and was not afraid to show his disapproval of Kip's father. Jess was sure his step-up or step-out attitude toward the man was why he had eventually left town. He wasn't comfortable being held accountable, and Grant Kendrick knew it. He had essentially run the man out of their lives, and she was grateful not to have him hanging around and causing problems. She and Kip were better off without him.

Grant seemed to want to have a place in the boy's life, and she was grateful since Kip would have no grandfathers around to look up to and be a mentor to him. He'd taught the boy a lot and been patient and kind with him. Now that he was gone, she knew a hole existed in Kip's life. She had tried to prepare him, but she hadn't done enough.

Now, she worried about her son more than ever. Not having a male figure in his life was tough on a boy of seven. Connor tried to be a friend to him, but somehow there wasn't a strong connection. Though he had always been kind to the boy, the two were too different. Connor was a bit formal and analytical. Kip was a free spirit who was creative and curious. It was part of the reason she'd never taken him up on his marriage proposal. If she was going to bring a man into their lives, it had to be a good fit in every way.

Which brought her thoughts back to Will. The other night in the tavern, when they'd talked about their partnership, she felt sure there was more to the situation than him needing someone he trusted to run the place. They would be tied together legally with a partnership, and it would take a lot to separate them. He wanted the connection. She just wasn't sure exactly why. But she felt something from him when he'd held her when she cried. What he wanted to do about it, she didn't know.

Becoming involved with Will was complicated, and bringing a child into it made it more so. Would Will have an interest in fathering the boy or not? If he didn't, it was a no-go. Connor may not have the most in common with the boy, but she knew he was interested in trying. She had no idea what Will's intentions might be. And what would she do about Connor? He didn't deserve to be cast aside just because Will had decided to come home after a decade away. And finally, how would any of it work? He lived in California, and her home was in Apalachicola. The situation seemed impossible, yet she couldn't keep her mind from going there. The connection between them was too real.

She decided she would maintain her wait-and-see attitude. Trying to figure anything out now was impossible. She would sign the paperwork for the partnership tomorrow and take it from there. After that was wrapped up, he had no reason to stay. What he did from there would tell her a lot.

Later, after she'd put Kip to bed and her mom was reading, she heard a text on her cell phone. It was Will.

Want to meet for a drink?

Sure, where do you want to meet?

How about the tavern? I'll buy.

Ha, very funny. Is Jimmy closing up now? It's after ten.

Already done. I helped so he could get home early. Just come to the front, and I'll let you in.

I have a key, remember?

LOL, okay. I'll be here.

She hopped in the shower, threw on some jeans, and told her mom she was heading back to the tavern for a little while. She didn't tell her why, and her mother didn't question her. Going back to the tavern at night wasn't unusual.

She felt a little unsure of herself. There was no other reason for Will to want her to come other than to spend time with her. That afternoon, they had covered all his questions about the tavern and its financials. And that he wanted to meet at the tavern meant he wanted to be alone with her. Her heart fluttered a little at the idea, and she realized how vulnerable she was to him. He could have her simply by asking, and she knew it. She needed to be strong until she knew exactly what was happening between them.

She decided to walk. It was only a few blocks, and she didn't want her car parked in front of the tavern at this hour. Even though it would not seem unusual for her car to be there to anyone passing by, with Will in town and staying there, she didn't want to stir up any rumors that might get back to Connor. He didn't deserve that.

The night air was cool and breezy, and she was glad for the light jacket she had grabbed going out the door. The passing storm had brought in a brief cold front, and she shivered a little as she wrapped her arms around herself. A misty fog was coming off the bay, and she knew it would be dense by morning. With it came the briny smell of the salt water and the feeling of dampness that would linger until midday tomorrow. The season was changing in Apalachicola.

When she got to the tavern, the lights were down low as they usually were after closing. As she approached, he opened the door, and she saw he had a bottle of whiskey and two glasses in his hand.

"Let's go upstairs where we can sit more comfortably," he said with a laugh as he locked the door behind her. "I've had enough of sitting on these barstools for one day."

She followed him to the stairs, where he stood aside and let her go ahead. When they reached the door, he reached around her to open it. When he did, he brushed against her, and the feel of him made her shudder.

The apartment was warm and cozy. She'd spent quite a lot of time up there in Grant's final days, but now it seemed so different with Grant gone and Will there. He set the whiskey bottle and glasses on the table and looked at her.

"I forgot to ask you what you wanted to drink. Is this okay, or do you want me to get you something else?" he asked.

"That's fine," she said with a laugh. "Have we made a whiskey drinker out of you, Will Kendrick?"

"I suppose so," he said, smiling. "I guess it's in my Irish blood."

He poured two glasses and motioned her over to the couch. They were quiet for a moment as they sipped, each collecting their thoughts.

"So," he said, "tomorrow's the big day."

"Yep," she said. "Are you having second thoughts?"

"Not at all, are you?"

"I'm not the one who called this meeting," she said with a smile.

"I just wanted to make sure you were comfortable and not feeling pressured or overwhelmed," he said as he eyed her.

"No, I don't feel that way at all. I still don't quite understand why you want to do this. Now I'm going to be hard to get rid of," she laughed.

"Who says I want to get rid of you?" he said, his tone a little more serious than she expected.

She looked over at him, and their eyes locked. He was sitting a little sideways, somewhat facing her with his arm on the back of the sofa. As they looked at one another, he reached over and pushed a strand of hair away from her face. His eyes traveled lazily over her features and then settled back on her eyes, and he had a slight smile that disarmed her. She felt paralyzed by the intimacy of the moment.

"How did I not notice what a beautiful woman you were turning into when we were in school together?" he said wistfully.

She blushed and looked away. His compliment made her feel shy and awkward, and she didn't know what to say. She glanced at the ceiling and then back at him, holding his gaze for a moment.

"I think you must have been too busy dating cheerleaders," she said, finally, a little sarcastically.

He thought about that, then let the comment pass. Looking back, she was right. He seemed to have left her behind when they'd gotten to high school. So much so that he hadn't even known when her father had walked out on them. Somehow, he hadn't seen her the way he did now. He guessed it was the familiarity between them, but he sensed from her comment it had hurt her. Looking at her now, he felt like a fool and an ungrateful bastard.

Their silence became uncomfortable, so Will tried to shift the conversation.

"So we are meeting at Connor's office at ten tomorrow morning?"

"Yes," she said as she glanced at her watch. "I better get going. It's getting late, and I have to get up early with Kip in the morning."

His heart sank. He'd been yearning for some alone time with her, if for no other reason than to talk to her. There was something about her that soothed his soul. He started to ask her to stay but thought better of it. If she felt uncomfortable and wanted to go, he should let her.

"Okay, where are you parked?"

"I walked. It's only a few blocks," she said.

"Come on," he said, "I'll walk you home."

CHAPTER NINE

Onnor sat in the conference room, arranging the paperwork for signatures before the ten o'clock meeting. While he was happy for Jess, something about the arrangement made him uncomfortable. In his opinion, it was far too generous and certainly not what he would recommend to a client. But Will could not be persuaded to offer her less.

Connor knew it was better for the town that Will decided not to shutter the place and sell the real estate. The old tavern had been at the heart of the community for a long time. It would be a blow to the people of Apalachicola, both young and old, but he wondered a bit about his motives. He'd like to think Will was doing it for the good of the community, but Connor suspected it was way more complicated than that.

He had long suspected Jess's reluctance to marry was born from her attachment to someone else. While Connor knew it was not Kip's father, he'd never had an idea of who it might be, at least not until now. She had always talked fondly about Will, and he knew they were childhood friends, but he'd never suspected it was him. But she had been different since Will had returned to Apalachicola. The two had been spending a lot of time together with the service, repast, and transition with the tavern. Connor hadn't seen much of her, but he'd felt a shift.

Losing her was something he didn't care to think about. He'd spent too many years trying to make her his, and he longed for a family of his own. Conner would welcome her and the boy into his life permanently if she would agree to a marriage, but he hadn't convinced her so far. He knew he would make a good husband, and though the boy seemed disinterested in him, he felt he could at least be a consistent factor in his life and a good role model. He'd tried to grow closer to him, but their relationship had always seemed awkward and forced. It bothered Jess, he could tell, but nothing he did ever appeared to make a difference.

Connor had grown up in a well-to-do family of lawyers, and while he could describe his relationship with his father as close, he couldn't exactly call it warm. There was a formality between them, and they were more like good friends than father and son. Connor had done what was expected of him, which seemed most important to his father. With his exceptional educational pedigree, he could have practiced law with any large firm in the South. Instead, he had come home to practice with his father and uncle for a few years and to continue the family practice after they retired. Though his parents had mapped out his life, he wasn't unhappy. He just wanted a wife and kids to complete the picture.

Connor realized that he probably seemed boring compared to Will and his exciting life in California. But with the boring part, he felt he could offer her stability and security. She would never have to worry about him having a wandering eye or gambling away the family fortune. If Connor was anything, he was predictable and consistent. He hoped that would appeal to her sensibilities at some point.

But one thing he knew about Jess was that she had never

longed for the status quo. She was always reaching to accomplish the next great thing, and she had a natural talent as a businesswoman. She would never be content to put on the apron and stay at home, and if he were honest, his vision of a wife was precisely that. He guessed it was because his mother had never worked. Though she was educated and held a law degree herself, she'd been content to be the wife of a prominent lawyer and fill her time with caring for her home and family and attending social events.

Still, his deep feelings for Jess could not be denied. She was a stunningly beautiful woman, but it was much more than that. To him, it was her inner beauty that was the most attractive. Jess had a big heart and a warm, genuine nature. She was also remarkably transparent, which he appreciated in a woman. He never had to guess what was on her mind. He knew if he asked her directly about the situation with Will, she would be honest with him. He just wasn't sure he was ready to hear it.

"ANOTHER WEEK?" Kate said, clearly exasperated. "What are you doing about your projects, Will? You've already been gone for weeks."

"My current project is wrapping up, and I've been able to work on any loose ends from here. I've told Tony to put my availability on hold, but keep me apprised of what may be coming down the pipeline. If something big comes up, I can work from here," he said, annoyed by her mothering demeanor.

"Well, I can't imagine what's keeping you there. Certainly, you could handle these things from here."

"It's not as simple as that, Kate, and I owe it to my father to do this right," he said, his annoyance growing. "I'm taking on a partner in the tavern, and I need to get that settled while I'm here."

"A partner? I thought you were going to shut the place down. Why are you taking on a partner?"

"I've changed my mind. The tavern meant a lot to my father and a great deal to this community. I think it should remain open, and I can't manage it from California. The woman I'm taking on knows the tavern inside and out and has been running it for a while."

"The woman? Who is she, Will?" Kate said, her voice full of suspicion.

"She's a childhood friend and someone I trust implicitly."

"You're not rekindling any old flames out there, are you?" she said with a shallow laugh.

"I've got to go, Kate. I have a meeting in twenty minutes. I'll call you later," Will said as he hung up the phone. He'd had enough of that conversation.

Being back in Apalachicola had changed him. He could feel the pretentiousness of Hollywood slipping away and the realness of the little town creeping back in. His perspective on life was changing, and even though it was a shock to his soul, he welcomed it. His conversations with Kate seemed to accentuate that, and he found himself thinking about her less and less. He also seemed to feel more relaxed without her and knew that, regardless of his current circumstances, that needed to be addressed. He guessed they had been together too long for him to remember what life felt like without her.

Now, he was potentially headed into something he knew would change everything. Though it should have unsettled him, he felt differently about it. It felt like a new beginning, and he welcomed it. What it meant for him and Jess in the long run, he didn't know, but it had somehow snapped his life into focus in a way he hadn't expected.

He looked at his watch and realized he had time to walk to Connor's office. It would do him good and give him a chance to blow off the steam from his conversation with Kate. He wanted to be in a good mood when they signed the papers, and he didn't want any overflow from the morning casting any doubt in Jess's mind.

He hadn't been able to shake the after-effects of their drink together the evening before. He had lost himself in her for a moment, and she'd seemed uncomfortable with it. He didn't know what to think about that, and it had been on his mind since he'd woken up that morning. Was he running headlong into something that was going nowhere?

As he stepped out onto the sidewalk, he shoved his hands in his pockets and turned up his collar. There was a brisk, cool wind coming off the bay and whistling through the streets of Apalach, and he was reminded of the harsh winter mornings out on the bay with his father harvesting oysters. It was a cold he hadn't experienced much in the last decade. Cold on the West Coast, even in the mountains of Colorado and Montana, where he often visited, didn't seep through to his bones as it did in Apalach. He was thankful for it, though. It seemed to clear his mind and heighten his senses immediately—something he needed.

He'd wanted to go to Connor's office with Jess, but she had declined. Mornings before ten a.m. were busy for her getting Kip off to school, and her day started. He knew she could have accommodated him if she wanted to, but he respected her decision to arrive at Connor's office alone. He suspected it had a lot to do with her relationship with Connor, which was something he had yet to contemplate. From his conversation with the lawyer, it seemed she was reluctant to commit. Would she feel the same about him if Will tried to move forward with her? After the night before, he wasn't sure.

When he arrived, he didn't see her car and experienced a moment of fear that maybe she had changed her mind. As the secretary greeted him and led him back to the conference room, he was relieved to hear her chatting with Connor, and his spirit lifted when he thought he heard happiness in her voice. He hadn't realized until then how much he had riding on her agreeing to the arrangement. He couldn't imagine how he would have felt if she'd backed out.

"Hello, everyone," he said as he entered the room.

Jess was sitting close to Connor, and they were clearly involved in an intimate conversation. She turned to him, smiling, and Will had a moment of unfamiliar jealousy. They knew each other better than she and Will did and had a history different from his childhood friendship with her. He couldn't help but feel like the third wheel as he sat down at the table.

He looked at her and smiled, but she seemed businesslike and detached. He suspected she didn't want to show too much familiarity in front of Connor. He suddenly realized how complicated things were between the three of them. Maybe letting his heart get too far ahead of his practical nature had been a mistake. She was unavailable, and the person she was involved with was his lawyer. Besides that, Connor was a nice guy. Will needed to put everything between him and Jess in its proper perspective. It was unlikely they could ever make it work between them, and who was he to try to upset the status quo? Getting between her and Connor and causing problems for them was selfish and inconsiderate. He needed to leave it alone and head back to California. His life was there, not in Apalachicola.

Connor passed the papers around, and as they signed, he kept his attention on the documents. It was time their relationship became more businesslike, he guessed. If they were going to make the partnership work, he couldn't let any misplaced feelings get in the way.

"Well, guys, that's it. You're officially partners," Connor said as he gathered up the documents, smiling at them both.

Will stood and extended his hand across the table to Jess. When she took it, the feel of her warm skin and the delicate bone structure of her hand sent a ripple through him, and he was reluctant to let go. When she smiled at him, he felt his heart constrict a little. Moving on from the idea of being with her wouldn't be easy.

He gathered his jacket, shook hands with Connor, and thanked him as he turned to go. He needed some fresh air and was grateful he had walked there alone and not together. He needed some time to process the myriad of feelings that had come over him since the day had begun.

He decided not to go straight back to the tavern and instead walk down to the waterfront. The coolness of the morning was dissipating, and the misty fog was clearing along with it. Will could see blue skies emerging, and it was turning into a warm, pleasant day in Apalach. He was thankful for it. He didn't need any gloomy weather to add to his mood. As he took up residence on his familiar bench, the smell of the bay and the breeze off the water seemed to help get himself in check. He hadn't realized how emotional the events of the morning had made him.

As he sat, watching the activity on the river as its waters spilled into Apalachicola Bay, he let the memories of his father come in. For years, he had squeezed his mind shut each time he thought about him. Now, some of the pain was gone, and he could remember things about his father that brought a smile to his face. He guessed he had Jess to thank for that.

CHAPTER TEN

J ess left Connors's office and headed to the tavern. She was
very eager to see Will. She hadn't had a chance to talk to
him while they were signing the paperwork, and his odd
mood struck her. He seemed somewhat sullen and withdrawn, which was in contrast to his mood lately. She wondered
what had him so preoccupied and hoped it had nothing to do
with her or their partnership. He had seemed relaxed the night
before but very uptight at the closing.

She'd decided to walk that morning rather than take her car
and was surprised to see Will had done the same. She hadn't
realized it until she'd looked through the window and watched
him go. She would have walked back to the tavern with him if
he hadn't left so quickly. It would have been a good chance for
them to talk.

She honestly didn't know where things would go with Will
now that they were tied together with the partnership. She'd
been surprised when Connor had gone over the agreement with
her and pointed out her generous exit clause. When she'd asked
if Will had requested such an easy out for himself, Connor told
her he hadn't. She didn't understand any of it.

As she turned the corner to the tavern, she saw Will sitting on a bench by the water. She stopped for a moment, contemplating whether or not she should approach him. Maybe he wanted to be alone. After his demeanor this morning, she couldn't gauge his mood. She decided to check on him. Perhaps something else was going on with him that had nothing to do with her.

"Hey," she said as she touched his shoulder. She saw him flinch a little as if she had roused him out of deep thought, then look up over his shoulder at her.

"Hey," he said softly, then turned toward the water again.

She moved around the bench and sat beside him, neither speaking for a few minutes.

"Are you okay?" she asked as she studied his profile.

"Yeah," he said. "I just have a lot on my mind."

Her heart clenched as her eyes raked over his features. He looked handsome with his collar turned up against the breeze and his features stoic as he squinted at the bright reflections off the bay.

"Anything you want to talk about?" she asked.

"Not really," he said but offered nothing more.

"Hey, listen," she said, looking to change the subject. "Kip is out of school tomorrow, and it's supposed to be a warm day. I was thinking about taking him over to St. George Island. I've got Jimmy covering the tavern. Do you want to come with us? I think you could use a break."

He turned to look at her for the first time since she sat down, his eyes catching hers with a look she couldn't gauge, and he paused for a moment before answering her.

"Sure," he said, finally. "That would be nice. I haven't been over there since we were kids."

She smiled at him, and his expression softened, but it was easy to see that whatever was on his mind was troubling him to the core.

~

As Will navigated the old truck over the Franklin Boulevard bridge that separated Apalachicola Bay from St. George Sound, he felt his mood lift. The beauty of the water, with the bright sun dancing off the ripples, captivated him in a way he hadn't experienced in a long time. California was a beautiful place, but it was hard to see past the hustle and hurry of LA with its hordes of people. There was a quiet, pristine beauty about the islands and waters around Apalachicola that touched a part of him he had forgotten existed.

He had suggested taking his father's old truck. It needed to be run, and aside from the ease of transporting their beach necessities, Kip seemed excited about riding in it. Now perched between them on the bench seat, he could hardly keep still. Will watched as he sat up straighter to peer out the window and over the dash as they crossed the bridge. He understood his excitement. As a boy, crossing the bridges and causeways around Apalach had fascinated him, too.

"So, Mr. Kendrick was your dad?" he asked Will as they exited the bridge onto the island,

"Yes," Will answered, "he was."

"Wow," Kip said. "He was so cool. You were so lucky to have a dad like him."

"Really?" Will said with a smile. "You thought my dad was cool?"

"Yeah, he used to let me help him fix things and take me fishing."

Will looked over at Jess, who was gazing out the window with a slight smile across her lips. He couldn't quite read her expression with her sunglasses on, but something told him she was paying close attention to their conversation.

"I miss him," Kip said, as his expression clouded. Jess put her arm around the boy and pulled him to her. She tussled his hair a little as she let out a sigh.

"I do, too, buddy," she said softly.

They were quiet momentarily, trying to let the emotions pass, especially Will. He'd had no idea the boy had been so close to his father, and he couldn't help but feel a pang of envy. His boyhood memories of his father didn't include things like that.

"Which way do you want to go?" Will asked as he approached the road that ran along the beach.

"Take a right," Jess said. "There's a beach walk-over down this way, and there is never anyone there."

As Will parked on the sandy shoulder and the three got out, Kip ran up the hill and started over the walkover.

"Kip, wait!" Jess called to him.

"You go ahead," Will said. "I'll grab everything."

"Are you sure?" she asked as she watched Kip disappear over the dunes.

"Yes," he said. "I'll be down there in a minute."

Will watched as she hurried after the boy. When he got to the beach carrying the chairs and Jess's beach bag, he saw a small pile of clothes where they had shed their shorts and T-shirts. They were chasing each other around in the shallow surf, and he smiled when he saw them go down, giggling and holding on to one another. The sight and sounds of them struck a chord in him, and it didn't take much for him to imagine having a place in their lives.

He tried not to stare at her from behind his sunglasses as she made her way up from the water. Her dark hair, wet from the sea, was pushed back away from her face, accentuating the delicate and beautiful bone structure of her face. Her smile was relaxed and absent of the hint of seriousness she always seemed to carry with her. Though there were remnants of the little tomboy he had once known, she was now a very beautiful woman, and as much as he tried, he couldn't tear his eyes away from her.

She seemed to sense his eyes upon her and grabbed a towel to cover herself as she sat down. She wiped the salt water from her face and turned to look at him.

"Hasn't changed much, has it?" she said as she surveyed the coastline.

"Hardly at all," he said. "There are a few more houses, but it's still pristine here. Not like California."

"I don't know how you live in LA, Will. All the people and the crime? Do you ever get tired of it all?" She looked at him, but he seemed lost in his thoughts.

Finally, he turned to her. "Yes, I do...I am, especially since I've been back here. Being home has been eye-opening."

She didn't question him. He suspected she knew what he meant. The next obvious question from her should have been how much longer he planned to stay, but it didn't come. He was glad about it. He didn't have an answer.

Yesterday, after they had finished signing the paperwork, he had been resolute in his decision to go back to California and put any thoughts of a relationship with her out of his mind. It had only taken her hand on his shoulder and their quiet conversation on the bench to put him right back where he'd been. Now, being there with her and the boy, he was rationalizing again, yet the situation was no less complicated than it had been the day before.

"So this partnership is still what you want?" she asked softly as she gazed over the blue water.

"Yes, of course," he said. "Why would you ask me that?"

"I don't know. Yesterday, you seemed a little...*something*. If you've changed your mind, it's okay."

"Absolutely not," he said as he turned to look at her. He reached for her hand and squeezed it. "I want this to work, Jess.

And besides, we've already signed. I'm afraid you're stuck with me."

Just then, Kip ran up and rummaged through Jess's beach bag. "Want play catch, Mr. Kendrick?" he said as he retrieved a football from the bag and tossed it to Will.

"Sure, Sport, take off down the beach, and I'll hit you with a long pass."

As Kip took off running, Will turned to Jess. "Can't he just call me Will?" he asked.

"No, it's too informal. It's not how I've taught him," she said.

"But don't you think it's hard for him to call me that after his relationship with my dad?"

She thought about that briefly as Will threw the football down the beach. "Okay, how about Mr. Will?" she asked.

"Jess, that makes me sound like a cartoon character. Can't it just be Will? Can we make an exception under the circumstances?"

As Kip came running back by, he tossed the ball to Will, then circled around, taking off down the beach again.

"Okay," she said with a frown, "I guess it's all right, just this once."

Will smiled at her. "You're doing a great job with him, Jess. He's a great kid, and he handles himself very well. Don't worry so much."

As THE OLD truck headed back west over the causeway, the sun was setting and lighting up the sky in a shade of orange that Will didn't think he had ever seen before. Of course, he had as a boy, but he'd somehow forgotten how beautiful and intense the sunsets were on the Forgotten Coast. The three of them were quiet, and when Will glanced over, Kip was leaning into his mother, trying to stay awake. Suddenly, he had some vague memory of his mother, but it was fleeting, and he couldn't hold on to it.

By the time they got to Jess's house, Kip was asleep, and as she tried to get him out of the truck without waking him, Will saw her struggle.

"Let me get him," he said softly, taking the boy from her. He followed her up the walk and into the house, where she led him down a long hallway to the boy's room. She motioned Will to the bed, where he carefully laid the boy down. Kip rolled over and was instantly asleep again.

They quietly left the room, and when they returned to the porch, Will could see the fatigue in Jess's eyes. She wrapped her arms around herself as the night air brought a chill, and the day's warmth dissipated.

"Thanks for a great day," he said to her. "You were right; I needed a break."

"Well, I'm glad you got one, Will Kendrick," she said, smiling up at him.

"I'll see you tomorrow?" he asked.

"Yes, I'll be working a double since Jimmy worked today. I'll be at the tavern all day."

"I'll help," he said as he smiled at her.

"Well, then, you better get your rest," she said with a chuckle as she started to go. When she reached the door, she turned. "Thanks for being so good with Kip. He doesn't have a lot of men in his life he can look up to. I appreciate you doing boy things with him today. I know it doesn't seem like much, but it's important."

Will nodded, smiled at her, and turned to go. As he left, he could feel her eyes upon him, and he resisted the urge to turn and look at her one last time. He didn't want the image of her standing there in his mind. He was already going to have a hard enough time falling asleep.

He pulled the old truck through the gate behind the tavern,

turned off the key, and sat for a moment. The level of uncertainty he felt threatened to overwhelm him, and he needed a moment to collect himself. The day had only heightened his feelings for her and now for the boy. He had vivid memories of being seven years old and envying other boys who had active fathers in their lives. The irony of Kip's comments about his dad haunted him and toyed with his emotions. Now, he longed to fill the gap in the boys' life and finish what his father had started. He was getting a second chance to frame things differently and to change long-held beliefs. He knew fate was playing with him, but he couldn't help but let it.

He realized then he wasn't going back to California any time soon. He didn't want to, and he felt in control of his destiny for the first time in a long time. He was no longer ruled by the reality he'd formed as a child and could finally let go of some of the hurt and disappointment of feeling unloved and abandoned. Instead, those feelings were being replaced by compassion and understanding. Yes, his father was a complicated man, but so was he.

As he sat listening to the ticking of the old engine cooling down and taking in the smells and feel of the old truck, he let his mind wander through forgotten memories of his boyhood. He remembered running down the beach with the wind whipping around his face. The feeling of absolute freedom and unbridled joy as his mother chased after him. He heard her calling his name and laughing and her footsteps falling on the sand behind him. Then, in his mind's eye, he saw his father scoop him up and nuzzle his face, his scratchy beard making him wince. He let the tears come. It was the only concrete memory of his mother he'd ever had.

CHAPTER ELEVEN

Will tapped lightly on the screen door and listened. He hadn't called to let her know he was coming and hoped he hadn't overstepped his bounds by showing up unannounced. She stopped and smiled through the screen door before opening it. It was as though the clock had stopped decades ago. Penny hadn't changed at all in the years since he'd seen her, other than the absence of her long brown hair.

She didn't say anything as she opened the door and held out a hand to him. When he stepped inside, she hooked her arm through his and walked him out to the garden off the back of the kitchen.

The place was quintessentially her. He could tell the little courtyard served as her sanctuary with its potting bench in the corner and pretty white wicker furniture. The abundant flowers spilling out of their beds and cascading down their pots gave the place a magical feel, and Will could see the love and care she put into it.

"Come sit with me, Will," she said. "I want to hear all about your life in California."

Will chuckled. "I'm afraid I'll bore you. LA is not as exciting as it's cracked up to be."

"I don't know about that. I hear you are involved in movie-making or something like that?" she asked.

"Yes," he said, "as a screenwriter. It sounds glamorous, but it's not. I enjoy the work, though, and I can control my time, so it suits me."

"Well, you always did enjoy telling a story," she laughed. Her eyes misted over for a moment, and he could tell she was remembering something from a long time ago.

"How are you, Penny?" Will asked quietly. "Are you okay? Are you holding up all right?"

"I'm doing okay," she said, nodding. "I'm getting through the treatments. Only a few more to go, and then we will see how things go from there. Thank goodness for Sawyer. He's been so strong and optimistic. I couldn't make it without him."

They were quiet again, the silence between them not at all uncomfortable.

"So I hear you and Jess are partners in the tavern now?" she asked.

"Yes, we are. She's put so much of herself into that old place, and I can't run it from California, so it seemed the right thing to do. I think my dad would approve, and she deserves it for all she did for him. She knows what she's doing, too. She's one hell of an operator."

Penny smiled. "You two always made a great pair, like peas in a pod, as I remember. Always off on some adventure."

Will chuckled and nodded.

"Any chance of anything else brewing between you two?" Penny asked, her voice hopeful.

Will didn't answer immediately as he thought about how best to explain. "That's a little complicated," he said, finally.

"Matters of the heart usually are," she said, "but good things are worth the trouble. You'll figure it out."

Will looked at her momentarily as he thought about what he wanted to say next. "Penny," he asked finally, "what can you tell me about my mother?"

He saw her visibly stiffen, and she cleared her throat before answering.

"What is it that you want to know, Will?"

"I want to know what happened to her. Nobody ever told me," he said, feeling the emotion rise in his throat.

She let out a long sigh. "Perhaps now is not the time for that conversation, Will. You've just lost your dad and are still sorting through those emotions."

"I'm almost thirty-five years old, Penny, and I have no idea how my mother left this earth over three decades ago. Why won't anyone talk to me about it?"

Penny looked down at her hands. "It's a hard thing to talk about. Everyone loved her, and we all felt we should have done more."

"More what?" he asked.

"More to help her," she said, "more to get her well."

"She was sick?" he asked

"Yes, she was, but probably not in the way you're thinking."

"What do you mean?" he said. "I'm not following you."

Penny sighed again. "She was emotionally unwell, Will, and there weren't many resources to help her. After she had you, she became depressed, and what we all thought would pass with time never did. Eventually, she could endure it no longer."

"I'm still not understanding, Penny. What *happened* to her?"

Penny looked at him for a long moment, then dropped her gaze.

"She took her own life, Will," she said as her eyes found his again. "I'm so sorry, honey."

Will felt the shock ripple through him as his heart tried to absorb what his ears had just heard. As often as he'd wondered, the idea that she had committed suicide had never entered his realm of thinking.

He abruptly stood and walked to the other side of the garden, where he stood with his back to her, his hands on his hips.

"So he blamed me," he said finally.

"What?" she asked. "Oh no, Will, he didn't..."

"Yes, he did," he said as he whirled around to face her. "You said it yourself. She was fine until she had me."

"Will, it was nobody's fault, especially not yours."

"I could never figure out why he was so bitter toward me. Now I know. Now it makes sense," he said as he sat down hard in the chair again.

"Honey, he loved you and your mother very much. He was devastated when he lost her. He just closed himself off to everyone and everything. It was the only way he could cope."

The two were quiet for a while, and Will was keenly aware of the birds chirping and the cicadas buzzing. The cool morning was dissipating, and the heat that had moved in over the last few days was settling in. He felt the sweat on the back of his neck.

"At least I know now. As hard as it is, at least I don't have to wonder anymore."

He stopped for a moment and put his head down to collect himself. "Thank you, Penny, for being honest with me and being there for me when I was a kid. You and Sawyer were always kind to me."

"I would have done anything for you and your mother, Will," Penny said as the tears rolled down her cheeks. "I'm sorry. I feel like I failed you all."

Will went to sit beside her on the little wicker couch. He put his arm around her and pulled her to him. "You did a lot more than you know, Penny, more than you'll ever realize."

He choked back his own tears as the two sat there for what

seemed like an eternity. Though the emotions were raw, they had clarity. That was a first for him in a while.

~

WILL TOOK his time walking back to the tavern. He needed some time alone. He was filled with an overwhelming sadness, not just for himself and the childhood he had, but for his mother and father too. What a true tragedy they had lived through, and even as a writer, he didn't think he could ever imagine something so intensely sad. They had all suffered in individual ways that no one else could ever understand.

He had a deep longing to go back in time like nothing he had ever experienced. It all seemed so senseless, and his heart begged to fix it even though his head knew it was impossible. Even so, he could not shake the desire. He was unsure if he ever would.

Will never dreamed, at the age of thirty-five, he would come face to face in such a way with his life as a kid and a teenager. It was amazing, he thought, how children could filter out some of the harshest realities and only let the tips of the struggles seep in. He'd known he'd had a lonely childhood with his distant father but hadn't had any idea of the depths of his father's anguish.

He realized then how important Jess had been to his young life. Without her, he would have had very little happiness as a child. She always seemed to know, even now after all the years, what he needed. His mind flooded with a thousand scenes between them as children, her always trying to make him happy and carry him along on new adventures. Even after he had abandoned her as a teenager and left Apalachicola without so much as a goodbye, she was still doing it.

Will slipped into the back of the tavern unnoticed and went up to the apartment. He couldn't face her at the moment, and if she laid eyes on him, she would know something was very wrong. It had always been her gift to him — sensing his pain and giving him some salvation from it. His heart couldn't endure it right now.

IT WAS a few minutes before opening, and Jess had yet to see Will. She thought she'd heard him coming through the back door earlier but couldn't be sure. It might have been Loretta. She had hoped they would have a few minutes alone before the crush of Saturday in the tavern set in, but as she unlocked the front door, she knew that chance was lost.

She kept herself busy cleaning and helping Loretta prepare the kitchen for the day's business. Still, she couldn't help but keep a watchful eye on the stairs. She wanted him to spend the day with her as he had promised. They'd had a good day before at the beach with Kip, and she didn't want them to lose any momentum.

By two in the afternoon, after the lunch hour had passed, there was still no sign of him. She had to admit the disappointment ran deep. She asked Loretta if she had seen him, and she said she had. They had passed in the hallway that morning as he came in. Jess couldn't help but feel a little angry at him. He had always been a little moody, even as a child, but she was having a hard time keeping up with him lately. When they were kids, she'd only needed to drag him off on some adventure. Now, she felt perplexed and somewhat exhausted by his ever-changing temperament.

She was stooped down, retrieving bar napkins from a cabinet, when she felt a hand on her back. When she realized it was Will and looked up at him, she knew something was wrong. She could see it in his eyes. He looked tired and sad.

"Hey," she said, her eyes searching his for some clue as to what might be going on.

"Hey," he said. "Sorry, I'm late getting down here. I got tied up with some work stuff."

She knew he wasn't telling her the truth, but she didn't press him. Whatever it was, she could tell it was something of importance. He looked like he was carrying the weight of the world on his shoulders.

"No worries," she said with a smile. "It was a pretty light lunch hour for a Saturday. Loretta and I got through it just fine. Why don't you just sit and keep me company while I do a little restocking for the evening? There's not much else to do right now."

"Okay," he said as he walked around the bar and slid up on one of the barstools. "You're sure there is nothing else you need me to do? I feel bad for letting you down earlier."

"No, there's nothing," she said as she studied him. "What's been going on, Will Kendrick? You seem a little down."

"Nothing," he said as he looked away. He started to say something, but the front door opened, and a man in a broad-brimmed hat entered, went straight to the bar stool next to Will, removed his hat, and sat down.

"Well, hello, Jess," he said with a broad smile.

"Hello, Father Hudson," she said, smiling back at him. "You remember Will."

She said it matter-of-factly, which Will took to mean they had met before, but he couldn't place the man. Upon a second, closer look, he realized it was the preacher who had performed his father's graveside service.

"The usual Father?" she asked as she retrieved a high-ball glass off the back bar.

"Why yes, Jess, thank you," he said as he turned toward Will. "How are you, son? Are you getting along all right?"

Jess poured the preacher a healthy portion of whiskey and

set it before him. Something seemed to pass between them, and she moved down the bar to converse with another customer who had just arrived.

"Yes, I'm doing okay. It's been a hard couple of weeks, but I'm getting through it." Will said, not sure why he felt compelled to be so frank.

"You know, son," the preacher said as he paused to sip his whiskey, "it's okay to take things in a little at a time. Some things are damn hard to accept. The good Lord doesn't expect us to always be strong."

Will was silent for a moment as he thought about what the preacher had said. "Penny told you," he said quietly. "She told you I asked her about my mother."

"She did," he said. "It broke her heart, and she's worried about you." He stared at his glass momentarily as he spun it slowly on the bar. "I reckon nobody had the heart to tell you along the way, and now, here you are, a grown man, and just finding out. I know it can't be easy."

"No, it's not. It was…unexpected. But it made a lot of other things make sense for me."

"Well, don't take too much into your heart right now. Let things settle on your soul a bit. You'll sort things out over time."

Jess passed by and set a glass of whiskey before Will but said nothing. The two men sat for a while, not talking, just sipping.

"It's hard not to feel betrayed," Will said, finally, "when you realize everyone knew but you."

The preacher thought for a moment, then nodded. "I can see how you would feel that way," he said. "Sometimes folks have the best intentions trying to save someone from hurt but end up hurting them all the same. You were just a child, Will. I'm sure your father was only trying to protect you."

Will wrapped both hands around his glass and stared at it for a moment, trying to sort out his feelings. A long moment of silence passed between them.

"I can't help but feel he blamed me for it," Will said finally as he felt the emotions start to take hold of him. He stopped for a moment to settle himself. "He seemed pretty bitter towards me," he continued. "I could never figure out why, but now it makes sense. Penny said my mother was well before I was born. It was only after she had me that she got so sick."

Father Hudson was quiet for a minute as he thought about what he wanted to say and chose his words carefully. "Will, I knew your father well. He was a good man, and he loved you. But he was only a man, flawed and incomplete. Grief has a way of dropping a veil over everything else, and sometimes, it takes a while to see clearly again. Unfortunately, time keeps ticking by, and the hurts can just get deeper. He didn't blame you, son. He blamed himself."

CHAPTER TWELVE

P enny sat amongst her flowers, listening to the distant thunder over the bay as an unseasonable afternoon rainstorm threatened to roll in. The air was thick with humidity, and even though the cool winds of the gust front were rippling through her garden, she felt warm and sticky.

She'd just gotten up from her nap but felt no less tired than when she'd laid down. The treatments were getting harder for sure, but it was the heaviness of her heart that was wearing on her. The emotion of the morning had been almost too much to bear, and if it hadn't been for Father Hudson, she might have broken down completely.

When Will had come to see her that morning, she was elated to see the boy she'd once known had grown into a striking young man. He was handsome and tall, but her heart had nearly imploded when he'd stepped through her door. *My God, he looks just like her.*

As the memories of her came rushing in, she felt a bit weak. It had been some time since she had allowed herself to think about Anna in such detail. For years, they had all suppressed the memory of her and the circumstances surrounding her death.

And, while Grant had shielded the boy from knowing the truth about his mother, she'd often wondered when it would rear its ugly head. When she saw Will through the screen door, she had an eerie feeling that the time had come and that things would never be the same. Not for him or any of them that were left.

Anna Kendrick was a fresh-faced beauty who seemed to capture the attention of almost everyone around her. But it was her childlike innocence that attracted everyone to her. She seemed unspoiled by the world's harsh realities, having grown up in Panacea, a tiny coastal town along Dickerson Bay. She was a breath of fresh air to the little town, and everyone thought her naïveté was incredibly charming. They all smiled when they discovered that to her, coming to Apalachicola from Panacea was like coming to the big city.

It was why Grant Kendrick had been completely swept off his feet the moment he saw her. Though she was more than a decade and a half younger than he, her presence seemed to consume him. To him, she was a perfection he longed to possess. To her, he was someone to look up to and to look after her.

For Penny, when Anna arrived in Apalachicola and dropped into all their lives, it was as though she had always been there. The two became as close as sisters when Grant hired her at the tavern. Anna had been raised in a family of boys, the only girl among the four siblings. As an only child, Penny had dreamed of having a sister her entire life.

They were decidedly kindred spirits. They were connected on a level different from any relationship Penny had ever known. If she'd believed in such things, she might have thought they'd known each other in a past life.

They shared everything, including their job at the tavern. Grant didn't need two full-time employees, so they worked part-time, trading off shifts and sometimes working together, one off the clock, to be together. When Anna needed a place to live, Penny invited her to share the cottage behind her parents' home. It was tiny, but the two managed to make it work.

The romance between Grant and Anna was intense and powerful, and he wasted little time making her his. In her mind's eye, Penny could still see Anna's smile as she gazed up at him in the sanctuary of Holy Cross Church the day they married. Though it all happened so quickly, it was as though it was meant to be, and they all seemed powerless to stop it. Not that any of them wanted to.

Penny and Sawyer had known each other their entire lives, and she had always expected they would marry. She had never known any man other than him, and it had never occurred to her that things would be any different. When her parents felt the time was right, they allowed her to marry, and they wed in the same church as Anna and Grant just months later. It all seemed so natural and perfect, and the four became inseparable. Looking back, Penny knew it had been a time of innocence. What would come later would change everything.

WILL SAT at the bar long after Father Hudson had said his goodbyes. It was a remarkably slow night at the tavern as the thunderstorms swept through, clearing the streets of tourists and locals alike. By eight-thirty, the bar was empty, and even though they were supposed to be open until ten o'clock, they contemplated shutting the place down early.

Jess was quiet as she cleaned the empty glasses and wiped down the bar top. She knew something had happened by the intenseness of the conversation between Father Hudson and Will. She wasn't sure what it was, but she had some ideas. Her heart went out to him if it was what she thought it was. She knew he must be devastated if the decades-long secret had finally found its way to his ears. She wanted to ask him about it but was afraid of stirring up his emotions and didn't want to intrude on his thoughts. She'd been sworn to secrecy as a child as everyone around the boy had sought to protect him from the terrible truth. She hadn't realized until their conversation some days before that no one had ever gotten around to telling him.

Will, his head heavy from the whiskey and the emotion of the day, didn't have the energy to make small talk, so he and Jess were silent. He wanted to talk to her about it but somehow couldn't find a way to start the conversation without bolts of anticipated pain echoing through his soul. *Had she known? Had everyone known?*

"It's been a long day," she said when she could endure the silence no longer. "Why don't you head up to bed? I'll finish up here."

He looked up at her and saw the sympathetic look in her eyes. He felt guilty. She was always making things easy for him.

"I was supposed to help you today. I'm sorry. Let me at least wash some glasses or something. You must be tired," he said as he started to get up off the bar stool.

"It's okay, Will. I'm mostly done. I'll be all finished in a few minutes. Then I'll close things up. You just get some rest, and I'll see you tomorrow." She went back to her work, leaving no room for him to argue with her.

He looked at her for a long moment, then reluctantly slid off the barstool and started to go. When he got to the end of the bar, he stopped and turned to her.

"I've never told you how sorry I am for abandoning you all these years," he said. "You always made things good for me, and without you in my life, I don't know where I would have been. Thank you for always being there for me, Jess, and I'm sorry I've failed at doing the same for you."

His confession stunned her, and nothing came out when she opened her mouth to speak. Instead, she went to him, and the two looked at each other face-to-face for a long moment.

Finally, she reached for his hand, and when she did, he suddenly pulled her to him, wrapping his arms around her. They stood that way for a while as he pressed into her and cradled her head against his chest. The feel of him threatened to overtake her, so she clung to him, lost in a moment where all her desires were suddenly manifested.

Slowly, he untangled himself from her and looked at her, his eyes misty and full of emotion. He didn't speak but slowly backed away from her and reached out to wipe a tear from her cheek that she hadn't even realized was there. Then he turned to go. She closed her eyes as she heard his footsteps on the stairs, and her heart broke into a million pieces when she heard his door close softly at the top of the stairs.

WILL LAY in the old bed in the guest room of his father's place, thinking. He knew he wouldn't be able to sleep, but he was too tired to do anything else. He let his thoughts drift, and for what must have been the hundredth time that day, he tried to conjure up a clear picture of his mother. All that came to him were fragments, like old photographs, torn into pieces, yellowed, and curled with age.

Even with the imagination of a writer, he couldn't form a mental picture of her. He knew she was light-haired and fair-skinned with blue eyes. Or was she? He wasn't sure. He could not recall ever seeing a picture of her. In fact, he didn't remember any photographs at all around the home he grew up in.

He thought that was odd, but when he contemplated it, it was in keeping with what he knew of his father. In his anguish and grief, he'd sought to rub out every fragment of her existence.

Sitting up, he turned on the light next to the bed, trying to ground himself, and looked through the bedroom door into the darkened apartment. Certainly, there had to be something somewhere. It wasn't possible to extinguish every hint of someone's presence on this earth, was it?

He clicked on the lamp by his father's chair and ran his hands through his hair as he looked around. In the corner was an old wooden desk Will remembered from his childhood home. He decided to start there.

He slowly opened the top drawer and looked without disturbing its contents. He saw nothing of interest there, mostly just receipts and ordinary papers. He opened the remaining drawers with more purpose and began searching in earnest, still failing to find what he was looking for. He moved on to other places in the apartment, rifling through cabinets and cupboards and slamming them shut in frustration. The more he looked without finding, the angrier and more frustrated he became, and when he was mentally and physically exhausted, he sat down hard in his father's chair. *Damn you for erasing every memory of her.*

His eyes wandered to the still-closed door of his father's bedroom, and he swore again under his breath, realizing that as much as he wanted to go in there, he couldn't make himself do it. The bottle of whiskey he'd taken from the bar the night he'd invited Jess for a drink was still on the table, and the sight of it stirred up memories of her. Another set of emotions came, so he quickly pushed her from his thoughts. He went to the kitchen for a glass, poured himself a drink, and sat back down in his father's chair. He couldn't remember another time in his adult life when he'd been so unable to control his emotions.

Sipping his whiskey and deep in thought, he let his eyes wander to the stack of books on the side table. As he gazed at the titles, curious about what his father had been reading, he was not surprised by the classic novels he saw there. Most nights, when his father was at home in the house they shared,

Will could remember him reading by the soft lamp light. When Will was of age, his father began to give him books or leave them next to his bed. More than once, he'd struggled to get off to school after reading late into the night, the likes of Moby Dick and Robinson Crusoe capturing his young mind.

He opened the drawer of the little side table, realizing he hadn't looked there yet. Inside, he found his father's Bible, its worn leather cover curling a bit around the edges. He knew his father to be a quietly religious man. They attended Church every Sunday at Holy Cross Church, and while others seemed to view it as a social event, their visits were quite utilitarian. When the service was over, instead of congregating with the others in the Parrish Hall, they went straight home, where his father would change and head to the tavern. Will would strip off his Sunday suit, grab a sandwich, and head out into the neighborhood to enjoy the last of the weekend before school on Monday.

He pulled the Bible from the drawer and studied it. It was a classic King James version, the gold edges of its pages still brilliant. As he thumbed through its pages, occasionally stopping to read a note his father had written in the margin, something slipped out and fluttered to the floor. As he reached for it, the image stopped him cold. It was a picture of his mother sitting on the front steps of the house he'd grown up in. She looked ethereal with her long, blonde, windswept hair, and her eyes were peaceful as they stared directly into the camera. He could tell by her posture that she was with child, and the little bouquet of garden flowers she held paled compared to her beauty.

He stared at the photograph for a long time, the image answering a lifetime of questions and curiosity. He wanted the picture imprinted in his mind so he would never again not remember what she looked like. He looked like her, and seeing his likeness reflected there changed something inside of him. He realized that, for the first time in his life, he felt like he truly belonged to someone.

He got up and went to the mirror hanging in the vestibule over the little table just inside the door. He held the picture next to his face and stared at his reflection. While the likeness was nearly startling, he saw a subtle difference that was oddly familiar. He thought it was probably his father's influence, but he wasn't sure. He hadn't seen his father in a decade and had most likely forgotten the nuances of his features.

He was still thinking about it as he drifted off to sleep. In his dreams, she came to him, walking towards him with an angelic smile. When she reached him, she stopped, lightly kissed his cheek, then looked him straight in the eyes.

"Don't believe them..." she whispered, her blue eyes clear and piercing.

The dream startled him awake, and as he lay there, he swore he could still feel her essence.

PART TWO

7 JUNE 1985

CHAPTER THIRTEEN

Anna gathered her long, blonde mane, twisted it, and tied it into a low knot at the back of her neck. It was June in Florida, and it had been scorching hot since early May. She felt the sweat trickle down her back as she walked with no destination in mind. She was just happy to have arrived in Apalachicola as she'd been dreaming of this day for a long time. It had taken her almost 28 years to get out of Panacea, and now that she was here, she felt like her life was just beginning.

Though Apalachicola was no metropolitan city, it was the biggest town she'd ever been to. In fact, she'd never really been anywhere. Growing up dirt poor in Panacea hadn't offered her many opportunities to escape. It took money and resources to leave, and she'd had neither. She'd tried to earn a little money here and there by working odd jobs where she could find them, but she'd never been able to find a good enough place to hide the money in the dingy little clapboard house. Sooner or later, her father would find it and spend it on rot-gut whiskey from the corner liquor store. He was always happy when he got home with his bottle, but as he got well into it, his mood would shift and become dark and angry. When he'd drained the last drop, he'd come looking for her, screaming her name over and over. She'd learned to hide under the porch behind the old brick columns until he fell silent. Then she would tiptoe past him, usually passed out in his chair, and retreat to her little single bed on the floor of the tiny bedroom at the back of the house.

Eventually, she stopped trying to build a nest egg and began to look for any opportunity to leave. Her brothers had left one by one as soon as they could with just the shirts on their backs. Her oldest brother, Ricky, had fled north to Tallahassee, and Jonah had gotten a job on a fishing boat in Carrabelle. The last one to leave, Tommy, the closest to her in age, had begged her to come with him to Georgia. He was sure they could find work on the peanut farms up there, but she had been too afraid to go. After he was gone, she realized that while her father was all too happy to get rid of her brothers, he had no intention of letting her go anywhere.

Her mother, damaged from years of abuse at the hands of her husband, had checked out mentally a decade ago. That's when her father had begun to focus his attention on Anna. When he flew into his rages, her mother would sit in her rocking chair on the porch and hum the same church hymn over and over until the house went quiet. Anna figured it was better that way. Her mother was defenseless, but Anna knew how to get away from him.

One afternoon, while picking up some rice at the little grocery, she heard some boys talking about Mexico Beach. One planned to ride his motorcycle there in a few days to visit friends. She waited outside, and when he came out, she followed him for a couple of blocks. When she was sure he was out of earshot of the other boys, she called to him. After flirting with him for a while, she asked him about Mexico Beach and if he would take her to Apalachicola on his way. She'd try to scrounge up a little money for gas to help out. He said he was happy to take her, and she only needed to meet him on Friday morning at the corner. He'd have her in Apalachicola by eleven.

In the two days that followed, she went through what little clothing she had and made sure everything was fresh and clean. She visited the community outreach center at the local church and found a few items to add to her small wardrobe so she didn't look entirely destitute. She stealthily went through the pockets of her father's jackets and pants, finding a few dollars here and there and some change. When she had everything ready, she carefully rolled it all up in a small blanket, stuffed it into a canvas bag, and placed it behind her pillow in the corner of the tiny bedroom, entirely out of sight.

At seven o'clock, Friday morning, she crept from her room down the hall to where her mother was sleeping, kissed her on the cheek, and went out her window, avoiding passing by her father, who was passed out in his chair in the front room. As she hurried down the streets to the meeting point, she kept glancing over her shoulder, sure she would see her father chasing after her. But when she reached the corner, the boy was there, and when she climbed on the back of his motorcycle, and he took off towards Apalachicola, she let out a long breath and never even looked back.

As she walked through the streets of the old town, she admired the beautiful red brick two-story buildings that housed the stores and other businesses. They were classy-looking to her, and as she gazed at the upper-floor windows, she imagined herself living there someday. She peered into the shops and strolled along the streets, keeping a keen eye out for any help-wanted signs. She wouldn't last long there without money. She took a stroll down the waterfront and sat on a bench there, watching the activity on the river as the fishing boats came and went. Down the street, she saw a tavern and thought it might be a good place to stop and ask if they knew anyone around town who might need help. People congregated in bars and had conversations about such things. Perhaps she would get lucky.

When she pushed the door open, the air inside the tavern was cool and comfortable, a welcome change from the sweltering summer heat. She sat and waited for someone to notice her, but whoever was tending the bar was not out front. She released her hair from the knot and shook out her locks, fluffing them up to look presentable. If she was going to be asking about a job, she didn't want to look disheveled. She had her eyes closed, trying to keep the stray strands out of her eyes, and when she opened them, a man was standing in front of her with a slight smile on his face. He placed his hands on the bar rail before him, leaned in slightly, and cocked his head in amusement.

"Hi," she said as she smiled back at him, a little embarrassed.

"Hello," he said, studying her, "what can I get you?"

"Oh, um...nothing really," she said. "I'm looking for work. Would you happen to know of anything around?"

Grant didn't say anything. Instead, he turned and walked to the back bar, where he drafted a cold beer and put it in front of her.

"It's on the house," he said. "What kind of work are you looking for?"

"Oh, anything really. I've just got to town, and I need money," she said as she took a sip of beer and eyed him over the rim.

Grant thought for a moment. "I could use some part-time help here at the tavern. Do you have any bartending experience?"

She shook her head. "No, is it hard to do?"

He laughed. "If you can pour whiskey and draft beer, you're about ninety percent of the way there. My evening help comes in at six. If you want, you can start tonight, and she can show you what to do."

"Really?" she said. "Oh my gosh, thank you! I can't believe I already got a job! Is it okay if I just wait here until six?"

Grant glanced at his watch. "Honey, it's only two o'clock. Do you really want to sit here for four hours?"

"I don't have anywhere else to go, and it's so hot outside. I can sit over there where I'm out of the way if it's okay," she said.

"Sit wherever you like. You aren't in the way. Did you say you just got to town? Where did you come from?"

"Not far," she said, "just Panacea."

He was surprised. He saw the little canvas bag on the bar stool next to her and surmised it contained everything she'd brought with her.

"So, what brings you to Apalachicola?" he asked.

She thought for a moment as she gazed wistfully out the window. "Everything and nothing," she said, finally.

It was then that Grant Kendrick knew that she was special. He'd never met another woman like her.

PENNY EYED THE YOUNG GIRL. She knew why Grant had hired her even though they didn't need help at the tavern. She was a beautiful girl, that was obvious, but something about her was intriguing beyond her physical beauty. Anna was an ingénue, and her innocence was a magnet to everyone who met her.

The girl may have been inexperienced, but she was smart, and Penny only had to show her things once. By the end of the evening, Anna was capable of at least running the bar. Whatever she didn't know, she figured out, and the patrons were exceedingly patient with her. Her gentle demeanor and sweetness charmed everyone.

"Where are you staying?" Penny asked her as they were closing up. "I know you only got here today."

"I'm not sure," Anna said, her brows furrowed. "I'll figure it out."

"Anna, It's ten o'clock at night. Unless you plan to sleep on the sidewalk, there is no place to stay at this late hour. Why don't you stay with me, at least tonight?"

"Really?" Anna asked. "You would let me stay with you?"

"Yes, of course," Penny said, smiling at her, "you can stay with me for as long as you need to."

Anna threw her arms around her, taking Penny a few steps backward. She hadn't expected Anna's reaction, but it made her laugh.

"Thank you," Anna said as she kissed her on the cheek, "you are so kind."

Penny didn't know what to say, so she just smiled. "We are pretty much done. Let's lock up and head out," she said.

The two women walked a few streets over to the cottage behind Penny's parents' house. When they got inside, Anna could not believe her eyes. The little house was neat and clean and the closest thing to perfect she had ever seen. She sat down in an overstuffed chair in the living room and put her face in her hands.

"What's wrong, Anna?" Penny said as she went to the girl. "Are you okay?"

"Yes," Anna said as she wiped away tears. "I'm just so thankful to be here, and everyone has been so nice to me. Your house is lovely, and I can't believe you would share it with me. I'm just so overwhelmed."

"Oh, Anna," Penny said as she put her arms around her. Her heart broke for the girl, and she knew something awful had brought her to Apalachicola. "Where did you come from, Anna? What are you running away from?"

Anna didn't answer, so Penny didn't press her. Maybe in time, she would find out more.

"I think I have a little wine. Will you have a glass with me?" She asked as Anna wiped away her tears.

Anna nodded, and Penny got two glasses from the kitchen and motioned Anna over to the couch where they sat and put their feet up on the ottoman together. When Anna had collected herself, they began to talk and tell stories, and Penny was glad to see Anna relax and laugh a little. Finally, in the wee hours of the morning, they collapsed onto the bed, exhausted from the work and the long day.

"Thank you again, Penny," Anna said as she settled under the covers. "I don't know where I would be now if it weren't for you."

Penny just smiled, her eyes heavy with sleep. Anna rolled over, pulled the covers over her shoulder, and fell asleep instantly. As Penny listened to the girl's deep and steady breathing, she could tell her mind was at peace for the first time in a long time. It seemed Anna felt safe there, but safe from what she didn't know.

GRANT WALKED THROUGH THE TAVERN, surveying the place, then went to see what restocking he needed to do from the night before. The bar was neat and clean, and he could see the girls had done a nice job closing the place. He was curious to find out more about how the night had gone. But if he were honest, he really just wanted to see her again.

She was like no other woman he had ever met, and as much as he tried, he couldn't stop thinking about her. Her long blonde hair and clear blue eyes were etched so vividly in his mind that he only needed to close his eyes to envision her. But as beautiful as she was, there was something else about her that had captivated him. She was like a cool glass of water, refreshing and transparent, and her unspoiled innocence fascinated him.

He was also curious to find out what brought the girl to Apalachicola. Though he knew Panacea was a small town and jobs were probably scarce, the girl had seemingly arrived with only a small bag of possessions. He didn't know if she even had a place to stay, and he'd spent a restless night thinking about it. He would get to the bottom of it later and ensure she wasn't on the streets. Though Apalachicola was a safe town, he shuddered at the thought of her being alone on the streets at night.

He didn't need another employee. He, Penny, and the young woman who ran the kitchen could handle things just fine, at least during the week. Another employee on the books would be somewhat of a strain, and he would need to figure out how to make it work. The weekends were busy, and he knew Penny would welcome having Saturday or Sunday off. Perhaps, if she could get up to speed behind the bar, she could work with him on the busy nights and only a night or two during the week. He'd make sure it was enough to sustain her.

He would do whatever it took to keep her. Now that she was there and in his life, he wouldn't be able to let her walk away. He knew if he did, he would never be able to forget her.

CHAPTER FOURTEEN

Anna could not believe her good fortune. She'd only been in Apalachicola a short time and already had a safe place to stay and some money in her pocket. She knew she couldn't live with Penny forever, but Penny had assured her she was welcome to stay as long as needed to get herself settled.

She loved her job at the tavern. The people in town had been so nice to her, and she had already made a lot of friends. She'd worked there almost daily, even on days she wasn't scheduled. She was eager to learn everything and loved being there with Penny. She'd never had a real job before, and working behind the bar made her feel important and valuable.

She noticed Grant had begun to look after her in ways she'd never experienced. Every day, he made sure she had plenty to eat and still had a place to stay with Penny. He offered to lend her money if she needed it, but she didn't. She kept asking Penny how she could help, but Penny said she needed nothing. She didn't have any expenses at the cottage, and having Anna there was like having a sister, something she had always longed for.

So, for a few weeks, Anna lived in a state of complete bliss. It was as if her life had been completely transformed, and she had never known such happiness. That all came to a complete halt one early evening when she was alone in the front. The tavern was empty as the place was transitioning into the evening hour, and the night patrons had yet to arrive. She looked up as the tavern door opened, and in walked her father.

Her heart nearly stopped as he approached her slowly, his eyes narrowed with anger.

"Just what in the hell do you think you are doing, Anna?"

She glanced over her shoulder to see where Grant was, but he must have been in the store room and out of sight. She said nothing but began carefully backing away from him. He trailed her slowly across the bar, keeping his eyes on her.

"Stay away from me, Daddy," she said in almost a whisper. "Leave me alone!"

"Leave you alone? Leave you alone?" he said in a low, angry voice. "You dare say that to me after I've taken care of you all these years. You walk out without so much as a goodbye?"

"I'm not going back!" she said, her voice a little louder.

"The hell you aren't!" he said as he moved toward her.

She took off running, but he quickly hopped the bar and caught her by the hair, yanking her backward. She stumbled and fell at his feet. He grabbed her arm, pulled her up, and drew back his fist. Anna screamed, and suddenly, her father let go of her. She slumped to the floor against the back bar as she saw her father stumbling backward, hands up.

"Woah, fella!" he said as Grant advanced on him, a pistol in his hand. "This is a private matter. Just put the gun down, and the girl and I will go,"

"I don't think so," Grant said, reaching down and pulling Anna to her feet. "Just who the hell do you think you are coming in here and assaulting her like that?"

"She's my daughter and a runaway. She's none of your concern."

"She's a grown woman and can make her own decisions. You have no say in what she does or doesn't do. Now I suggest you leave. My trigger finger is getting itchy," Grant said as he motioned toward the door.

Her father wiped his mouth and pointed at her. "You haven't seen the last of me, Anna. Sooner or later, you and I are going to have a serious talk, and you aren't going to like it," he shouted.

Grant lunged at him, grabbing him by the collar and dragging him to the door, the gun to his head.

"Get out of my bar!" he shouted as he opened the door. "Don't let me catch you in Apalach again. If I find you here, I'll put you in a hole so deep even the devil won't be able to find you."

He pushed the man out the door and onto the sidewalk, where he lost his balance and fell. Grant slammed the door, locked it, and watched through the glass as the man stumbled away. When he was sure he was gone, he turned to Anna.

"Are you okay? Did he hurt you?" he said as he walked toward her.

"No, not really," she said, rubbing the back of her head.

He went to her and put his hands on her shoulders, examining her closely. "Are you sure? Did you bump your head? You went down pretty hard."

"I'm okay. I'm used to that from him," she said with disgust.

He sighed. "Is that why you are here, Anna, to get away from him?"

She looked at him for a long moment. "That and other things," she said as she looked away.

"Anna, look at me." Slowly, she returned her gaze to him, her eyes full of uncertainty and fear. "He will never hurt you again. I promise you. I'll make sure of it."

"How can you do that?" she asked, her voice shaky. "How can you keep him from coming back here again?"

"Just trust me, Anna. I can protect you," he said as he secured the gun and slid it under the register. "From now on, you don't go anywhere alone. When you leave here, I'll take you home, and I'll come and get you when you are ready to come in. It won't be forever, just until I can make sure he is no longer a threat to you."

"How will you do that?" she asked.

Grant didn't answer her, so she went back to work setting up the washed glasses on the back bar. They worked in silence for a while. Each lost in their thoughts.

"Can you stay and have dinner with me after work?" he asked quietly. "I'll have Loretta prepare something for us. We can eat upstairs, and then I'll take you home."

"Sure," she said, smiling at him. "That sounds nice. Penny will be out late tonight with Sawyer anyway, and I don't think I'd be comfortable at the cottage alone after today."

Grant nodded but didn't speak. His dark expression told Anna he was still thinking about the incident with her father. She didn't know what Grant intended to do but could tell he was planning something. She put it out of her mind. Whatever it was, it was clear he wasn't going to tell her.

"So, how long have you owned the tavern?" she asked as she took a bite of roast chicken. She'd never eaten food as delicious as she had in the last few weeks, and the meal Loretta prepared for them was no exception. Growing up, she had survived on very little sustenance and had learned to be satisfied with some grits or rice, vegetables she'd managed to grow behind the house, and the occasional piece of cheap meat. Now that she had enjoyed having a good meal every day, she vowed never to go hungry again.

"A little over ten years now," Grant said. "I bought the building, and it took about a year to build it all out. I was working during the day, so I could only work on it at night and on the weekends."

"Oh," she said. "What did you do for a living before you opened the tavern?"

"I was a fisherman, oysters mostly," he said as he poured her more wine. "Now, I only go out on the bay when I can get a free afternoon or evening, mainly just to fish a little and harvest oysters to serve here. What I can't catch, I buy from a local supplier."

"I love to fish," she said. "My brother Tommy and I used to fish off a little finger dock in the marsh on the bay. We'd bring our catch home, and Tommy would filet it in the backyard, and I'd fry it up on the porch over the old propane burner. That way, Daddy wouldn't get mad about the smell in the house. He hated the smell of fish."

She trailed off, and Grant could tell by the look in her eyes that she was remembering something unpleasant from a long time ago.

"Anyway," she said, "those were some good times and some of the best meals I remember as a kid."

"If you like to fish, I'll take you sometime when it's not so hot. I've got a boat I keep over on Scipio Creek at the marina there. It's a quick ride out to the bay."

"Oh, I would love that," she said, smiling at him. Their eyes locked for a moment, and he saw the happiness in them cloud over. She lowered her gaze. "Thank you for today. I'm not sure what would have happened if you hadn't been there."

Grant felt his heart constrict. This girl was such an open book, and what he saw there pulled at his insides. When he'd seen her father laying his hand on her, he'd been overcome with a desire to protect her. He hadn't thought twice before getting between them, and now that he knew there was a threat out there, he didn't want to let her out of his sight.

"Where are your brothers?" he asked. "Are they still in Panacea?"

"No, they all left when they could. I'm not sure where they are except for Jonah. He's in Carrabelle, I think, unless he's moved on."

"And your mother? Where is she?" he asked.

"She's still there. She's not mentally well, so my father leaves her alone. That's why he came looking for me. I was the last one he had to beat up on."

Grant felt the anger rise in his throat. He'd been repulsed by the man who reeked of liquor and sweat, and the thought of him hurting Anna made him furious. He would have to find a way to ensure it never happened again.

"Do you have any relatives? Aunts, uncles?" he asked. "Anyone who could check in on your mother there?"

"I have an aunt up in Wewahitchka, my mother's sister, but I haven't seen her since I was a kid. I don't think she's been in touch with my mother in years."

Grant nodded. "Do you remember her name?"

"Yes," Anna said with a smile. "Her name is Darlene, Darlene Sikes, but I don't know if she ever got married. She was so wonderful to me as a child, but my father didn't like her around us, so she eventually quit coming to visit."

Grant thought for a moment, then decided to change the subject. "How was your meal? Did you enjoy it?"

"Oh, yes!" she said, her eyes lighting up. "It was delicious! You are going to spoil me if you keep feeding me like this."

He couldn't help but smile. She was innocent, like a child, and completely transparent. She had obviously had a hard life, yet she wasn't hardened by it at all. Somehow, she had managed to keep her sweet nature, and he'd never met anyone so pure of heart. He glanced at his watch and saw that it was close to midnight and thought he should probably get her home soon.

"Do you want me to take you home now? It's almost midnight," he said.

"Oh, I didn't realize it was so late. Have I overstayed my welcome?" she asked as she got up quickly.

"No," he said with a chuckle. "Of course not. I just thought you might be tired. Better call Penny, though, to make sure she's home. I don't want you there by yourself." He gestured toward the phone on the table by the chair.

She dialed the cottage, and he waited as she listened. Finally, she hung up the phone and turned to him.

"I don't think she's home yet," she said with a frown. "But it's okay if you want me to go. I'm sure I'll be all right."

"I don't want you to go, Anna," he said as he got up and went to her. "Listen, I have a guest room. Why don't you stay here tonight, and I'll take you home in the morning?"

She looked at him and smiled. "You would let me stay here?"

He brushed the hair away from her face and pulled her into him, kissing her forehead. "Come on," he said. "Let's get you settled."

HE LEFT his door slightly ajar so he could see her's across the apartment. The door was shut, but he could see her shadow moving around in the light coming from under it. He was glad she had agreed to stay. Since the incident with her father that afternoon, he'd had an uneasy feeling in his gut. He would see about taking care of that tomorrow, but until it was settled, he didn't want her out of his sight.

She was too young for him by anyone's standards, and he was sure his pursuit of her would raise some eyebrows, but he couldn't help himself. Something about her vulnerability reached into the very core of his soul. Not only did it stir up his protective instincts, but it also seemed to bring out a tender and gentler side, a part of him that he realized had been buried for a long time.

Much to his surprise, he wasn't eager to bed her. Not that he wasn't attracted to her. She was stunningly beautiful and captivated him more than any woman he had ever met. It was just that he recognized a naïveté there that he didn't wish to overpower. If something were to happen between them, he wanted her to find her way there on her own. He would find no satisfaction in conquering her innocence.

When he contemplated the situation, he realized he hadn't had a genuine interest in a woman in a long time, at least not one who seemed to matter. His life had been mostly superficial, just going about running the tavern and indulging in mundane pleasures. Now, the possibilities before him seemed endless, and he had to stop and calm his mind now and then. He'd known her only a few weeks, yet he could completely imagine spending the rest of his life with her. The feeling both elated him and put a pit in his stomach. If the sentiment wasn't shared, it would be a long time until he would be able to forget her, if ever. Loving Anna could end up being a blessing or a curse. He just didn't know which yet.

CHAPTER FIFTEEN

G rant sat in his truck and stared at the rundown clapboard house with its cluttered front porch and dirt yard and tried to imagine what it had been like for Anna to live there. The images that came to mind were horrifying, and he had to squeeze his eyes shut to push them out. How she had endured, he didn't know.

Darlene Sikes seemed relieved to hear from him that her sister was still alive, even though she was not well. When Grant explained the situation to her, she didn't hesitate to agree to meet him there to take her into her care. Whatever the situation was, she seemed ready to meet it, and though Grant didn't know either of the women, he was more than ready to do this, if for no other reason than for Anna.

He hadn't seen any activity at the house since he'd been sitting there, which had been the better part of an hour. He was beginning to think Darlene had changed her mind when he saw a car turn down the dead-end dirt road where the house sat. She pulled alongside him, and the two acknowledged each other. When she rolled down her window, he told her to turn the car around, point it toward the way out, and wait for him. While she was maneuvering, he pulled out his pistol, checked for a round in the chamber, and clicked off the safety. When her car was in place, he got out and walked slowly toward the house.

He carefully and quietly climbed the steps to the front porch and stopped and listened. When he heard no sound, he opened the screen door. The inner door was open, and as he stepped inside, the smell of rotting food and garbage nearly overwhelmed him. Annas's father was asleep in a dirty and worn recliner in the front room, and from what Grant could tell, he was passed out drunk. He slipped by him and started down the hall, wincing every time the floorboards creaked under his feet.

When he got to the first bedroom on the left, he saw a woman asleep on the bed facing him, curled up on her side. He went to her, and when her eyes opened and went wide with fear, he held a finger to his lips and put his other hand on her shoulder. She seemed to understand, and the fear in her eyes dissipated. He motioned for her to sit up, still signaling her to be silent, then helped her to her feet. Taking her by the hand, he led her out of the bedroom and into the hall, where he paused and looked into the front room to be sure Anna's father was still asleep. When he saw he had not moved, the two crept silently past him, out the screen door, and down the steps into the yard. Then, as her sister stepped out of the car, the woman seemed to snap out of her catatonic-like state and ran to her. The two women embraced, and though Grant was reluctant to break them apart, he urged them to get in the car and leave as quickly as possible.

"I'll follow you to the highway to make sure you get on the road okay," he said quietly through the window.

Darlene nodded and put the car in gear. "Thank you," she whispered, tears brimming in her eyes.

Grant nodded and walked to his truck. He followed them to the highway and watched as they turned north, setting a course for the quickest route to Wewahitchka. When the car was well out of sight, he turned the truck around and headed back to the house.

~

"OH MY GOODNESS! " Anna exclaimed. "Look at all these beautiful things!"

Grant smiled as he watched her go from one rack of clothing to the next, holding up dresses and fitting them to her form in front of the mirror. He then realized she had probably never been in a dress shop or bought anything new. He'd been heartbroken when he'd noticed her wearing the same things over and over, realizing her wardrobe only consisted of a handful of items. Though Penny had offered to let her borrow anything she needed, Anna had refused, feeling like Penny was already too generous towards her.

When Grant offered to take her shopping, she had given him a definitive no. He told her it was only a loan to buy some clothes and other things she needed, and she could pay him back later out of her wages from the tavern. She had agreed then, though Grant never intended to deduct anything from her pay. He felt sure he could make it seem as though he had.

He was worried she might balk at the prices of the things she chose, but she hadn't. Instead, her enthusiasm seemed to overtake her practicality, and Grant delighted in watching her choose one beautiful dress after another. When she was finished at the dress shop, he sent her across the street to the woman's boutique, where she could be fitted with some proper undergarments without him, and he waited until she was out the door before paying the bill. Later, they would purchase some shoes for her to wear instead of the worn and tattered sandals she'd shown up in.

When they were finished, they put the bags in the truck and walked down the block to a little cafe on the corner for lunch.

Anna had never been to a place as big as Tallahassee and was full of questions. When he promised to ride by the Capitol on their way out of town, she'd giggled like a teenager.

The restaurant was a bit upscale with a sophisticated menu, and Grant could tell by Anna's look of trepidation she had probably never been to a nice restaurant. To make her feel more comfortable, he asked her what she wanted to eat and ordered for her, including a glass of wine to make her feel more relaxed.

"Thank you so much for doing this for me. I've had a wonderful day," she said, eyeing him over the rim of her wine glass. "You'll take the money out of my pay, right?"

"Yes," he said. "No need to worry. We'll work it out." He paused and smiled at her for a moment. "I've been thinking. Would you like to go to the hotel for dinner one night? It's very nice. We could invite Penny and Sawyer, and you could wear one of your new dresses."

Her eyes opened wide. "Really?" she said. "That would be so fun. Like a double date," she said, laughing.

"Yes," he said, laughing with her, "like a double date."

He almost felt guilty about his interest in her. Even though she was in her late twenties, she was far from mature. But Grant realized there were parts of her that had seen the world's harshest realities and had survived some of the cruelest conditions he could imagine. One look inside that house confirmed it. So he soothed his doubts by thinking about the life he could give her if she let him. He could right some of the wrongs if she gave him the chance.

They enjoyed a lunch of delicious crab cakes and a sophisticated, delicate salad. He enjoyed watching her eat, suspecting every meal was a new experience. Her ravenous appetite and thinness clearly showed that she wasn't accustomed to having plentiful, nutritious food and most certainly had never had anything gourmet. He knew he could spend a lifetime spoiling her.

She was quiet on the way home, and Grant kept glancing at her, trying to determine the reason for her pensive mood.

"Will you teach me to drive?" she asked, finally. He was completely surprised at her question. It had never occurred to him that she didn't know how. He thought back to the dingy little clapboard house and how desperate she must have felt, having no way to get herself out. The fact that she had found a way to escape was a miracle, and he admired her resourcefulness.

"Of course," he said. "Do you want to learn right now? We will be on the backroads all the way home. There won't be many cars."

"Now?" she asked, her eyes fearful. "Oh, I don't know. Do you really think it would be okay?"

He turned off the hard road onto a lime rock road, went a little way down, and stopped.

"We can start here, and when you are ready, we'll head back to the hard road," he said, smiling at her.

"Okay," she said breathlessly as she watched him get out and walk around the front of the truck.

He opened her door and instructed her to slide over behind the wheel, and after a minute or two of instruction, she carefully put the truck in gear and started slowly forward. For the next hour, she drove around the dirt roads in the little community of trailers and vacant lots, giggling whenever she made a successful turn or started again after stopping at a crossroads.

"Ready to hit the road for home?" Grant asked, feeling upbeat after watching her for the last hour.

"Do you think I'm ready?"

"Yes," he said, "you are definitely ready."

"Okay," she said as she headed for the way out.

He watched in amusement as she looked up and down the asphalt to see if any cars were coming, biting her lip in intense anticipation. As she pulled out onto the hard road and got the truck up to speed, she looked over at him and smiled, the look on her face one of pure joy and happiness, and Grant was sure he had never seen a more beautiful sight.

"I THINK this one is the prettiest," Anna said as she showed Penny her new clothes.

"Oh, it's gorgeous and looks so beautiful on you!" Penny said. "Did Grant buy all these things for you?"

"Well, he paid for them, but it's only a loan. He's going to take the money out of my pay at the tavern."

Penny didn't comment, and Anna looked at her.

"What?" she asked. "What are you smiling about?"

"I think Grant is sweet on you. Sawyer thinks so, too." Penny said with a sly smile.

"Really? You think so?" Anna said as she admired herself in the mirror.

"Yes, I've never seen him so...attentive," she said with a laugh.

"Well, he did kiss me the night I stayed at his place," Anna said.

"What? He kissed you?"

"It wasn't a real kiss, actually, only on the forehead, but he said he wants to take me on a date. A double date with you and Sawyer."

"Oh, and where are we going on this date?" Penny asked, laughing.

"To the hotel for dinner," Anna said, her eyes sparkling.

"Very fancy," Penny said. "The hotel has the nicest restaurant in town. It seems Grant is looking to wine and dine you."

Anna couldn't help but feel flattered. Grant was older than her, but he was extremely handsome with his tall, well-built frame, salt-and-pepper hair, and blue eyes. And he was very sophisticated in her eyes. What he saw in her, she didn't know. She was just a poor girl from Panacea who didn't know much about anything. But Grant was patient and kind and seemed so willing to help her learn new things. When he'd taught her to drive that afternoon, he never once seemed impatient, even when she'd braked too hard or started off too fast.

She had never had the attention of a real man, only the occasional flirtation of one of her brother's friends. Grant's attention made her feel like a real woman, and she hoped he wouldn't tire of her lack of sophistication.

If she were honest, she had never pictured having a man in her life after suffering at the hands of her father. After watching him abuse her mother and the cruelty he showed toward her brothers and eventually her, she never imagined there were men who treated women well. Even her brothers, whom she dearly loved and would never harm her, showed signs of pent-up rage. She knew why, but she just assumed all men had those tendencies.

Now, Grant was showing her a different side of life, and she couldn't get enough of it. She was realizing that having a clean, safe place to live and enough food on the table was the norm and not the exception. And that most people were kindhearted and willing to help if you needed it. Had she known that ten years ago, she would have left then. Since she had only known poverty and cruelty inside the little house, she assumed the rest of the world was much the same, and no one had ever shown her things were any different.

She couldn't remember when she had stopped going to school. Staying home was easier than enduring the ridicule from the other kids about her tattered clothes and shoes. She never had lunch money, but one of the lunchroom ladies was kind enough to give her a peanut butter sandwich and a carton of milk most days. She was too ashamed to eat with the other children, so she would find an out-of-the-way place to sit far enough away from them so she didn't have to listen to their snickers and insults.

To hear that a man as good as Grant might have feelings for her was almost unbelievable to her. Never in her wildest dreams would she have believed her life could change so much in just a few short weeks. Even her fears of her father coming after her had begun to fade. Grant had told her he could protect her from him, and she believed him. He had not shown up in Apalachicola since, and Anna had a feeling she had seen the last of him.

CHAPTER SIXTEEN

Anna finished up her makeup and slipped on her dress. She'd never even worn makeup until a few weeks ago when Penny had shown her how. She didn't like the feel of a lot of it on her skin, but she liked how her lips and cheeks looked with a little color and how mascara seemed to accentuate the blue of her eyes. She wanted to be as beautiful as possible for Grant.

He was taking her for dinner at the hotel with Sawyer and Penny, and she was nervous. The restaurant was expensive and elegant, and she didn't want to look foolish in front of Grant by not knowing which fork to use or committing some other breach of etiquette. She'd gotten a book at the library to study such things. She only hoped she could remember what to do.

"You look beautiful, Anna," Grant whispered as he reached over and squeezed her hand. "Let's have some champagne to celebrate being together," he told the group.

As the waiter poured the champagne, Anna giggled with delight. She'd never had champagne before, but she loved how sophisticated she felt when she drank it. It was hard for her to imagine her life just a few months back. She would have never believed it if anyone had told her she'd soon be wearing beautiful clothes and dining in a fancy restaurant. Grant had changed her life, and as much as his generosity sometimes made her feel uncomfortable, she knew she would never tire of his kind treatment of her. She had a lifetime of sadness and cruelty to make up for.

~

"WOULD you like to come back to my place for a nightcap?" Grant asked her as they headed down the front steps of the hotel. "I think Penny and Sawyer would like some time alone." He looked at her and winked, but she seemed pensive.

"Oh, okay," she said with a frown. "I hope I haven't intruded too much on Penny's privacy by staying with her. She always tells me not to worry about it, but I can't help but worry all the same."

Grant took her hand and squeezed it. "She adores you, Anna, and would do anything for you. You have to know that," he said, giving her a sympathetic smile.

"I do, and I adore her too. I'm just not used to people being so generous towards me. Sometimes it makes me uncomfortable."

Grant could tell she was becoming emotional, so he tried to change the subject.

"Did you enjoy your dinner?" he asked.

"Yes, I did!" she said, smiling up at him. "Thank you so much for taking me there. I've never been to such a nice place, and I don't think I've ever had such a good meal. Lobster is wonderful!"

He loved showing her new things and giving her new experiences. It was like watching a child open Christmas presents. The joy and delight was contagious.

They reached the tavern, and he retrieved a bottle of port

from the bar before going to the apartment. Once upstairs, he poured a couple of glasses, sat on the couch, and patted the cushion next to him.

"Come sit with me, Anna," he said, smiling at her. She settled in next to him, and they were quiet momentarily, sipping their wine.

"I've been thinking," he said. "Since Penny's place is so small, why don't you move in here with me?"

He watched her, searching her eyes, trying to gauge her reaction.

"No pressure, Anna. I have the guest room, and you can move in there if you want to. At least you would have your privacy and not have to worry about being in Penny's way."

Anna looked at him for a long moment. "Are you sure, Grant?" she asked quietly, the knowing in her eyes entirely transparent.

"I'm sure," he said, not taking his eyes off her.

"What does this mean?" she asked, her clear blue eyes reflecting her uncertainty.

"It can mean whatever you want it to, Anna."

He saw a slight smile cross her lips, and she reached out and touched his cheek. He took her hand and pulled her to him, feeling no hesitation from her at all. Tenderly, he kissed her lips and then drew back. When he saw the desire in her eyes, he leaned in again, kissing her more urgently and feeling her yield to him. Before he lost himself in the moment, he pulled back again.

"It doesn't have to mean this, Anna, not if you don't want it to," he said, searching her eyes. "Being here doesn't have to mean this."

"I want it to," she whispered.

He kissed her again, and when he felt the passion rise in both of them, he stood and held out his hand to her. She took it eagerly, and he picked up their wine glasses with his free hand

and led her to his bedroom. In the hours that followed, Grant felt his world shift and his fate become sealed. He knew then Anna's presence or absence would forever determine his happiness.

~

PENNY LAY awake in the empty bed, thinking about Anna. When she'd come home that morning and told her she was moving in with Grant, the news had sent a feeling through her she didn't recognize. Now, as she thought about it, she realized it was a strange mixture of loss and jealousy.

Anna had a way of getting under one's skin and staying there. From the moment she saw her, she recognized her beauty, but there was so much more to her essence than that. It was why she'd asked her to share the cottage with her and had let her stay for so long. Anna always seemed to leave everyone wanting more.

On the nights that they had slept together in the small bed, she'd had feelings that were new to her. Now and then, she would wake up, and Anna would be nestled up against her. The warmth and the smell of her were intoxicating and made her want to reach for her, but she never had. The impulses made her feel strange, fearing that acting on them might cause a cataclysmic shift in her world. Instead, she would lie there in a kind of sweet agony, imagining what it would be like to caress her soft skin or taste her kiss, but knowing she never would.

Even when she and Sawyer had come home alone from the restaurant and had the place to themselves, she'd felt different. Though they had been together for a long time, the attraction between them was still intense. He had taken her virginity some time ago, but somehow, being with him always felt new and exciting. But as he had made love to her that night, she'd found herself thinking about Anna. She hoped it was a simple infatuation that would fade with time, but somehow, deep down, she knew that was wishful thinking.

With Anna gone and living with Grant, she tried to imagine the future, but all she felt was sadness. She would never again have Anna in such close proximity to her, and her attraction to her could mean a lifetime of unfulfilled desire. Anna's coming to Apalachicola had changed everything, and she knew their worlds would never be the same again.

GRANT PULLED the truck through the gate behind the tavern and headed for the coastal highway. He had decided to take it all the way to Mexico Beach before heading north to his destination. It would take longer to get there, but the drive was beautiful and romantic, and he looked forward to Anna's undivided attention.

"Where are we going?" she asked as the truck got up to speed. Grant was always taking her to new places and showing her new things, so she had no idea where they were headed.

"You'll see," he said, smiling at her. He watched with amusement as she unconsciously pouted and sat back in her seat, turning her attention to the landscape out the window.

They drove along in silence for a while, and when they passed the turn-off to Cape San Blas, he saw her head turn toward the bay as they rejoined the coast again. Her eyes reflected the turquoise of the water, and he thought she had never looked more beautiful. Her expression was ethereal as she took in the beauty of the expanse of coastline ahead, its white sand beaches curving softly toward Shipyard Cove.

"So beautiful," she said just above a whisper. "I've never seen anything like that."

It occurred to Grant that she'd probably never been farther west than Apalachicola and seen the beauty of the Gulf there. Once you passed the cape, the waters became clearer and bluer and took on a magical quality different from the dark blue waters of the bays.

"Are you hungry? Do you want to stop for lunch?" he asked.

"Yes," she said, turning toward him with a smile. He really hadn't needed to ask. She was always hungry. He suspected that was left over from the years she spent in poverty. It was almost instinctual, like a built-in reflex.

He remembered there was a little seafood restaurant in the heart of Port St. Joe where they could sit outside. Even though it was late summer, the temperature was tolerable in the shade with the steady off-shore breeze.

"You still haven't told me where we are going," she said as they sat, sipping a cold beer and enjoying the views.

"It's a surprise," he said with a smile.

"Is it a good surprise?" she asked, her head tilted.

He chuckled. "Of course, it's a good surprise."

She smiled but said nothing more for a while as she gazed over the bay. She'd pulled her hair up and away from her face to get some relief from the heat, and her face was framed with little wisps of hair pulled loose by the breeze. As he noticed them and her natural beauty, he could not believe she was actually his. Suddenly, he had an overwhelming urge to make it permanent.

Her eyes traveled over the coastline and slowly found their way back to him, and she smiled. He took it as an unspoken sign confirming what he'd been thinking.

"Can we invite Penny and Sawyer over for cards Friday night after we close the tavern?" she asked.

"Sure," he said. "We can do dinner before if you want. I can get Billy to work in the evening. He's always looking to pick up a shift,"

"Oh, that would be fun. Can we go to the oyster bar?"

Oysters were a delicacy she couldn't get enough of, and Grant delighted in watching her eat them. She had a habit of eating them so voraciously that eventually, he would have to dab at the cocktail sauce dribbling down her chin.

"The oyster bar sounds perfect. I'll call Sawyer when we get home."

After lunch, they continued on to Mexico Beach before finally heading north. Less than an hour later, Grant pulled the truck to a stop in front of a small but neat house with a brick path leading to the front porch. Anna gazed at the house, clearly confused, then back at Grant with an inquisitive look.

Grant tooted the horn, and moments later, the front door opened, and two women stepped out and hurried down the front steps. Suddenly, Anna jumped out of the car and ran up the walk, nearly tripping as she ran into the embrace of the two women.

Grant sat in the car, smiling as he watched Anna's mother wipe the tears from her eyes and cradle her daughter's face in her hands. He could hear excited chatter but couldn't make out what they were saying. He could only imagine.

Finally, the women waved him in as they started back toward the house. He slowly got out of the truck, reluctant to intrude on the reunion. He didn't want to talk about things, and he didn't want any accolades. Just seeing Anna happy was enough.

ANNA STARED out the window at the bright orange colors of the setting sun and tried to process all the events of the day. Seeing her mother safe and sound and not in the near-catatonic state she'd been in for so long was unexpected, and seeing her aunt again was something she'd long since believed would never happen. But what was occupying her heart at the moment was what she knew Grant had done for her. She could not imagine what it must have taken to get her mother out of that house and safely up in Wewahitchka. He seemed reluctant to talk about the details, but her aunt told her he had arranged everything. Maybe her father had let her mother go willingly, but Anna doubted it. She knew better.

No one had ever done anything so brave and honorable for her, and the pure unselfishness of it was so moving it threatened to break her down. She didn't deserve that level of kindness. She wasn't worthy of it. She glanced at him as he drove along the darkening roads, his profile stoic as she realized he was deep in thought.

As if sensing her thoughts, he reached over and gently took her hand. He didn't look at her, but she knew he was thinking about her. It seemed he was always thinking about her.

"Thank you," she said in a near whisper.

He didn't answer but glanced over briefly, giving her a slight smile and her hand a squeeze.

She turned her gaze back to the bay and tried to imagine what it had been like for Grant to see the shabby, filthy house she'd grown up in, the thought of it making her squeeze her eyes shut with shame. With her gone for several weeks, she could not imagine the condition of the house. Left to his own devices, her father had no sense of self-preservation.

Since she'd snuck out of that hellhole early that morning, her life had changed immeasurably, and she owed it entirely to Grant Kendrick. It was at that moment that she knew she loved him. She was ready to give herself over to him if he would have her. She was his for however long he wanted her.

CHAPTER SEVENTEEN

Anna stood in front of the mirror in the choir room of Holy Cross Church and adjusted her veil. Though her dress was simple, it was the most beautiful thing she had ever seen. Grant had taken her to Tallahassee to shop for it and had sat for hours in the waiting area while she tried on dozens of dresses. He'd told her to choose whatever she wanted and not be concerned with price. In the end, the dress she chose was a perfect reflection of her.

Anna didn't want to walk down the aisle; she didn't want that much attention on her. Instead, she and Grant entered the sanctuary from opposite sides, coming together in front of Father Hudson, Penny as the maid of honor, and Sawyer as Grant's best man. It was simplistic yet elegant and more than Anna had ever dreamed of.

Afterward, they'd had a large and lively reception at the old hotel where Grant had arranged for spectacular food and drink and a wedding cake that mesmerized Anna with its intricate design of scrolls and flowers. It was all too perfect and a dream come true.

Grant hadn't told her where they were going for their

honeymoon, so when they arrived at the little cottage on the cape, Anna could not have been happier. There, they would spend a blissful week taking in the spectacular sunrises and sunsets and their days enjoying the deserted strip of sand that stretched a mile in front of the cottage.

"Are you happy, Anna?" Grant whispered as her beautiful naked form lay beside him, glistening with sweat from their morning lovemaking.

She rolled over to face him, her cheeks flushed. "I am so happy, Grant," she said, smiling at him.

He caressed her face, his eyes traveling lazily over her features. Lying there with her felt like a dream, and in the years that followed, he would remember that week as the happiest of his life.

ANNA WAS behind the bar when the front door opened, and two men walked in and approached her.

"Are you Anna?" one of them asked. Suspicious, she was reluctant to answer them.

"Let me get my husband," she said as she hurried back to the store room where Grant was putting away the supplies delivered earlier that morning.

"May I help you?" he said as he came out of the back, wiping his hands on a rag.

"We're looking for Anna Samuels, but we understand she's recently married," the taller one said.

"Anna is my wife. State your business, please," Grant said as he moved between her and the men.

"I'm Detective Paulson, and this is my partner Detective Richards. We're from the Wakulla County Sheriff's Office. We're looking into the disappearance of a man named Cash Samuels from Panacea, the girl's father."

"I see," Grant said, stepping aside. "Anna? Would you like to speak with these two gentlemen?"

"Okay," she said, her voice a little hesitant. "What do you want to know?"

"When did you last see your father, Anna?" Detective Richards asked her.

She paused for a minute, thinking. "I believe it was in July," she said, finally. "My husband and I went to help my mother prepare to move to my aunt's house in Wewahitchka."

The detective made some notes and then looked up at her. "And your father was there at that time?"

"He was," she said, her clear blue eyes steady and sure.

"And your mother is still in Wewahitchka?" he asked.

"Yes," Anna said, "she's not well, and my father could not care for her properly." She was quiet for a moment. "So my father is missing?" she asked innocently.

"Yes," the detective said. "We aren't sure for how long. He stopped showing up for work, and after a week or so, his friend went looking for him. He hasn't contacted you or shown up here?"

"No," she said, "he came to see me in June to talk about my mother and what could be done about her care, but I haven't seen him since we were there in July."

Grant's heart was pounding. He hadn't discussed with her what had transpired the day he rescued her mother, and he had no idea what she was doing, but to try to do anything to stop her now would be foolish.

"Did you take your mother to Wewahitchka?" he asked.

"No," she said, "my aunt came and picked her up."

"And you were needed there why?" he asked, looking directly at her.

"As I said, my mother isn't well and wasn't capable of packing her things. Also, my father was sad my mother was leaving, and I wanted to reassure him she would be okay. It was a difficult time for my family, detective."

"I understand," he said as he folded his notebook and put it in his shirt pocket. "Any idea where he might have gone, Mrs. Kendrick?"

"I'm sorry, detective, I don't," she said. "But this isn't the first time he's disappeared. He's had a habit of leaving. But I'm sure he'll be back. He's always come back in the past."

"Thank you, " he said. "We'll be in touch if we need anything more,"

"Yes, please," she said sweetly, "please let me know if you find out anything."

When the men were gone, the two were quiet for a while, each contemplating what had just happened. Grant was stunned at how Anna had been so quick on her feet, and it had never occurred to him that she had any inkling of what he had done. Now that she had lied to protect him, they needed to talk.

"Anna," he said. She had her back to him and didn't answer but turned around to him with a piercing stare.

She slowly shook her head and put her finger to her lips to signal him to stop talking.

"We should talk," he said, trying to gauge her state of mind.

"No," she said, "talk is dangerous."

They both went quiet again, and Grant's mind was full of worry. Now, it would be terrible for them both if the truth ever came to light.

She grabbed a broom and began to sweep behind the bar.

"Remember that day, Grant? When we went to help Mama? It was such a hard day, and Daddy was so sad. So sad that when you walked Mama to the car, I had to stay inside with him to comfort him. I didn't even get to see Aunt Darlene before she left. After you made sure Mama was okay, you came back in and got me, and we headed home. Do you remember, Grant?"

Grant stared at her and slowly nodded, stunned at what he had just heard. She knew.

"Do you think they will ever find him, Grant? Do you think he will ever reappear?"

He looked at her for a long moment. He knew what she was asking. "No, I don't, Anna," he said. "I'm sure he won't."

She nodded and returned to her sweeping. She would never speak of it again.

GRANT LAY awake that night thinking about what had transpired that afternoon. Anna was sleeping next to him, and he could tell by her steady breathing she was deeply asleep. He was still trying to process the risk she had taken. To say he was surprised at her bravery was an understatement. But what had startled him the most was how she had done it so effortlessly.

He had tried not to think about what he'd done that day in the months since. In his mind, it had been necessary to protect her, and he had let that take the forefront of his thinking. Now that the situation had become dangerous again, he was forced to contemplate the details of it.

When he'd turned the truck around that day, he'd known exactly what he would do. Anna's father had made it easy on him by being drunk and passed out in the chair. When he'd pulled his truck around the back of the house up next to the porch and come through the back door, he could see that he had not moved from his position in the chair. He quietly approached him from behind and pulled the rope taut between his hands. He stopped and waited for a moment, and when the man didn't move, he quickly slipped the rope around his neck and pulled the noose tight. The man's eyes flew open, and he clawed at his neck, but it was already too late. Grant watched as he thrashed and grunted, but in his condition, he couldn't put up much of a fight. When he finally went still, and the light went out in his eyes, Grant let go of the rope. He checked for a pulse, and when he was sure he was dead, he began his work.

He'd brought a large tarp he had stored in the shed behind the tavern. Although it was a struggle, he'd managed to tie the body up in such a way that its form was unrecognizable. He wrapped it up in the tarp and dragged it to the back porch, where he'd heaved it into the bed of his truck. He went back inside to ensure nothing looked askew, then left the house, got into his truck, and started back toward Apalachicola. He took his time. He needed to compose himself and calm the bile that rose in his throat now and then, threatening to overtake him.

The sun was setting when he arrived at the marina where he kept his boat. He parked the truck and made sure the tarp was obscured by the burlap oyster bags he kept in the bed. He said hello to the bait shop manager, who was closing up and leaving for the day, then busied himself on his boat until it got dark. To anyone watching, nothing would have appeared out of the ordinary.

When he was sure no one was around, he backed his truck up to the dock, slid the tarp off the back of the truck into the service cart at the marina, rolled it leisurely down the dock, and dumped it into the back of the boat. He moved in an orderly fashion, measured but not hurried. It was important that, if someone were watching, it would appear that he was only preparing for a night fishing trip on the bay, something he'd done many times.

When night had fallen entirely, he fired up the diesel engine, patiently let it idle for a few minutes, then backed out of the slip. As he headed down Scipio Creek toward the Apalachicola River, he relaxed a little. When he finally entered the bay and put the throttle to the firewall, he knew he was home free.

Remembering it in detail was hard, but it was important now that her father's disappearance was being looked into. He wouldn't change anything about what he'd done and how he'd done it. But just in case someone had seen something, he needed an explanation for every move he'd made. Now that they'd had a visit from the detectives, he needed to think through all the details.

Anna stirred and rolled over toward him, sighing softly in her sleep. In the darkness, he could just make out her features but could see her expression was relaxed and free from the worry he had seen on her brow earlier. Somehow, she had been able to leave the trouble of the day behind. He thought that was probably from growing up like she had, amid violence and poverty. If one carried that into the night, there would never be any restful sleep. But he was still stunned that she had so effortlessly accepted that he had murdered her father. He guessed she had developed a survival instinct so strong that doing anything to stay safe was acceptable.

He realized then that was one of the things that made her so different and special. She had the ability to live entirely in the moment and garner happiness from the smallest of things, regardless of what might have happened before or might happen after. No matter how tragic and awful yesterday might have been, she was able to leave it behind. There was promise in the present, and no amount of terribleness could snuff out her optimism. In all his years, he had never known anyone like her.

She hadn't mentioned the visit from the detectives or the fateful day he had rescued her mother again that evening. Instead, she'd chatted happily through dinner about the curtains she wanted to hang in their bedroom. He had tried to match her lighthearted mood and enjoy the meal with her but had been unable to shake the fear he'd felt when the detectives had questioned her.

He wasn't worried about himself. Whatever happened to him was worth what he had done to keep Anna safe. But now that she had lied to cover for him, there was a danger he couldn't protect her from. If any of it were ever revealed, she would be considered an accessory, and there would be nothing he could ever do to keep her from suffering the consequences.

They would never find her father. He knew exactly where he was going when he'd headed into the bay that night. Navigating by the stars and the shore lights, he'd taken the body to the deepest part of the bay. After stripping the body of any distinguishing clothing and removing the St. Christopher medal from around his neck, he'd weighted the body down with cinder blocks and pushed it overboard. The crabs and the fish wouldn't take long to do their work. Every trace of her father was undoubtedly gone from this earth now.

He glanced over at the valet on his dresser, where he had carefully hidden the St. Christopher medal. He'd kept it for her, thinking she might want some remembrance of him someday. It was foolish, he knew. She despised everything about him, but he couldn't make himself toss it into the bay as he should have.

He watched as the occasional passing car interrupted the light coming through the window, his eyes becoming heavy and tired. In the moments before sleep consumed him, the visions that had haunted him for months visited him again. In the watery depths of the bay, he saw him, his arms outstretched and desperate, the medal glistening around his neck.

At that moment, he envied Anna. He knew he would never be able to leave it behind, and he would never be able to move on from the trauma. What he had done would haunt him for the rest of his life.

CHAPTER EIGHTEEN

I n the months that followed, Grant took solace in the fact that they had not heard anything further from the detectives. He guessed they had surmised that her father, having been freed from the burden of his sick wife, had taken off. And with no one pressing them for answers, the case had probably gone into a drawer along with the other cold cases in Wakulla County.

With that seemingly behind them, he'd been able to focus his attention on Anna again. Their relationship was still fiery and intense, and he began to wonder why, with all of their frequent lovemaking, she had not yet become pregnant.

He knew she longed for a child, and when their marriage had stretched to nearly a year without her conceiving, he became concerned that maybe something was wrong. He decided to see his friend, a local doctor, to discuss the matter and find out what they should do to get to the bottom of whatever was happening.

"Well, the easiest thing to do right away is to check you out," Dr. Thompson said. "We can have a sample analyzed to see what your counts are. If all is well there, we can move on to Anna."

"Okay," Grant said, "and if we need to see a specialist, you can recommend one?"

"Yes, there are a couple up in Tallahassee, but let's take it one step at a time. There could be nothing wrong. Sometimes, these things just take time."

A week later, Dr. Thompson called. The message said there was no need to make an appointment, just to come in whenever he had a free moment. Grant headed to his office on foot the following day, and after a brief wait, the nurse took him back to Dr. Thompson's office.

"The news isn't good, Grant," he said, looking at his chart. "We got your counts back, and they were basically zero. I know this isn't easy to hear, but I'm afraid you're sterile."

Somehow, Grant wasn't surprised, but the confirmation of it set his mind going in a thousand different directions. Mainly searching for ways to fix it but also knowing nothing could be done.

"There are lots of options these days, Grant," the doctor continued. "There is an excellent fertility clinic up in Tallahassee that specializes in artificial insemination of donor sperm. They are also making great strides with IVF, and there is always adoption."

"Thank you, Bill," Grant said. "I'll speak with Anna about it, and we'll get back to you."

Instead of returning to the tavern, he left the office and took a long loop through town, ending up on the waterfront. As he sat staring out over the river and listening to the calls of the gulls, he tried to imagine Anna's reaction to the news. She very much wanted a baby, and Grant suspected it was an unconscious effort to give a child the stable upbringing she never had. Somehow, that would right some of the wrongs done to her and help her wipe out the memories of her miserable childhood. Now, he wouldn't be able to give her that. The thought of her carrying another man's baby, even through an anonymous donor, crushed him inside, and he couldn't imagine it. Adoption never seemed to work out for anyone he knew, and the process was painful and took years. He would do whatever he needed to keep her happy, but he couldn't think of any scenario he was comfortable with.

He wondered if the news would change the way she felt about him. Would she be sorry she married him? Would his age now become a sore point between them? Would she yearn for a younger man who could give her what she wanted? His worst fears could materialize, and he shuddered at the thought. He couldn't tell her now. It was too risky. He would wait awhile until he'd had a chance to think through every possibility. After everything, he couldn't lose her now. He wouldn't survive it.

~

"OH, PENNY, IT'S BEAUTIFUL!" Anna said as she walked around her, admiring her wedding dress. "You are going to be such a gorgeous bride."

"I can't believe the wedding is only a week away. I'm so nervous!"

"Don't be Penny. It goes by so fast. Just soak it all in," Anna said, remembering her own wedding. "Try to remember every detail."

"Are you happy, Anna?" Penny asked. "Are you glad you got married?"

"Oh, yes, I'm so happy with Grant. He treats me so well. I could never dream of anything better," Anna said as she fluffed Penny's train and let it fall to the floor. "I know you'll be happy too, Penny. You and Sawyer are meant for each other."

Penny was quiet for a few minutes.

"You know," she said finally, "I've never dated anyone but Sawyer. He's the only man I've ever, you know, *known*."

Anna wasn't sure what to say. It sounded as if Penny had a few regrets or some cold feet jitters.

"Well, you couldn't do any better, Penny," Anna said finally, taking her hand. "He's kind and sweet and very handsome, and it's obvious he loves you very much."

"You really think so, Anna?" Penny said as she tilted her head and studied her reflection in the mirror.

"Yes," Anna said, " I do. So you should stop worrying and enjoy the moment. Before you know it, you'll be chasing little ones around!"

Penny smiled at the thought. She and Sawyer had always talked about having a big family.

"Speaking of babies," she said with a sly smile, "when are you and Grant going to start trying?"

"We've been unofficially trying since we got married. But so far, nothing has happened. We haven't talked about it, but I know Grant really wants a child. I hope he doesn't get impatient with me."

"Oh, Anna, it will happen! Just give it some time," Penny said as she hugged her. Anna hugged her back and tried to put the worry out of her mind.

When Anna returned to the tavern, Grant was behind the bar and busy preparing the place for the evening crowd. She kissed him and wrapped her arms around him, still a little emotional from her conversation with Penny. He kissed her back, then put his hands on her shoulders.

"Did you girls have fun?" he asked as he pushed a strand of hair away from her face.

"We did," she said. "Penny looks gorgeous in her dress. She's going to be a beautiful bride," she said, smiling up at him. "What have you been doing?"

"Just getting the bar all set for the evening. I'd like to do some night fishing tonight if it's okay with you. I'll get Billy to work the bar with you and help you close. It shouldn't be too busy. Would that be all right?" Grant asked her.

"Yes, of course," she said. "Will you be gone all night again? Like last time?"

"Yes," he said. "I'd like to. I'll head back in the morning, but If I have fish to clean, I won't be back here until ten o'clock or so."

Grant had always liked to night fish, but he had been drawn to the bay more than ever since the night he'd dumped the body. He didn't know why. He guessed it was the same reason that murderers usually returned to the scene of the crime. He didn't expect to see or find anything. The creatures of the bay had long since consumed her father's remains. Yet he felt compelled to go anyway. He would navigate to the same spot and sit there, listening to the waves lap against the boat. After a while, he would move on, never understanding exactly why he needed to do it.

In the long months since the detectives had shown up, Anna had never mentioned anything about her father again. Grant wondered if, through the years, she had found a way to reframe things into how she wanted to remember them. Maybe she had developed it as a coping mechanism during the years of awfulness. That day, she had "retold" the story and asked him twice if he remembered. It was as if she was imprinting the memory upon him. *Do you remember Grant?*

As he exited the mouth of the river and headed into the bay that evening, the sun was setting, the bright orange sphere taking its last gasps as it sunk behind the dark blue waters of the bay. With the wind in his face and his eyes on the colors of the sky, he tried to remember how coming out on the bay at night used to make him happy. Now, it had lost its joy and had become a dark obsession, and he was terrified he would never be able to shake it.

∽

WHEN GRANT RETURNED to the apartment the next morning, he found Anna sitting in a chair by the window. It surprised him that she didn't seem to hear him come in, but she wasn't startled when he put his hand on her shoulder. Instead, she covered his hand with hers and looked up at him.

"Are you okay, Anna?" he said, a look of worry across his face.

"Yes," she said. "I'm just a little tired. I didn't sleep well. I never do when you're not here."

He smiled at her and squeezed her shoulder. "I'm going to take a quick shower," he said. "I need to head downstairs soon to get the tavern ready to open."

While he was showering, she prepared a simple breakfast, sat at the kitchen table, and waited.

"Are you sure there is nothing wrong, Anna?" he asked as he came out, drying his hair with a towel. "You don't seem yourself."

"I'm sure," she said but added nothing more. "How was your fishing trip?" she asked. "Did you catch anything?"

He chuckled. "I always catch something," he said, smiling at her. "But yes, I caught some nice fish. They are cleaned and in the walk-in. I'll ask Loretta to fry some up for our dinner this evening. Would you like that?"

She smiled at him, and he was glad to see her brighten up a little. He could tell something was bothering her. She wasn't so reflective often, and if she was, he usually knew why. Whatever it was, it was something she didn't want to share with him, which troubled him.

"I think Penny is having some wedding jitters," she said, changing the subject. "She told me she's never been with anyone but Sawyer, so I think she's just thinking maybe she should have dated around a little more or had more experiences. But she loves Sawyer, and he adores her. They'll work it out,"

148

"Well, I sure hope so," he said, hoping that was the cause of her worry. "It's only a few days until the wedding,"

"I remember being so excited before we got married and looking so forward to the honeymoon. She's just nervous, I think. She'll be okay."

"I've been thinking," he said. "When Penny is back after their honeymoon, and we have some coverage with the tavern, why don't you and I go away for a few days for our anniversary? We can make it like a second honeymoon."

He saw her break out with a huge smile. "Oh, Grant, that would be wonderful. Can we go back to the cottage on the cape?"

"Sure," he said. "I'll call today and see when it's available. It would be nice to get away and spend some alone time with you."

"Oh, I can't wait," she said, wrapping her arms around his shoulders.

Grant was glad to see a shift in her mood and hoped some time away might help her cure the melancholy plaguing her. It might be a chance for him to leave some things behind, too.

GRANT AND ANNA stared at each other across the sanctuary as they listened to Father Hudson recite the vows for Penny and Sawyer.

Grant smiled at her when he saw the tears on Anna's cheeks. He knew she was sentimental, but he'd noticed she'd been particularly so the last few days. He hoped the wedding would lift her spirits. He didn't often see her that way, but he didn't pretend to understand everything about her. Though she was the most transparent woman he had ever known, he knew there were dark parts of her that he would never understand. Whatever was bothering her would pass. He was sure of it.

Grant had offered to host the reception at the tavern since it was a small wedding, and they didn't have much money to spend. As a wedding gift, he supplied all the libations and convinced the restaurants around town to send in food. Loretta had spent hours making and decorating their wedding cake, and Anna thought it was one of the most beautiful cakes she had ever seen. The generosity had allowed Sawyer to plan a lovely honeymoon.

Anna stood behind the bar watching the young couple laugh and talk with their guests, envying them for being on the cusp of their lives together. Grant came up behind her and wrapped his arms around her.

"How are you, darling?" he asked, kissing the back of her neck.

"They look happy, don't they?" she said wistfully. "Wasn't that a wonderful time, Grant, the night of our wedding?"

"It was," he said as he remembered it. "So I guess Penny came around then," he chuckled. "I could tell Sawyer was nervous up at the alter before she came down the aisle. I think he was a little afraid she wouldn't show."

He'd expected Anna to laugh with him, but she didn't. He couldn't see her face, so he couldn't gauge her thinking, but he felt her mood shift again. Whatever had been on her mind for the last few days was back again, making him uneasy. It wasn't like her to dwell on things. If there was one thing about Anna, she could compartmentalize. Whatever it was, it was bigger than that.

CHAPTER NINETEEN

T he little cottage, perched above the dunes on the cape's bright white sugar sand beach, was exactly as Anna remembered it. She adored the feel of the place with its overstuffed furniture, chintz fabrics, and pretty antiques. She didn't know its age, but the charming little house held a palpable nostalgia, and as they sat on the porch swing watching the sunset colors paint the Gulf, Anna hoped to feel again the magic they shared on their honeymoon.

Cape San Blas, breathtaking with its turquoise waters and gentle surf, was largely undiscovered by tourists, so they saw only a few people. The long strip of land attached to the Florida Peninsula had only a smattering of houses, and the long, wild coastlines on either side were beautiful and pristine. St. Joseph's Bay sat within its gentle curve, where she hoped Grant would take her scalloping. He'd taken her there on their honeymoon, and she'd enjoyed a whole day of searching and gathering up the little mollusks. Afterward, he had cleaned and cooked up the tender morsels, and they had dined outside on the porch, watching the spectacular changing colors of the Gulf. It was one of her favorite memories from that week.

She hoped this time away spent in the romantic little cottage might help her pull out of the emotional tailspin she'd been in for the last few weeks and be fruitful in other ways besides just getting a break from the everyday grind of running the tavern. She very much wanted a child, and she thought Grant did too. Maybe something would happen as a result of their frequent lovemaking there. Hopefully, the timing would be right.

They hadn't discussed that, despite it being a year since they'd married, she had yet to become pregnant. She'd tried tracking her cycle and thought she had timed things right several times, but it didn't seem so. She'd decided a couple of months ago to stop trying to figure that out. She wasn't sure she was doing it right, and it just seemed to add to the pressure. It was probably better to try not to worry and let nature take its course. Still, she feared something might be wrong. If she were unable to conceive, it would be devastating to her.

Now, with Penny and Sawyer married, she was afraid Penny would turn up pregnant before she did. That would make it glaringly apparent that something could be wrong and might raise questions in Grant's mind. She prayed it would happen for her soon. She worried Grant wouldn't want to stay with her if she couldn't give him a child. Losing Grant was something she couldn't think about.

"What are you thinking about, Anna?" he said as he smiled at her.

"I'm remembering our honeymoon and thinking about how happy I am to be here with you now," she said, smiling at him.

"Are you sure?" he asked. "You looked a little pensive for a moment."

"It's just so bittersweet to be back here with you, Grant. It was such a magical time. It seems so long ago, but it's only been a little over a year."

"I feel the same way," he said, looking out over the waters of the Gulf. "But a lot has happened in the last year."

She knew what he was thinking about, so she left it alone. She'd made a vow to herself never to bring it up again, but now and then, she saw the same look in his eye she'd seen when the detectives came to visit, and she knew it was on his mind. She sensed it still haunted him, but talking about it wouldn't help him. It was better to try to forget about it.

They were quiet for a while, watching the little seabirds chase the tide back and forth, and the setting sun cast its magnificent array of colors on the surf. Every sunset on the cape seemed more beautiful than the last, and even though the little cottage faced the east, the colors on the surf made the evenings beautiful. In the moment's serenity, it seemed to her like nothing bad could ever touch them there, and she wished they could stay forever.

GRANT WAS VERY worried about his wife. Even though she seemed happy to be at the cottage for the week, whatever was clouding her mood had yet to dissipate. He had no idea what was bothering her, but she clearly didn't want to talk about it. It wasn't like her. In all the time he'd known her, he'd never seen her closed off. Something had happened that had shifted her.

He could feel it. It was like a whisper from her soul that he couldn't quite hear. He was desperate to rescue her from it, but he felt powerless. All he could do was try to lift her spirits and pray it would soon pass.

He spent the days trying to occupy her mind. They took long walks on the serene beach, where he tried to engage her in interesting conversation, and at night, he would cook for her and pour her wine until she seemed ready for sleep. Then he would take her to bed, tenderly make love to her, and hold her until she fell asleep.

As the days went by, her mood seemed to lift a little, but as their time at the cape began to draw to a close, he worried that without the beautiful scenery of the coast and the magic of the little cottage to soothe her soul, she would slip backward.

He watched her carefully as they were packing up to go home, looking for any indication of her mood, but he could find none. If she was feeling sad or emotional, she wasn't showing it. As they headed back to Apalachicola, she was quiet yet serene. He hoped the week at the cottage had brought her back to herself. He didn't think he could bear to see her so melancholy much longer.

As they settled back into the day-to-day of running the tavern and living above it, she seemed to pull out of whatever emotional slump she'd been in and returned to her usual happy and sweet-natured self. Grant was relieved and vowed to provide her with a change of scenery more often. Perhaps their mundane life was not enough stimulation for her and allowed ghosts from her past to sneak in. He had no idea if that was the case, but with the abundance of beautiful scenery around them, it wouldn't be hard to change her view now and then.

He also made it a point to take her out for a nice weekly dinner. Loretta was an excellent cook and made them delectable meals nearly every evening, but he felt it was good to get Anna out of the tavern and away from the apartment now and then. New places and people seemed to make her happy. As the days since the cottage stretched into a month, Grant breathed a sigh of relief that his wife seemed to have left behind whatever was bothering her for good.

ANNA SAT DOWN HARD on the barstool with a sigh.

"What's wrong, Anna?" Penny said. "Are you okay? You look exhausted."

"I am," she said. "I've just felt drained lately. I've had a little stomach bug, and I think that's been taking all my energy away."

"Oh, honey," Penny said, "you go on up and rest. I'll finish up here. You should see Dr. Thompson tomorrow and have him check you over. You do look a little peaked."

"Thank you, Penny. If you could finish up, that would be wonderful. And I think I'll take your advice. I'm going to call him in the morning. Goodnight," she called over her shoulder as she started up the stairs.

"Goodnight, Anna. I hope you feel better," Penny said as she hurried to finish the closing. She didn't want the noise to disturb Anna's rest. She was suddenly worried about her. Penny didn't know what she would do if she were really sick. She couldn't lose Anna.

She hoped it was just a passing virus or perhaps a little food poisoning. She knew those types of things could hang around for a while. Still, she had a nagging worry that it was something more than that. She'd never seen Anna sick or even heard her complain. Something was definitely wrong.

"How long have you been feeling unwell, Anna?" Dr. Thompson asked her as he scribbled notes into her chart.

"A few weeks," she said. "I came down with some stomach upset, and I haven't been able to get rid of it. It makes me so tired, too."

"Okay," he said. "I'd like to run a few tests and see what might be going on. Have you ever had anything like this before?"

She shook her head no. She was never sick and couldn't remember being sick as a child. How she managed to stay healthy in the environment she grew up in, she didn't know.

"I'll have the nurse draw your blood. It will take a few days to get everything back. In the meantime, you should rest and eat a bland diet," he said. "I'll call you when we have your results."

She watched him go, and as she waited for the nurse, she thought about Grant. She hadn't told him she wasn't feeling well because she didn't want to worry him. But as the illness seemed to linger, she began to get nervous and thought she might need to talk with him about it. But now that the doctor was going to run some tests, she felt it was probably better to wait until she got the results back and talked to the doctor again. A couple of days more wouldn't matter.

She stopped by the market on her way home to pick up a few things they needed. She hurried, thinking Grant might already be home from his night fishing trip on the bay and be worried about where she was. Perhaps he'd caught some nice fish for their dinner that evening.

"I was wondering where you were," he said as she came through the door with her shopping bags. He crossed the room and took them from her as he planted a kiss on her lips.

"Just needed to pick up a few things from the market," she said. "How was your night out on the bay?"

"It was good. I have some nice fish for your favorite dinner," he said with a smile. "Did you sleep okay? You look a little tired again."

"I slept okay," she said. "We had a hectic night in the tavern last night, so it took a while to close. Penny was nice enough to stay later and help me finish up."

"I'm sorry you had a tough night. I didn't expect it to be that busy, or I wouldn't have left you girls on your own."

"It's okay," she said as she smiled at him. "We managed okay."

Anna didn't want him to worry about her, so she put on a brave face. But, deep inside, she was consumed with worry. Whatever was wrong with her was like nothing she'd ever felt before. She just hoped it was nothing serious.

~

WHEN ANNA HUNG up the phone with Dr. Thompson's office, she struggled with understanding everything he told her and the questions he'd asked. She thought some of them were odd, and she wasn't sure what to make of them. She knew she had to talk to Grant that evening about everything. It wouldn't be fair to keep anything from him longer than necessary. They had plans to go out to dinner at the hotel. She thought it would be the perfect place to have the conversation she needed to have with him. She wasn't sure exactly how he would react.

They were seated at a lovely table for two by the window. It was their favorite table, and Grant always requested it when they dined there. She let them settle in for a little while before bringing anything up. She wanted him to be relaxed when they talked. The conversation needed to go well.

"You look lovely, Darling," he said, admiring her beauty in the soft candlelight. "You seem better rested today."

"I am," she said as she smiled at him. "Today was a better day."

She looked at him momentarily, then dropped her gaze to her lap.

"Grant," she said, "I have something to discuss with you." She paused for a moment. "I haven't felt well for the last few weeks or so. I've been having a lot of stomach upset and got a little worried when it didn't go away. I'm sorry I should have told you. I didn't want you to worry."

She paused again, trying to gauge his reaction. She could see the alarm on his face, but he wasn't saying anything.

"So," she said, "I went to see Dr. Thompson to see if he could figure out what was wrong."

"Anna," he said as he leaned forward and took her hand, "are you all right? Is everything okay?"

"They ran some tests, and he called me this morning to let

me know the results," she said. She wasn't sure exactly how to tell him. He looked so worried.

"I'm okay," she said as her face broke into a serene smile. "We are going to be parents, Grant. I'm expecting our child."

CHAPTER TWENTY

G rant could not begin to fathom what was happening. Seeing Anna's face when she told him the news told him everything. She was thrilled with the pregnancy and believed wholeheartedly that the baby was Grant's child. But how could that be?

He began to wonder if the test results were wrong. Maybe they had mixed up the samples, or something else had happened that had given the wrong result. The baby had to be his. He couldn't imagine another scenario that made sense.

Anna was a very loving wife and fiercely loyal to him. These were things he was sure of. The thought of her being unfaithful was something he could never comprehend. He felt he would know somehow if she was. There had to be an explanation.

He decided to just put the bad thoughts out of his mind. Anna was thrilled, and there was no way he would do anything that might dampen her joy. Being pregnant and the impending birth was all she wanted to talk about. And even with the lingering doubts, he enjoyed seeing her so happy.

"I think we should look for a house," he said one evening as they enjoyed a late dinner together. Anna hadn't been feeling well enough to work in the tavern much, but she took long naps during the day to stay up late to eat with Grant after he closed for the night.

"Really?" she said. "Why? I love our apartment here."

"I'm worried about you on the stairs. It will only get harder for you, and I worry about you taking a fall. Besides, having more space and a yard for the baby to play in would be nice."

"And a garden?" she asked, her eyes dancing like a child's.

"And a garden," he said with a chuckle.

"Okay," she said, "how do we go about looking for a house?"

"I'll set you up with my friend, a realtor here, and he'll take you around to see everything available. When you find something you like, we'll go see it together."

"Thank you, Grant," she said as she looked at him, her expression one of gratitude and love. "I never dreamed I'd have a real home and a family growing up. This means the world to me."

He reached over and pulled her to him, caressed her face, then gently kissed her lips. He decided then that nothing else mattered. As long as he had Anna, he had everything.

"I JUST THOUGHT I would call and check on you, Grant. I assume by now Anna has told you the news," Dr. Thompson said, his voice full of concern.

"She has," Grant said. "I think the test results must have been wrong, Bill. There is no way this isn't my child."

"It's possible, I guess, that maybe something happened with the sample. Do you want me to order another test so you can be sure?"

"I probably should," Grant said. "But we are happy, so I'm just going to leave things alone for now. Anna has been through too much and deserves this happiness."

"Are you sure, Grant? Don't you want to know?"

"I'll think about it, Bill. I'll be in touch with you next week."

Grant knew he should pursue another test. Any man would want to know, but he couldn't think about destroying their happiness. He couldn't put the possibility that it could be his child out of his mind, and he wanted to hold on to it for as long as possible. In the end, would it make a difference? If Anna loved him and wanted to be with him, even if she had made a mistake, would he not forgive her? Would he not raise the child as his own if that's what she wanted? Maybe God had planned for this. If Grant couldn't give her a child, perhaps someone had been put in her path, making it possible for them. He might be rationalizing, but it was all he knew to do.

They found a beautiful historic home just a couple blocks off Market Street that Anna fell in love with. It had classic Southern architecture with a wide porch and a pretty garden off the back that bordered a large yard. She adored the high windows, the bath with a clawfoot tub, and the sunroom where she planned to grow ferns and orchids. It was like a dream come true for her, and never in her wildest dreams had she thought she would live in such a place.

Her days were filled with packing what they planned to take and shopping for furniture and necessities they would need for the new house. She decided to fill the old house with things that reminded her of the cottage on the cape, where she was sure the baby had been conceived, so she perused the local second-hand shops and antique stores. Grant took her to Tallahassee for the things she couldn't find in town.

They decided to keep the apartment over the tavern rather than rent it out. It would be a place to retreat to if needed while working or to help someone who needed temporary shelter, so there wasn't much to do there to prepare for the move. When the time came, they would only need to gather up their personal things.

During the busy time, Grant tried to keep the creeping thoughts out of his mind. He wanted the baby to be his, and as much as he was tempted to assume it was, he couldn't help but let the doubts come in. Even though he knew he would never leave her, no matter the results of another test, he still had a nagging inclination to find out.

"I wish I had better news, Grant, but I'm afraid the results are pretty much the same. I don't think it's possible that this is your child," Dr. Thompson said with a big sigh. "So what are you thinking? What now?"

"I don't know. I just don't understand how it couldn't be mine. Anna isn't that way, and I've never had an inkling of suspicion. Hell, I can't think of a time when she's been out of my sight long enough for her even to get to know anyone else like that. I just can't believe it. Are you sure, Bill?"

"See for yourself, Grant," he said as he handed the results to him. "I'm afraid the numbers don't lie."

Grant stared at the piece of paper in his hands. He wasn't a doctor, but interpreting the results didn't take much.

"I'm not going to say anything to Anna," he said as he stood to go. "I want this baby for her and for us. I'll just have to learn to live with whatever happened."

Dr. Thompson dropped his gaze to his desk and sighed again. "I feel for you, Grant. I know this can't be easy, and I admire you for wanting to stick by Anna. I've seen you two together, and I don't think I've ever seen a happier couple. I don't know what happened, but I'm here if you need anything."

Grant nodded and shook the man's hand before leaving. Walking home, he tried to imagine the fallout if he confronted Anna. He couldn't fathom it. His mind wouldn't go there. It seemed impossible that it could be true. Anna loved him. He was sure of it.

He realized he had the test results still in his hand, so he carefully folded them into a small square and tucked them into the top pocket of his shirt. He needed to let the reality of things go. If he wanted to keep Anna and everything they had together, he would have to be strong and push it from his mind.

"Congratulations, you two," Mason West said to them as he wrapped up the paperwork on the closing of their new house. "That's a wonderful home. I know that you two will be happy there."

"Thank you, Mason," Grant said as he smiled at his wife. "We are excited to get settled. Our baby is due in just a few months, and I know Anna is eager to get the nursery ready."

"What are you two hoping for? Girl or boy?"

"Just a healthy baby," Anna said as she smiled back at Grant.

"Of course," Mason said. "Here are your keys, Grant. As you know, the seller is the estate of the former owner, so if you have any questions about the house, call me, and we'll get them answered for you."

Grant nodded, then turned to his wife. "Are you ready, darling?"

She nodded as he helped her out of the chair. Although he always thought she was the most beautiful woman he had ever known, he was awed by how being with child gave her an ethereal glow. She was handling the pregnancy well, and the doctor assured them that all was progressing nicely, but he worried about her constantly. The thought of childbirth terrified him, and he dreaded having to watch her endure the pain. But, each day that passed that she was happy and healthy made him grateful.

After the closing, Grant and Sawyer moved the furniture and what Anna had collected into the house. Three days later, Grant closed the apartment door for the last time and took Anna to her new home a few blocks away.

As they started up the walk, Grant asked her to wait and walked up the steps where he gathered a bouquet he'd picked from the garden. She smiled as he presented the flowers and led her to the front steps, where he carefully helped her sit down.

"I want a picture of you, Anna," Grant said. "You look so beautiful, and I want to remember this day forever."

As the days passed and they prepared for the baby's impending arrival, Grant had never seen Anna so peaceful and serene. As she carefully and thoughtfully prepared the nursery, he liked to watch her carefully folding the tiny clothing and blankets or rearranging the baby's things on the built-in bookshelves. Now and then, he would find her sitting in the rocker in the little room, gazing out the window. When she'd catch him looking at her, she'd reach out her hand and pull him to her for a kiss.

"Soon, Grant," she'd say. "Soon, we will be holding our baby."

One night, not too long after, she woke him by gently rubbing his shoulder.

"It's time, Grant," she said softly in the darkness.

As Grant quickly gathered their things for the hospital, Anna sat calmly on the couch, managing her breathing. It was a long way to the hospital in Tallahassee, and Grant feared they had waited too long. But Anna seemed to instinctively know what she was doing, and they arrived well before the baby came.

Grant's insides would churn every time Anna had a strong contraction. He was amazed at her strength as she managed through the pain, and when it was finally time to push, he held her hand as she bore down with everything she had. Moments later, baby Kendrick arrived. Grant heard Anna laughing and crying at the same time as he gazed upon the baby the doctor held in his hands.

"It's a boy!" the delivery nurse exclaimed, and Grant felt all the air go out of his lungs at once. They had a son.

As Grant stood staring at the baby in the bassinet wrapped

in a blue blanket, all he could see was Anna. The boy looked exactly like her, and Grant could find nothing about the baby that wasn't familiar to him. He once again told himself that the baby had to be his. No matter what the test results said, there was no way this wasn't his child.

They decided to name the child after Grant's father, William, and give him Grant's name as his middle name. As he gazed at the baby, he repeated the name in his mind over and over. *William Grant Kendrick.* It was a beautiful and noble name, and Grant was proud to have passed it to him. He tried to imagine the boy as a young man with Anna's light hair and blue eyes. He realized then that it didn't matter if the child was his. As long as he was Anna's, that was enough for him.

ANNA LAY on their bed and stroked the blond peach fuzz on little William's head. He was perfect in every way, and sometimes, she spent hours examining his little features or entwining his tiny fingers with her own. He was a beautiful child. Everyone who saw him admired his exquisite features and remarked how much he looked like Anna. She could not believe she had created something so perfect.

She marveled at every little milestone as the weeks after his birth stretched into months. He was a big boy and tall for his age. She knew that had to come from Grant, as no one on her side had extraordinary height. Grant, on the other hand, was six feet four and broad-shouldered. But aside from the baby's size, everything about little Will was her.

He did everything early, from rolling over to sitting up to walking, and she loved sharing and showing all the accomplishments of the day with Grant when he came home at night. While she loved being in her home, she delighted in taking Will to the tavern and showing him off to all the patrons. By the time he was two years old, he had captured the hearts of everyone and was a regular sight, running around the place and making the patrons smile with his adorable good nature.

One evening, one of the old timers slipped a gold coin into her hand and put his arm around her shoulder.

"Put that away for the boy in case he needs it someday," he said with a chuckle.

"Thank you," she said as she hugged him, "that is so kind of you."

"He's an Apalach boy," he said as he kissed her on the cheek. "He's special, and he's family."

The kindness the people showed towards her and now Will always filled her heart with joy. She had never known people who cared so much about one another.

When she got home later that evening, after she put Will to bed, she remembered the coin and wondered where she should put it for safekeeping. When she perused their bedroom, she saw Grant's valet on the dresser and thought that would be the perfect spot. She opened the small drawer on the bottom and looked inside for a suitable place. When she did, she saw something gold glittering toward the back of the drawer as the light hit it. When she pulled the drawer out further, what she saw shocked her. She recognized it instantly and slowly pulled it from the valet and held it by the chain as it dangled and spun in front of her eyes. It was her father's St. Christopher medal, and the reality of what it meant threatened to overcome her. Even though she had always known the truth, the proof made her knees weak. She slowly turned it over in her hand, hoping the ultimate evidence wouldn't be there. Her heart clenched when she saw the initials engraved on the back. She put her hands to her face and wept, not for her father, but for Grant's innocence.

After a while, she stood, went to the valet, and pulled the drawer out to put the medal back where she found it. When she did, a small piece of folded paper fell out. It intrigued her, and even though it felt like snooping, she slowly unfolded and read it. At first, she didn't understand, but as she comprehended its meaning, she thought she would collapse. As she let the paper flutter to the floor, she knew then that nothing would ever be the same again.

CHAPTER TWENTY-ONE

Anna slept on the little single bed in the baby's room. She couldn't bear to be in their bed. When Grant came home and found her there, she told him the baby had felt warm earlier, and she wanted to be near him if he became ill in the middle of the night. But the real reason was that she couldn't face Grant, and she knew she wouldn't be able to sleep. There were too many things she needed to think through.

Finding the medal had stirred up some memories and old fears. It also brought home the stark reality of what Grant had done for her. It wasn't that she didn't know the truth. It was just that the medal told a bit of a story that she had never wanted to know. It was also the only evidence that could tie Grant to her father. She wondered why he'd kept it, and the possibilities of what that meant frightened her. Was it a souvenir? Had he meant to discard it and forgotten about it? She didn't know.

But as difficult as all of that was to process, it was the other information she discovered that rocked her to the core. The implications of it were stunning. That Grant was incapable of fathering a child was hard to comprehend and led her down dark roads she had hoped never to revisit. But the hardest thing for her heart to realize was that Grant knew that baby Will was not his child but had accepted him as his son all the same. That could only be born out of his love for her. It was heartbreaking to think about what he must have gone through when he realized it, and yet she'd never noticed him being moody or withdrawing from her. Grant was the kindest, most loyal, and most loving man she had ever met. She didn't deserve him and was now riddled with guilt and shame.

From the date of the test results, he knew the baby could not have been his from the beginning, yet he had forgiven her without ever knowing what happened. He had provided her with a beautiful home, an abundant life, and a father to her child when he could have shunned her from his life. That kind of love and sacrifice was almost too much to comprehend.

Realizing now that little Will was not Grant's child devastated her and brought the events of a night she had pushed from her mind back in a way that threatened to crush her. She was afraid the secret would be revealed eventually, and the thought made her physically shake with fear. So many lives would be affected, potentially ruined, and she could not bear the thought. But as painful as it was, she forced herself to remember.

She had been finishing up a few things in the bar after Billy had gone home for the night when she heard a tap at the front door. Looking up, she saw a familiar face and immediately knew something was wrong. She hurried to the door, unlocked it, and let him in.

"Hey, Anna," he said. "Is Grant here?"

"No," she said, "he's out night fishing. What's wrong?"

The troubled look on his face alarmed her. He said nothing momentarily as he looked at her, then looked away.

"I just need someone to talk to," he said.

The anguish in his voice made Anna's heart break.

"Come sit down," she said as she slipped behind the bar, grabbed a highball glass, and poured him a whiskey. She grabbed another glass off the back bar and poured herself one, and the two sat quietly for a while, just sipping and thinking.

"Women are so complicated," he said finally.

"Oh, and men aren't," she said, laughing.

"No," he said, laughing too, "not like women."

"How so?" she asked, eyeing him over the rim of her glass.

He thought momentarily, his eyes narrowing, trying to find the right words. She reached over the bar, refilled his glass, and then refilled her own.

"I never know what they're thinking. I try, but I never get it right." He chuckled as he shook his head. "You're not that way, though, Anna. You are so honest and open. It's like looking into a clear glass of water."

"I thought I was supposed to be mysterious," she said, waving her glass around. "Grant will probably get tired of me then."

"No," he said as he drained his glass. "You never have to worry about that."

They were quiet again and a little subdued, the whiskey and the emotions taking a toll on them. She realized she hadn't had anything to eat all evening. The bar had been too busy, and she'd had no time.

"Are you hungry?" she asked. "I'm starved. I could make us a little something in the kitchen."

"Yes," he said. "That would be great, Anna."

She grabbed her glass, dimmed the lights in the tavern, and headed to the kitchen. There, she made them a light dinner of sandwiches and fruit. He followed and stood watching her as he leaned against the large refrigerator.

"Do you like living here, above the tavern, Anna?" he said.

"Yes," she said, smiling over her shoulder at him, "we're happy here."

When she finished, the two sat at the little table in the kitchen and had their simple meal. Anna made small talk, trying to keep the conversation light. He'd gotten quiet and broody, and she guessed being a little drunk had gotten him thinking about his troubles again.

She'd set the fruit bowl between them, and she watched as he grabbed an orange and slowly peeled it. His brow was furled, and she could tell he was deep in thought.

She got up, gathered their plates, and took them to the sink. She stood there momentarily, her back to him as she finished her drink. The silence between them had become long, and she suddenly felt awkward. Although he was a friend of Grant's, she had never been alone with him. She didn't want to give him the wrong idea. It was time for her to say goodnight and send him on his way.

When she turned, she hadn't realized he'd silently come up behind her. Her uneasiness grew, and she stepped backward and leaned against the sink. His demeanor was suddenly serious, and he had a look in his eye that she didn't recognize. She took a shaky breath and tried to tamp down the uncomfortable feeling rising inside of her.

"Beautiful Anna," he whispered as he stepped toward her and pushed her hair away from her eyes. She turned her head away in defiance and averted her eyes.

He reached for her, gently touching her waist and pulling her towards him. She stumbled and fell against him.

"No," she said as she tried to push herself away from him. "We can't do this."

As if he didn't hear her, he bent and kissed her, his lips soft and tasting of orange. Then he pulled her to him, wrapping his arms around her. She felt powerless, his large frame more than twice her size.

"Please," she whimpered.

"Please, what?" he whispered as his kiss lingered on her lips. She tried to push him away again, but his weight had her pinned against the sink. She felt his hands on her breasts, then move up under her dress. Her breath caught in her throat as he

171

unbuckled his belt.

"Do you want me to stop, Anna?" he asked as his lips traveled down her neck. She wanted to say yes and stop the moment's madness, but no words would come. She felt like she couldn't breathe as his lips returned to hers, and when he lifted her onto the counter, pulled up her dress, and took her, she cried out in anguish. Her mind swirled with thoughts and feelings so intense she thought she would lose consciousness, and then, as quickly as it began, it was over.

They stayed there for what seemed like an eternity, Anna feeling the heaving of his chest slowly subside. When she could breathe again, she drew back and looked at him.

"You have to go now," she said, her eyes fiery and angry.

"Anna," he sighed, "I'm sorry."

"You have to go now," she repeated a little louder.

He buckled his belt, tucked in his shirt, and started to back away from her. She grabbed his collar and pulled him back, staring at him.

"This never happened! Do you understand me?" she said through her teeth. He nodded as he looked down at his feet.

"Say it! This never happened!" she said as she shook him by the collar. "Say it!"

"This never happened, Anna."

She released him, and he staggered back a few steps. She put her face in her hands so she didn't have to look at him.

"Please go now," she whispered.

She listened as he quietly left the kitchen. When she heard the tavern's back door close, she slid off the counter and onto the floor. She sat for a while, the tears sliding silently down her face and running down to the front of her dress. Finally, she pulled herself to her feet, locked the back door, and went upstairs. She undressed, showered, and climbed into bed. When she saw the light of the dawn through the windows, she closed her eyes to sleep. She had to put it out of her mind. Grant would be home for breakfast soon.

As she returned to herself, the shame of the moment washed over her in a giant wave again. How could she have let it happen? Why didn't she do more to stop him? But she then realized that had it not happened, she wouldn't have baby Will. At that moment, she had the perplexing thought that she would do anything, yet nothing to change what had happened. It put an awful angst in her soul. It was a terrible place to be.

She cried silently at the thought of what Grant must think of her and longed to tell him the truth. Doing so might make him realize that it was unintentional, innocent in a way. But then what? He would know he was not Will's father, which might be too much to bear. At least with how things stood, he could hope that Will was somehow his child. As long as Will's paternity was unconfirmed, he seemed to be able to accept things the way they were. Was she willing to risk that?

Revealing the truth would destroy so many lives. How would Will's true father react if he discovered the boy was his son? Would he demand his rights as a father? He was a married man. The fallout was too terrible to contemplate.

She had to be strong now. She had to help Grant believe that Will was his son, and she vowed to herself never to let the truth be known. She would do whatever it took to protect what they had, and she would need to put aside her desires to purge her sins through confession. To do so would be selfish. She had to put it out of her mind forever. She got up, crept across the hall to their bedroom, and climbed into bed with her husband.

"Is everything all right, Anna?" Grant asked as he rolled over towards her.

"Yes," she whispered. "Everything is fine, darling. Go back to sleep. Your son is well."

CHAPTER TWENTY-TWO

It was a beautiful spring day in Apalach, and though it was sunny and warm, the breeze still held a hint of coolness. Anna had cultivated her garden into an idyllic setting with an abundance of hydrangeas and chrysanthemums and beautiful ground covers. Grant had built her a pretty picket fence around its border and a brick patio so they could enjoy temperate evenings there. With the giant live oaks as a canopy, it was exquisitely perfect and picturesque. Anna seemed to spread her beauty to everything she touched.

Grant watched as she brought the cake to the table in the garden. It was Will's third birthday party, and Anna had been planning it for weeks. He delighted in her bright smile, and she looked beautiful in the pretty sundress she had chosen for the occasion. Her long golden locks blew gently in the wind as she arranged the table, and when she unexpectedly looked up, she smiled at him. This was his Anna, the one he longed for constantly.

Still, something was just under the surface of her smile that had been gnawing at him for weeks, maybe months. In the three years since the baby had arrived, she had been happy and serene and noticeably content, but something had happened in recent months to change that.

She was the Anna he'd always known if she was engaged in conversation or socializing. But, left to her own thoughts, she quickly became sullen and withdrawn. It was a pattern he had become all too familiar with.

He only saw pure, unbridled joy when she was playing with little Will. As a mother, she was everything he could have asked for and more. She was loving and attentive and delighted in every little thing he did. Every day, he became more and more convinced that Will was somehow his child. Anna always pointed out little things about him that reminded her of Grant. An expression or a mannerism that she saw that was exactly like his. And he could always see it if he tried hard enough.

Will was growing tall, and though he was the mirror image of his mother, Grant took solace in his size. He was a big man who always pictured having big, strapping boys. He daydreamed about taking Will to harvest oysters or fish on the bay. He looked forward to that in a way he wouldn't have if he'd had only daughters. But, if he were honest, the thought of having a little girl just like Anna intrigued him. Was it possible they could conceive another little miracle?

He wondered if Anna's occasional bouts of depression were just remnants of her past returning to haunt her now and then. She'd dealt with things he couldn't even comprehend. Still, her melancholy troubled him even though he assumed it probably had nothing to do with him. He hadn't seen much of it since she found out she was pregnant, but it suddenly reappeared one day a few weeks back.

He was told not to worry too much when he spoke to Dr. Thompson about it. Sometimes, women suffered a slight depression on and off after childbirth, and it would probably pass on its own. As long as she was functioning normally and Grant observed times of happiness as well, the doctor felt he would see some improvement over time with a bit of patience. Still, Grant couldn't help but be concerned.

Penny and Anna were close, and Grant felt sure Penny would come to him if there was something she thought Grant should know. He had thought about talking with her but had never found the right time. Perhaps the doctor was right. Letting things take their natural course was probably better.

As they gathered around the table to light the candles and sing, Grant focused on his son. The boy, handsome and beautiful with his perfect features and coloring, was a picture of happiness, his little hands clasped together in anticipation as he gazed upon the cake. Any man would be proud to have such a beautiful family, and Grant could not hold back the joy he felt at that moment.

"Make a wish!" he heard Anna whisper as he blew out the candles. He watched her eyes light up as the boy huffed and puffed at the three candles, finally extinguishing them with great fanfare.

Grant moved around the table beside his wife. She leaned against him and slipped her arm around his waist, pulling him close for a moment as everyone clapped and cheered. Were it not for his nagging worry, it would have been a perfect moment.

PENNY COULD TELL something wasn't right. In the five years she'd known Anna, she'd only ever seen her in this state for a short period, right before she'd found out she was pregnant. Unbeknownst to them all, she'd been suffering from morning sickness and exhaustion, and once they'd found out a baby was on the way and had put her to bed for a few weeks, she had returned to her sweet and happy self in short order. What was happening now was different.

When she first noticed it, she hoped that Anna was pregnant again. Penny had yet to be able to conceive a child, and even though they could find nothing wrong with either her or Sawyer, she had begun to lose hope. As Godparents to little Will, they were very much involved in his life, and as best friends to Anna and Grant, they intended to stay that way. Penny felt there was nothing that could ever separate them.

The relationship between Penny and Anna was born in those first few days after Anna came to Apalachicola. Anna was naive and innocent despite the trauma she had suffered growing up, and her openness and sweetness drew Penny to her. Living in the little cottage together in the following weeks had forged an iron bond between them. Once they became close, Penny knew she could never live without Anna, and her attraction to her had never waned.

Now that something was going on with her, she felt desperate to make it go away. She was concerned about Anna's well-being, but the feeling that Anna was keeping secrets from her really bothered her. Whatever it was, Penny felt a kind of jealousy about it that she couldn't quite place. Aside from Grant, Penny was the closest person to her. The thought that there was something that Anna was keeping from her tore her apart.

"Let me help you with these," she said to Anna as she gently pushed her to the side. "I'll get these dishes finished up. You go enjoy your son's birthday party."

"Thank you, Penny," Anna said, putting her arm around her and kissing her cheek. "I don't know what I would do without you. But why don't we leave them for later and have a glass of wine on the patio? Let's enjoy a few minutes of quiet time."

Penny grabbed a dishtowel and dried her hands. "Sounds lovely, Anna," she said as she hooked her arm through hers. "I feel like I've barely had a chance to talk to you all day."

The two women were quiet for a few minutes, taking in the garden's serenity. Most of the guests had gone, and the day was waning, the sun moving low in the sky and casting long shadows through the live oaks.

"Is everything okay, Anna?" Penny asked tentatively. "You don't seem yourself lately."

Penny wasn't sure her friend had heard her. Anna was staring across the garden, seemingly lost in thought, her eyes fixed on Grant, who was talking to Sawyer.

"Anna?" she said, reaching for her hand and squeezing it.

"I'm sorry," she said. "What did you say?"

"Just that you seem a little down lately. Is everything okay?"

"Oh yes, I'm sorry," she said. "I've been very preoccupied with the party. I wanted it to be perfect for Will."

"Well, it was, and so are you," Penny said, smiling at her.

Anna returned the smile, but it quickly faded, and Penny watched as the dark cloud she'd seen before crossed over the light in Anna's soul. Something was definitely wrong, and as soon as she got a chance, she intended to speak with Grant about it.

THE OFFSHORE STORMS that frequented the Gulf in the spring moved through Apalachicola for several days, leaving cloudy skies and everything slow to dry out. Business in the tavern had been slow as the residents of the coastal enclave hunkered down against the storms and were reluctant to venture out amidst the downpours and the lightning and thunder. Though there was still some rumbling from the thunderheads offshore, even after the inclement weather moved on, cabin fever eventually caught up with them.

Grant was short-staffed and struggled to handle the packed tavern that was unusual for a Wednesday night. Anna stopped by with Will early in the evening to see Grant for a short while, but when she saw the crowd, she got behind the bar with little

Will on her hip to help out. As it got later in the evening, Will fell asleep in her arms even with the place loud and in full swing, and Anna laid him in the little cot in the back that they kept there for just such occasions.

When the crowd finally died out and Grant shut the doors for the night, they had a lot to finish up. Anna gathered the glasses and retreated to the kitchen to start running the dishwasher. With the busy night, there were several tubs of dishes, too. It was tiring work, especially at the end of a long night, and Grant could see the fatigue on her face,

"Why don't I take you and Will up to the apartment, and I'll come back down and finish up? We can spend the night here and go home in the morning."

"No," she said, "I want to help you so we can have a few minutes together before we have to go to bed," she said with a smile.

"There's not much left to do. I won't be long. Let's get Will settled and get you off your feet. " he said as he pulled a bottle of port off the rack and set it on the bar.

He retreated to the back room, where he gathered his son in his arms and slowly ascended the stairs, taking great care not to wake the boy. Upstairs, he laid the boy in the bed in the second bedroom and kissed Anna on the cheek.

"I won't be long," he whispered.

Anna showered, wrapped herself in a bathrobe, and curled up on the couch to wait for Grant. She hadn't been up to the apartment in quite some time and not since she'd learned the truth about Will's paternity. Sitting in the near darkness, with just the light from the lamp next to Grant's chair, she was overcome with shaking fear that her life could all come crashing down around her. It was a secret that threatened everything, and one she wasn't sure could be kept hidden forever. The cracks in her soul were starting to show.

Grant returned and headed for the shower as well. The pace

of the evening had left them both exhausted and sweat-stained. Anna was glad for the opportunity to collect herself. She wasn't sure she could've held herself together had Grant noticed her state.

"Would you like a glass of port?" he asked as he emerged from the bedroom and crossed the apartment to the kitchen. She nodded, and he opened the wine and poured their glasses.

"What a night," he said as he handed her one and sat down hard on the couch beside her. "I don't know what I would have done if you hadn't shown up."

"Well, at least it made up for the slow nights earlier this week," she said as she slowly sipped her wine.

"Yes, I suppose so. I guess everyone was eager to get out and about after the last few days of rain."

She studied his profile. His expression was contemplative, and she felt regretful for being so withdrawn from him the last few months. She reached out, took his hand, and pulled it to the side of her face, where she nuzzled it, then kissed his palm. When she opened her eyes, he was smiling at her, and she recognized the passion in his eyes. His hand cupped her cheek, and he leaned to kiss her.

"Where have you been, my beautiful Anna?" he asked as he moved closer, gently pushing her back onto the couch. He moved over her and let his hand travel to her neckline, where his lips tasted the tender flesh.

"Anna," he whispered as he languished in the feel of her. Before losing himself completely, he stood and scooped her up in his arms, cradling her for a moment before taking her to their bedroom. He slid the robe from her shoulders, shed his clothing, and pulled her into the bed with him. As he made love to her, she tried to respond to him, but a part of her refused to be awakened even though her mind was consumed with passion.

Afterward, as they lay together in the darkness, he felt her pulling back from him again, and when he heard her softly crying, his heart sank. She was slipping further away.

"Anna," he said, his voice full of desperation, "please tell me what's wrong. What's happened to make you so sad?"

She rolled away from him and curled up on her side. She couldn't find her voice, so she didn't answer.

"Please, Anna," he said, pulling her over to face him. "Whatever it is, it will be okay."

"No," she said, "it will never be okay. It will destroy us, Grant. Please just leave it alone."

Grant had an idea what it was. In the past months, he'd spent hours retracing their days, trying to remember the first time he'd noticed Anna's change in demeanor. It took him a long time to put the pieces of the memory together, but once he did, everything fell into place for him. Now, it was time to know the whole truth so they could forgive and forget. It wasn't about him. He'd already forgiven her for whatever she'd done. It was now a matter of her forgiving herself.

"Something happened while I was out night fishing, didn't it, Anna?"

He felt her stiffen, but she didn't answer.

"It's okay. We can talk about it, Anna. I will never let it destroy us."

"You don't understand, Grant. Things will never be the same again."

"Anna, they haven't been the same since anyway. At least if we talk about it, we can accept what happened and put it behind us. Did you have an affair, Anna?"

"No!" she said, her voice full of anguish. "It wasn't like that!"

Her answer changed the trajectory of his thinking, and panic started to rise in his throat. He thought he knew what happened. He supposed she had done something impulsively and was now racked with guilt and shame. But something else had happened. Perhaps something worse.

He knew who it was, or at least he thought he did. Through his questioning thoughts and remembrances of that time, he had figured out who had come to the tavern that night. Somehow, he had framed it in his mind as a kind of blessing, an intervention from God to give them the child they both wanted. In his more lucid moments, he realized the insanity of his rationalization, but it was the only way he could accept what had happened and forgive her. He was sure there had been no ongoing affair and that whatever happened had been a one-time lapse in judgment between them. Now, because of her reaction, he was suddenly terrified.

"Did he force himself on you, Anna?" he asked as he pulled her up by her shoulders. "Look at me, Anna! Did he rape you?"

She didn't answer but collapsed in his arms, sobbing. He held her, knowing he needed to soothe her, but his soul was seething. She needed him now, but all he could think about was ending the life of the person who had hurt her.

"I'm going to kill him," he said finally in a low voice as he slowly untangled himself from her and got up from the bed.

"No, Grant, Please!" she cried. "I should have stopped him. I just, I just..." She broke down again in sobs.

Grant began to dress as Anna watched helplessly, and when he reached into the top drawer of his dresser and pulled out his handgun, she lunged at him and clung onto him, trying with everything she had to stop him from going.

"Please, Grant! Please don't do this! It's not what you think!"

As if he didn't hear her, he pried himself away and headed for the door. He turned and took one last look at her before slamming the door and running down the stairs.

Loretta had fallen asleep on the couch, reading as she often did after a long night in the kitchen at the tavern. When she heard the banging on her door, it jarred her out of her sleep and startled her. She jumped up, wrapped her robe tightly around herself, and went to the door. She cracked it open, and when she saw Anna holding a sleeping baby Will in her arms, she opened it wide.

Anna was sobbing and a disheveled mess. Her hair was uncombed, and she had on a summer dress that was inside out. Her feet were bare, and her hands were shaking. Loretta could not imagine what was going on. The Anna she knew was always calm and beautifully put together. Something awful was happening.

"Loretta, please take my baby! I need you to take him," she said as she pushed the child into her arms.

"Anna, what's going on? What's wrong?"

"Please," she cried. "Please just take him!"

"Okay, Anna, please calm down. I will, but tell me what's happening."

"I can't, Loretta. Please just tell me you'll take care of him."

"Of course I will," she said as Anna turned to go. "Where are you going?" she called after her.

Anna didn't answer, and Loretta listened as she ran down the stairs, through the tavern, and out the front door, slamming it behind her. Little did Loretta know what horrors the night would bring and that it would be the last time she would ever see Anna Kendrick alive.

PART THREE

7 OCTOBER 2022

CHAPTER TWENTY-THREE

W ill sat on the little concrete bench in the cemetery. The season had changed in Apalachicola, and the rusty-colored leaves swirled at his feet. He watched the leave's ever-changing patterns as the cold wind swept through in gusts and let his thoughts drift. The impending winter was starting to show itself, and though he should have been longing for the warm California weather, he wasn't.

He'd woken up that morning tired after a long, restless night that had afforded little sleep. The events of the last couple of days had shifted things again. Now, he wasn't sure about anything.

Everything he had believed for years about his childhood, his father, and especially his mother, was now fluid and elusive. He didn't know what was truth and what was not, and he wasn't sure where to begin to sort it all out.

When he'd left Apalachicola on the cusp of becoming a man, he thought he had it all figured out. His mother had died young, and his father was a bitter old man. He'd been cheated out of a normal family and childhood, and he was ready to make a whole new life in a place as far away as he could get. California seemed new and shiny. There were no briny creeks or muddy oyster beds. The sunny beaches, tanned legs, and tall royal palms were a welcome change, and he did everything he could to put the memories of where he came from behind him. He deserved a better life, and California looked ripe to give it to him.

He had no idea he had talent as a writer. He'd never had much interest in it or considered it as a career choice. It wasn't until he'd taken a creative writing course as part of his under-graduate curriculum that he discovered his talent and love for it. Under the advice of one of his professors, he'd quickly shifted gears to a career path that would cement him in California. He had no reason to go back to Apalachicola anyway.

Back then, he'd never realized the sacrifices his father must have made to send him to college in California. Most of his friends attended state universities and colleges where affordable tuition and living expenses were manageable. Sending Will to USC for his undergraduate degree and then onto film school for his master's must have been an enormous financial burden, yet his father had never complained. A check arrived on the first of every month, and Will had never even thought about where the money came from. Looking back, he felt ashamed and ungrateful about his sense of entitlement and his lack of appre-ciation for his father's generosity. He guessed back then he felt his father owed it to him.

They would talk every couple of months in brief phone calls, and occasionally, a letter would arrive. He came home one time for Christmas, his first year away. Upon realizing that nothing had changed between him and his father, he'd given up on the idea that it ever would.

After he graduated, he did not come home again, and over time, the communication between them became less and less and eventually stopped altogether. When his career took off, he'd had little time to think about his father or his life growing up. That had suited him fine. Remembering only brought up feelings of sadness and abandonment.

He stood and took one last look at the gravesites. He'd come because he didn't know the exact date his mother had died. As he gazed at her headstone, etching the date of her birth and death into his memory forever, he realized he knew so little about her. It was a piece of his soul that was absent, and now every little thing he learned about her restored a part of it. It was something he hadn't even known was missing.

WILL FLIPPED through the microfiche in the library, searching the archives for stories in the local papers about his mother's death. He'd searched for some time on the Internet but had found nothing. He guessed the incident was too old and not very publicized for anything to be found there.

He could find nothing in the local paper and suspected that was out of respect for his father. Apalachicola was a small town. There was no need to publicize such an awful tragedy. But he found a couple of articles from nearby towns mentioning it. None were very long or included much detail.

It was believed that Anna Kendrick leaped from the Apalachicola Bridge after suffering a breakdown resulting from a prolonged bout with depression. Her body was discovered up the Apalachicola River due to the incoming tide. Otherwise, it might have been swept out into the bay. No one witnessed it, and the articles didn't mention how it was determined that's what happened, but every story carried the same circumstances. Will knew finding out the details of what happened might be difficult. There weren't very many people left who would remember.

Though the storms since had altered the tidal charts, he was able to find old ones that could give him an idea of how the water might have moved back then. When he studied them, doubts began to creep in about the theory. He was no expert, but he was a quick study, and something about it didn't jive.

It could be that his doubts were born out of the dream he'd had of his mother. After all, he'd been an emotional wreck after Penny had told him how she died. Maybe the dream was his subconscious driving him to discover the truth, but it had felt too real. He wasn't one to believe in such things, but he couldn't shake the feel of her kiss on his cheek or the sound of her voice when she'd whispered to him. Her essence was still with him, and her words haunted him.

He wasn't sure what to do next. He was reluctant to upset Penny by asking her about the details. Father Hudson had told him how distraught she had been after their conversation. Penny was going through enough, and certainly, facing her own mortality brought any regrets she had in her life to the fore-front. Stirring them up further seemed like the wrong thing to do.

He hadn't asked Father Hudson any details about the tragedy. At the time, he'd been in shock and trying to reconcile things. His imagination had conjured up a lot of ideas over the years. He'd always thought she must have died from some awful disease. Her perishing by means of a violent death had never occurred to him.

Perhaps he should talk with Father Hudson. He'd known his parents since before they were married, and he seemed kind and caring. He was easy to talk to, and Will felt he would tell him what he knew and do it compassionately. He may not have all the answers, but at least it would be a start.

FATHER HUDSON WAS PREPARING his sermon for the following Sunday in the rectory library. When he felt the time was right, he would retreat there to take in God's message and put the words to paper. Sitting quietly with his bible, reading through his favorite passages, and meditating on the words always brought forth what he felt God wanted him to pass on. It had been his way for decades.

He heard a soft knock at the door and thought perhaps he was getting a delivery. When he opened the door, he was surprised to find Will Kendrick there, but what struck him was the young man's demeanor. Father Hudson could see he was struggling with something and had a pretty good idea of what it was.

"Hello, Father," he said softly. "Would you have a few minutes to talk with me?"

"Why certainly, Will," he answered, "please, come in."

Will followed him to the library, where Father Hudson offered him a seat in one of the big leather reading chairs while he sat in the other. They were quiet momentarily, and Will took in the room's beauty. The woodwork was exquisite, and the place had a reverence that seemed to calm him. On the big leather top desk, he saw the open bible and the notebook beside it. It seemed Father Hudson did his work there, and Will could see why.

"I hope I haven't disturbed your work, Father," he said, gesturing toward the desk. "If you're busy, I could come back another time."

"No, of course not, Will. You're not disturbing me at all. I'm happy to talk with you anytime."

Will was silent for a minute as he gathered his thoughts. He wasn't sure where to start the conversation, and even bringing up the subject was hard. Father Hudson sat waiting patiently, and Will guessed he'd long since perfected the art of listening. He seemed in no hurry to find out why Will was there.

"I'm trying to find out more about my mother and what happened to her," Will said. "I've read some of the old newspaper articles, but there's not much information there. Since it was so long ago, I'm having a hard time getting much information. I don't want to upset Penny again with a lot of questions. She's dealing with enough. So, I thought perhaps you could tell me what you know."

Father Hudson rubbed his chin and glanced toward the ceiling. Will could tell if he was trying to bring in the memory of her and waited patiently for him to begin.

"Your mother was a lovely woman, and when I think about her, I remember her beautiful smile and sweet disposition." He paused for a moment as he intertwined his fingers, then rested his hands in his lap. "She was much beloved by everyone, and in the years I knew her, I never heard her say an unkind word about anyone. She had a true servant's heart and was always looking to help whoever she could. She was such a bright spirit. It was such a tragedy when we lost her."

Will nodded and was quiet again for a moment. He'd known it would be a difficult conversation, but he'd been unprepared to hear her described in such detail.

"The articles in the newspapers said it was believed she jumped off the Apalachicola Bridge after suffering a breakdown of some kind that night. Do you know anything about that?" he said finally.

"Unfortunately, no, I don't. I heard later that she had suffered from depression, but I never saw any signs of that when I was around her. The last time I saw her was at church the Sunday before, and we had a lovely conversation. She was holding you and was very excited that she and your father were taking you to the beach for the afternoon. You were the absolute light of her life, Will."

Will swallowed hard, trying not to let the emotions overtake him. Hearing Father Hudson talk about his mother in such a personal way was heart-wrenching, and he realized she'd never felt as real to him as she did then.

Feelings of anger swept over him. She deserved to be remembered and not have the memory of her rubbed out like she never existed. She deserved better. He deserved better. Why couldn't anyone have shared these things with him growing up? Even if he'd formed memories of her based on the memories of others, at least he would have felt he'd known her.

"The papers said there were no witnesses, so I'm wondering why it was assumed she jumped. She wasn't found near the bridge, and the tidal maps suggest that she might have been found in a different part of the river if that had happened. I know this might sound unreasonable, but I feel like none of this makes any sense."

"As I remember, someone passing through town came forward a day or two later and said they saw a woman running on the bridge that night. It was dark, obviously, so all they could see was that she had long hair. They couldn't remember anything else about her."

"Oh, I didn't know that. None of the articles mentioned it. I don't know, Father Hudson. Maybe I'm just still processing, but it all feels wrong to me. Do you know anything about her breakdown and what might have precipitated it?" he asked.

"I wish I could be of more help, Will. I do know Loretta saw her that night and said she was distraught."

"Loretta saw her? Where?" Will asked.

"At the tavern, I think. I'm sure she could tell you more if you asked her."

They sat for a few minutes in silence, Will deep in thought and Father Hudson trying to figure out the best advice to give the young man. When it seemed Will had run out of questions, Father Hudson reached over and patted his shoulder.

"I know this is hard, son, and I wish I could do or say something to make it easier. I understand your need to know. You'll get there, and when you do, you'll resolve many of these feelings. Just be patient with yourself."

"Thank you, Father. I appreciate you taking the time to talk to me. You're right. This is hard, but it's something I feel like I need to do to move forward. Honestly, I feel a little stuck right now."

"Perfectly understandable, son. I'm always here if you need me."

Will nodded and got up from his chair. Father Hudson patted him on the back as he turned to go. When they got to the door, Will turned, and the two men shook hands.

Father Hudson watched him go through the sidelight of the door, and when he was sure he was gone, he went to the phone and called Penny.

CHAPTER TWENTY-FOUR

W
ill turned his collar up against the wind as he walked through the streets back toward the tavern. He'd spent a few minutes in the memorial garden across from the church trying to sort out his thoughts. It was a beautiful place, with the live oaks and the magnolias, and it comforted him that his mother had probably spent time there. She felt closer with every little thing he learned about her, and he was even more determined to find out what happened to her. He didn't know why, but he couldn't accept that she'd jumped off that bridge.

Maybe it would just take some time to wrap his mind around the idea. But, with every attempt he made to get closer to what happened to her, he seemed to have more questions. His conversation with Father Hudson, while enlightening and comforting in many ways, had raised more doubts in his mind. He couldn't help but feel something was being kept from him.

He found it increasingly odd that the memory of his mother had become a taboo subject not just by his father but by everyone else in town. Suicide was a terrible reality and something that no one cared to contemplate, but that everyone had been sworn to secrecy made him wonder. Was it out of respect for his father, or was remembering his mother wrapped up in some stigma? Did everyone whisper about it among themselves, just not around him? Anything was possible, he supposed, though the thought raised his anger again. Still, something about the situation didn't sit right with him.

As he opened the tavern door, he saw Kip at the little table in the back, his elbow on the table with his chin in his palm. By his posture, he could see that he was contemplating something and was so deep in thought that he didn't hear Will come up behind him.

"What are you up to, Sport?" Will asked as he gripped his shoulder.

"I'm trying to write a paper," Kip said, sounding defeated.

"What's it about?" Will asked as he sat down across from him.

"That's the problem," Kip said. "I don't know what to write about."

"Is this a homework assignment?"

"Yes," Kip said, "and it's due tomorrow."

Will could see the boy was having a hard time and that his anxiety over the assignment was growing.

"How long does the paper have to be?"

"Two pages," Kip said as he pushed the notebook away and put his head in his hands.

"Okay, this is something I think I can help with. Put your pencil down, and let's just talk for a minute, okay?"

Kip put the pencil down on the table, and Will watched as he rolled it back and forth with his finger, his frustration evident.

"What does the paper have to be about? Anything?"

"Yes," Kip answered, "anything."

"Well, that makes things easier," Will said as he smiled at him. "What's something you really like, Kip?"

"What do you mean?" Kip asked as he stopped fiddling with the pencil and looked up at Will.

"You know, like a sport, a book, or a movie?"

"I like football," Kip said, a little confidence returning to his voice.

"What is it that you like about football?"

"Everything," Kip said with a smile.

Will laughed. "Well, that's good. That means you'll have lots to write about then."

He saw Kip frown again, but he pressed on.

"Every story needs an introduction. So, you might begin by describing what football is. You know what I mean?"

Kip smiled and nodded.

"Then pick three or four of the coolest or most exciting things about football that you can think of and write a paragraph about each one. Maybe something like how touchdowns are worth 6 points, but you have to kick the ball through the goalposts to get an extra point. Or that each team gets four downs unless they can earn a new set by advancing the ball ten yards. Are you following me?"

Kip smiled again and reached for his pencil.

"Then, when you have written enough words to fill up nearly two pages, you'll write your conclusion. That's the last paragraph, where you wrap everything up in a bow by summarizing all the great things about football. Does that make sense?"

"I think so," he said as he picked up the pencil and pulled the notebook toward him.

"Give it a shot, Sport, and when you've got a draft, I'll give it a read for you, okay? I'm headed upstairs for a few minutes, but I'll be back down in a little while."

Kip nodded as he bent his head over his work again, and Will smiled when he heard the sound of his pencil on the paper, writing as fast as he could.

~

JESS WAS in the back putting away some supplies from the morning delivery when she heard the front door open. The tavern wasn't busy, and Loretta was keeping an eye on the small number of patrons and on Kip, who she could see from the kitchen where she was prepping for the evening. He was doing his homework at the small table in the back while waiting for his mother to finish her work.

When she heard Will's voice, she peeked around the corner and saw him talking to Kip, his back to her. When she realized what was happening, she retreated a bit to avoid distracting either of them. She was interested to see how the interaction would go.

She felt the tears prick in her eyes as she listened to Will. He was patient and kind, and she could tell he genuinely wanted to help. He seemed to be able to connect with him, and there were similarities between them for sure.

Kip, like Will, was creative and curious. Will was shy as a child, something he was sure he could relate to in Kip, who was also slow to warm up to people he didn't know. After he went upstairs and left Kip to his work, she stepped out into the tavern and was happy to see him, head down, writing furiously in his notebook. Will's words had inspired him, it seemed.

She hadn't seen much of Will since he found out the truth about his mother. He'd been elusive after his conversation with Father Hudson at the bar and the moment they'd shared in the tavern two days ago. She hadn't seen him coming or going until a few minutes ago.

She wanted to talk to him and let him know she was worried about him, but she sensed he was angry that no one had told him before now. She couldn't blame him. Finding out that sort of thing three decades after it happened was terrible. She knew his father had been trying to protect him, but it had gone on long past the time he should have been told.

Jess wondered how all of this might affect his thinking about Apalachicola. Now that he knew the truth, would it push him away again? Would the thoughts be so painful that he couldn't bear them if he stayed? She hoped not.

She had begun to think that maybe Will was on the fence about leaving Apalachicola. She sensed something in him, especially at the beach, that he was tired of living in LA and longed for a deeper connection to people and a place. Now, with this news, she feared he would retreat again. She knew it would end any chance for them if he left now.

She couldn't think about him leaving him again. She'd spent so many years holding on to the idea that they might still have a chance that living without that seemed impossible. A wave of hopelessness washed over her at the thought. Was there life for her after if she had to let him go? She didn't know.

She was so deep in thought that she didn't hear his footsteps on the stairs, and when she looked up, he was sitting on the barstool in front of her. Having had such intimate thoughts about him just before startled her a bit, and he seemed to notice.

"Hey," he said softly. "Are you okay?"

"Hi," she said, trying to keep things light. She avoided his gaze. "Yes, I'm fine."

"Have you been watching the news?" he said. "There's a tropical storm heading our way."

"Really?" she asked. "I thought that was going west of us, more toward Louisiana."

"No," he said. "Looks like it's coming this way. Not much of a wind threat, but it's slow-moving, so there's some concern about the amount of rainfall and the tides."

He paused to gauge her reaction. She just nodded, so he went on.

"I remember the streets down here by the river flooding

when I was a kid. Is that something we need to worry about?" he asked.

"It depends on how much rain we get and if there is a storm surge at all. If it really looks like it's coming this way, we might want to put some sandbags out front. I've seen the water lapping at the front door before."

"Okay," he said. "I'll take care of that. Anything else we should do?"

"No," she said. "I don't think so. Talk to Mike at the hardware store. They usually have bags and sand for everyone."

He nodded, and they were quiet for a minute.

"Are you sure you're okay?" he asked. "Is something bothering you? You don't seem yourself."

"I'm fine," she said, finally looking up at him. "I think the real question here is how you are doing. I know you've had a tough couple of days."

Their eyes locked for a second, and he looked away first.

"I'm okay," he said softly. "I'm getting there."

She saw Kip come up behind him and tug at his sleeve.

"I've finished my paper, Will," he said. "Can you read it now?"

"Of course," he said as he winked at Jess. He got up, went to the little table where Kip had been working, and sat down. Jess watched as he took the paper from the boy and began to read, his hand rubbing his chin. Kip watched him closely, chewing on the eraser of his pencil and fidgeting as he waited.

"Well," he said as he finished and sat back in his chair. "It's good."

Kip smiled and looked at his mom.

"In fact," Will said, "it's quite good. You have a couple of things to address. A couple of periods and commas to add, but overall, it's a great paper."

Jess watched as Will leaned in, head to head, with the boy going through the paper, circling the corrections, and explaining them. When he finished, he sat back, and the two exchanged smiles.

"I'm headed to the hardware store," Will said as he got out of his chair. "Do you want to come with me, Kip?"

The boy looked at Jess expectantly, and she nodded. There was no way she would break up the connection between them now.

WILL SMILED when he saw the sweat on Kip's brow as they shoveled sand into bags behind the hardware store. It was hard work, but the boy's enthusiasm for the task wasn't letting up. As he watched the boy, a look of determination on his face, he realized how much he was like his mother. He had a seriousness about him that Will realized was a perfect reflection of her.

They loaded the bags into the back of the truck and headed back to the tavern. The storm would be rolling through during the night, so Will and Kip stacked the bags on the sidewalk up against the building, then some across the street in front of Jess's shop. Later, when the tavern closed, he would move them in front of the door where they could offer protection if the water began to rise.

Jess watched through the front window at the two of them working. She was overcome with longing for a life she was getting a glimpse of. They could make it work. She was sure of it. She felt Will had feelings for her but probably had the same worries. Maybe if they just talked about it, things would become clearer. She contemplated initiating a conversation, but the thought of it made her uneasy. What if he didn't share her sentiments? Then what? It would be devastating to her, and things would become unbearably awkward. But at least she would know once and for all and could move on if that needed to happen. She felt she needed to do it soon if she was going to do it at all.

"Mom!" Kip said as he and Will entered the tavern. "The lady at the hardware store said there's no school tomorrow because of the storm!"

"Oh really?" Jess asked as she looked at Will.

"That's what she said," Will said as he shrugged his shoulders.

"Okay," she said as she smiled at the boy. "I guess you get a free day tomorrow, then."

"Will said he's going to stay up all night here at the tavern. Can I stay here tonight?"

Jess looked at Will and then at the boy, a little confused.

"I thought we might camp out here tonight. Make a night of it. I'm going to stay up to be sure no water gets in. The rains will be starting soon, so we might close early."

"I don't know, Kip, maybe you should stay home with Nana," she said.

"There's no harm in him staying. We could make it fun. You know, play cards and eat junk food," Will said with a chuckle.

"Am I invited to this little party," she asked with a smile, "or is this strictly boy's night out?"

Will looked at Kip, who nodded his head.

"Little man says yes, Moms allowed."

CHAPTER TWENTY-FIVE

J ust after midnight, Will stepped out of the tavern's front door to check on things. He could hear the palms rustling as the wind came in gusty spurts and saw water accumulating in the street. It had been raining for several hours, and some fast-moving squalls had brought torrential downpours. With the most intense part of the rainfall still offshore, he thought significant flooding was a real possibility.

He stepped back in and quietly closed the door behind him. Kip was asleep on the little folding cot he'd found in the storeroom that afternoon. Jess had made it up with some sheets and a blanket from the apartment, and even with all the excitement, the boy hadn't made it to midnight.

"How is it out there?" she asked as he brushed the wind-blown rain off his sleeves.

"Well, there's already water halfway up the curb. If the rain keeps up, and I feel certain it will, we could have a problem."

"I've seen water over the sidewalk before, but I've never seen it get in here. Do you think it's possible?"

"This is a very slow-moving storm, so the rainfall predictions are huge. I guess it's possible with the flooding that could cause."

They were both quiet for a moment, thinking about the implications.

"Listen," he said, "you don't have to stay up. Let's take Kip upstairs, and you guys can sleep in the bedroom. I'll take the couch if I need to lie down for a while."

"I'm okay," she said. "I'd like to keep you company, at least for a while. You've got a long vigil ahead of you."

"Well, let's get Kip settled, and we can hang out upstairs where it's more comfortable. I can monitor things from the window and come down here to check on things throughout the night."

He scooped the boy up and quietly carried him up the stairs. They got him settled in the bed and then left the room, leaving the door open a crack.

"That's one tired kid," Will said with a chuckle as he settled onto the couch next to Jess.

"So much for staying up all night," she said, smiling at him.

"Well, he worked hard today. Filling those sandbags and carrying them around is hard work. Especially for a boy his size."

"Thanks for letting him pal around with you today and helping with his homework assignment," she said. "He's really proud of that paper."

"He should be," Will said. "It's very good for a kid his age, and I'm not just saying that. He's very bright, Jess, and I'm impressed with his work ethic."

"I heard you talking with him about that. He's kind of in awe of you, you know. Your compliments mean a lot."

Will smiled, and the two looked at each other for a moment. As if unconsciously, he reached over and pushed her hair out of her eyes. She felt a ripple of trepidation run through her. Unexpected intimacy from Will always unsettled her.

Things got quiet between them, and she knew the moment was right for the conversation they needed to have. If she didn't take the opportunity, then it might never come again. As if he sensed something was coming, the smile faded from his face, and his expression turned serious.

She looked at him for a long moment.

"Is there something happening between us, Will Kendrick?" she asked almost in a whisper, her voice thin and shaky.

He looked away, rubbed his chin then looked at her again.

"Is there Jess? Is that something you want?"

"Should I want it? Or is my heart going to be broken...again," she said, the tears pricking at her eyes.

"Again?" he asked. She could tell he was genuinely confused.

"Never mind," she said as she looked away.

He moved over closer to her.

"No," he said. "Don't shut this down."

He reached for her hand and pulled her to him, and they looked at each other for a long moment before he leaned in to kiss her. He drew back, his eyes searching hers. When he saw tears, he leaned in again and kissed her more passionately.

"Now I'll ask again, Jess," he whispered. "Is this something you want?"

She hesitated as she studied his eyes—the answers to a thousand questions there.

"Yes," she said, "very much."

He smiled at her, and as he moved to pull her close again, they heard Kip's voice from the bedroom.

"Mom?" he called, sounding frightened.

"I'm right here, Kip," she called as she got up to go to him. As she passed by Will, she let her hand trail over his cheek.

Will could hear the boy crying softly and Jess talking and reassuring him. Soon, things got quiet, and when he peeked through the door, he saw Jess lying on the bed with the boy in her arms, both of them asleep. He lingered there, the sight of them moving something deep inside his soul.

He could see himself with them, and the thought stirred up feelings of protectiveness and a strong desire to care for them. The emotions were new to him, and he realized he'd never felt about a woman the way he did about Jess.

The boy was a bonus, and he realized fate was handing him a chance to heal a part of his soul he knew was broken. He could give this boy a whole family and be the father he never had. He could visualize it, and at that moment, he'd never wanted anything more.

He looked out the window to check the status of the water, and seeing little had changed, he laid down on the couch and let his thoughts drift.

He and Jess were a perfect fit. She knew him in ways no one else ever could, and she had a way of seeing right through him. It unnerved him, but it was genuine, something he didn't realize he missed. The world he lived in out in LA felt plastic and fake. Jess was the most real person he'd been around in a long time. Maybe ever.

The question was, could they make it work? Was he willing to stay in Apalachicola? He was beginning to think he was. He realized how exhausted he was from the rat race he'd lived in for the last ten years. If it weren't for his career, he wouldn't even hesitate. Was he willing to give that up? He wasn't sure. Could he commute to LA when needed and work from Apalachicola? He thought he might be able to work that out.

Then there was Kate. She deserved more than just being dumped from afar, but the thought of having that conversation with her face-to-face made him feel claustrophobic. He had no idea how she would take it, but he guessed her pride would bear the brunt of it. After being away from her for a while, he realized that so much of their relationship was about appearances, especially to her. Did she really love him, or was it that they made such a beautiful couple? He suspected the latter.

As he contemplated his situation with Kate, his mind drifted to Connor, probably the most difficult thing to think about. He genuinely liked Connor, and he knew he cared deeply for Jess. Will couldn't imagine how losing her would feel to him after the years he'd been in her life. For him to stick around after her rejection of his marriage proposals meant he wanted a life with her. The thought of taking that away from him hurt. He didn't want to be that guy. Somehow, he knew Connor would handle it gracefully, but that only made it harder for him to think about.

He got up and quietly left the apartment to check on the water. When he checked his watch, he was surprised it was nearly three a.m. He didn't realize how long he'd been lying there thinking about things and thought he may have drifted off for a little while.

He crept down the stairs and across the tavern to the door, where he looked through the glass. He was relieved to see the water had still not breached the sidewalk. Looking at the radar on his phone, he saw that the bulk of the storm had already passed over. With some luck, they may come out on the other side unscathed.

WHEN JESS OPENED HER EYES, the morning light was coming through the blinds on the windows. She lay there for a moment, grounding herself and thinking. It was quiet out. The pounding rain had ceased. She hoped that meant the threat of flooding was over.

Waking up in Will's bed instantly brought back the events of the night before. It had been an enormous turning point for her and Will, and the feel of his kiss lingered. Now that she was standing on the threshold of everything she'd always wanted, she was suddenly terrified.

Their evening together, even before they were alone and he'd kissed her, had made her believe that, given the chance, they could be a real family. Will's interest in Kip and his ability to connect with him was better than she had hoped. She'd enjoyed watching them make hamburgers together in the kitchen and Will teaching him how to play poker as they passed the time early in the evening. But was it all an illusion? Would they ever be able to make a life together a reality?

She looked at her son, who had slept peacefully for the rest of the night after she'd comforted him. He had occasional nightmares that seemed brought on by being in unfamiliar places. Even though he lived a very secure life with his mother and grandmother, she suspected they were born out of fears of abandonment. Knowing he had a father out there who had walked out on him seemed to linger in his subconscious even though he didn't remember him. She understood those feelings. They weren't easy to deal with and were impossible to forget.

She untangled herself from Kip and slid quietly out of bed. Will was asleep on the couch, and she took a moment to admire his long frame. She suspected it had been a long night for him and felt bad he'd had to spend it on the couch. His feet hanging off the end told her he couldn't have been comfortable.

Peering out the window, she was relieved to see that while some water was still flooding the street, it did not look like it had breached the sandbags Will had put in front of the door of her shop across the street or in front of the tavern. She guessed the tides had been in their favor and that rainfall totals had not matched the predictions.

She gently roused Kip and smiled at him when his eyes fluttered open.

"You don't have to get up," she said. "I just wanted you to

know I'm headed downstairs to the tavern. Will is here with you. He's sleeping on the couch if you need anything. Okay?"

He smiled at her, nodded, then rolled over and settled into sleep again. She quietly left the room and slipped out of the apartment. Something about leaving them sleeping in the apartment together comforted her. Something about it felt right.

She put the coffee on in the kitchen, put away the clean dishes from the night before, and smiled as she thought about the night they had all spent together. It felt like a glimpse into the future, and she could tell that Kip felt it, too. Did Will see it that way? She wasn't sure, and her doubts made the fears begin to creep in again. If it didn't work out, it would be tough on Kip, especially so soon after losing Grant.

Part of her wanted to pull back again and maintain her wait-and-see attitude, but she knew she couldn't play it safe anymore. Whatever was going to happen between them needed to be resolved one way or another. She couldn't spend her whole life in limbo.

They had so much to resolve to make it work, and she couldn't help but feel overwhelmed by it all. In so many ways, it seemed like an impossible situation. But in others, it seemed easy. If he loved her and wanted to make a life with her and Kip, then it was just a matter of logistics.

The sound of footsteps pulled her out of her deep thoughts, and when she peeked out of the kitchen, she saw Will and Kip coming down the stairs. Glancing at her watch, she saw it was a little before ten a.m. The long vigil had been tiring for them all.

"Good morning," she said, smiling at their sleepy demeanor. "You both look a little tired."

Kip just nodded and scratched his head, clearly not ready for conversation.

"You look exhausted," she said to Will as she set a cup of coffee in front of him. "How much sleep did you get?"

"Not a lot," he said, "but enough to get me through."

"Looks like we dodged a bullet with the water," she said. "It doesn't look like it got to the door."

"We did," he said with a smile. "How about you? Did you get enough sleep?"

She nodded and smiled at him. "Sorry for not staying up with you," she said. "I really wanted to."

Will smiled back, and the look in his eyes sent a ripple of emotion through her.

"Anyway, it's my turn to cook," she said as she looked between them. "What can I make you guys? Eggs? Pancakes?"

Will looked at Kip, who just shrugged and then turned back to Jess.

"Anything is fine with me," he said. "Whatever you think Kip would like."

"Pancakes and bacon it is," she said as she went to the kitchen cooler and gathered what she needed. As she worked, Will came through the kitchen to refill his coffee. When he passed behind her, he put a hand on her waist and kissed the back of her neck. It was a casual yet entirely intimate moment that sent a shiver down her spine. It was a feeling she didn't think she would ever get used to.

After breakfast, Will took a walk around town to assess the flooding. He suspected that most businesses would remain closed for the day since there was little access to the heart of town. He contemplated opening the tavern, but since everything in town had ground to a standstill, he decided against it.

The sky displayed remnants of the storm with its fast-moving scud clouds, and the persistent rain had slowed to a light drizzle. Will pulled the hood of his jacket over his head and shoved his hands deep into his pockets as he started down toward the waterfront. As he stood, looking at the angry bay, he saw that the water was beginning to recede.

"Good morning," said a voice from behind him. Will turned

to see Sawyer Hayes coming up behind him. "Looks like this one's almost over for us. Things okay at the tavern?" he asked.

"Yes, things are fine. I was worried there for a few hours, but the water never reached the door."

"Good," he said. "I've walked most of the town. I think everyone came out okay."

The two men were quiet for a minute, just watching the bay. Though the winds were still blustery, Will could see some clearing skies on the horizon.

"How's Penny?" he asked. "I hope my visit with her didn't upset her too much. It wasn't my intention."

"She's okay, and she was happy to see you. She was worried about you after you left, though. Are you doing okay with everything?" Sawyer asked.

"Yes, I suppose. It was just hard to learn something like that after so many years. I'm still trying to come to grips with the fact that everyone knew but me. I'm a little angry about it."

"I can see why you'd feel that way. It was never anyone's intention to hurt you. You were just a little boy when it happened, and it was a terrible thing. I guess as time went by, it was easier not to tell you. We all knew it was wrong that you didn't know the truth, but none of us knew what to do about it."

Will thought about that for a moment, the anger and the hurt welling up inside him

"I'll be honest with you, Sawyer. Something about the whole thing doesn't seem right to me. Not how she died, where she was found, and certainly not all the secrecy. I know I was just a little kid when it happened, but still. It's been over thirty years."

Sawyer didn't say anything, and when Will turned to look at him, his expression stirred something deep within his subconscious. Sawyer was staring out over the bay as if he hadn't heard him, and from the look on his face, he looked like he'd seen a ghost.

CHAPTER TWENTY-SIX

J ess was at the end of the bar reviewing invoices and writing vendor checks. As Will came in, she looked up from her work and smiled at him, but something about his mood immediately telegraphed to her.

"Where's Kip?" he said, looking around.

"My mom came and got him. She was able to walk over. The streets are pretty clear now. He got bored with me after you left," she said with a smile.

Will smiled, too, but it quickly faded. From his serious expression, she could see something was on his mind.

"Is everything okay?" she asked.

He walked to her, turned her barstool towards him, and studied her eyes for a moment.

"How is it that you can always see right through me?" he whispered.

She said nothing for a minute as she returned his gaze.

"What's wrong?" she said, her eyes searching his. "Something's wrong."

He sighed and sat down on the barstool next to her. He thought momentarily, unsure he wanted to tell her what was on his mind. He was afraid it wouldn't sound rational to her. He wasn't even sure it sounded rational to himself.

"I've been looking into my mother's death," he said, looking away momentarily. "Something *is* wrong, Jess. It just doesn't add up. The more questions I ask, the more it doesn't make sense to me."

"Tell me what you're thinking," she said, her expression serious.

"I don't know," he said as he ran his hand through his hair. "The secrecy around everything really bothers me. It goes beyond just trying to protect me. It feels...coordinated."

He paused to judge her reaction, but she didn't say anything, so he continued.

"Whenever anyone talks about her, they just want to tell me how wonderful and loved she was. Don't get me wrong. I appreciate people sharing their memories of her with me. I grew up knowing almost nothing about her. But no one seems very forthright about her supposed illness or what precipitated this breakdown she had the night she took her life. It all just feels very wrong to me."

She nodded and reached for his hand to encourage him to go on.

"Anyway, I've read the newspaper reports, though there aren't many, and no one actually saw her jump off the bridge. Someone reported seeing a woman with long hair on the bridge that night but couldn't really identify her. I don't know. Maybe I'm just having a hard time accepting what happened to her."

"You're smart, Will, and you have good instincts. I think you should keep digging. Even if it turns out to be nothing more, at least you will feel satisfied in your heart that you know the truth."

Will nodded as he thought about what she was saying.

"You know, Jess, This may sound crazy, and I'm not one to

believe in such things, but I almost feel like my mother is pushing me to learn the truth. I've dreamt about her."

Jess's serious expression didn't change. If she thought his line of thinking was ludicrous, she wasn't showing it.

"Tell me about the dream," she said.

Will looked away. He didn't know how she would react and felt he was already on thin ice. If she didn't already think he was crazy, certainly, this would do it.

"She told me not to believe them."

Will watched as Jess's eyes filled with tears, and she reached out and stroked his cheek.

"Keep going, Will," she whispered. "You have to keep going."

WILL KNOCKED TENTATIVELY on Loretta's door and listened. He was sure she was home because he hadn't seen her leave after the storm. When she didn't answer after a couple of minutes, he tapped lightly again.

"Just a minute," he heard her call from inside the apartment. A moment later, she opened the door, her hair in a towel and a bathrobe wrapped tightly around her.

"I'm sorry," she said. "I was just getting out of the shower. Is everything okay?"

"Yes, I'm sorry to disturb you. I just wanted to talk with you for a few minutes, but I can come back later if now isn't a good time."

"No, it's fine," she said, opening the door wider. "Just give me a minute to throw on some clothes. I'll be right out."

While Will waited for her, he glanced around the apartment. Jess told him Loretta had lived there since the tavern opened. She was the first and only tenant ever to occupy it. When she found out Grant was looking for someone to run the kitchen, she quit her job at a local restaurant to work for him. In fifty years, nothing had changed.

"Would you like some tea or a cup of coffee?" she asked as she returned to the living room.

"No thanks," he said. "I just had a cup downstairs. Are you sure I'm not disturbing you? I just wanted to ask you a couple of questions."

"Of course not, Will. How can I help?"

Will hesitated. He wasn't sure how to ask her what he wanted to know.

"I spoke with Father Hudson a couple of days ago, and he mentioned you saw my mother the night she passed away. I was hoping you could tell me about it," he said.

Loretta went visibly pale as she slowly sat down on the couch. She took a minute to gather her thoughts before she spoke.

"I haven't thought about that night in a long time, Will. It was a terrible time. I think I was the last person to see her alive."

Will said nothing. He didn't want to interrupt her thinking.

"She came to my door. It was late, and I had fallen asleep on the couch. She was crying, very distraught, and she had you in her arms. She asked me to take you but wouldn't tell me why. Then she ran downstairs, through the tavern, and out the front door. I never saw her again," she said.

"Why was she here so late? Where was my father?"

"They would sometimes stay in their apartment if it had been a long night at the tavern. We'd had a busy night, and she had stopped by with you earlier like she often did. She stayed to help out because Grant was shorthanded. You eventually fell asleep, and we put you on the little cot they kept for you in the back," she said. Will could tell by the faraway look in her eyes that she was remembering details she hadn't thought about in many years.

"Your father left after the Tavern closed, but I don't know

where he went. When he came back much later, and she wasn't in the apartment, he came to my door looking for the two of you. He took you, and nobody knew what happened to your mother until she was found a day later."

"Do you have any idea why she was so upset? Could they have had an argument or something? Did you hear anything?" Will asked.

"I don't know, and I didn't hear anything, but I can tell you that I never once heard a cross word pass between them in all the time I knew them. Your mother was as sweet as the day is long, and your father adored her."

"Had you ever seen her upset like that before? Penny told me she suffered from depression. What can you tell me about that?"

"I never saw any signs of depression. She was always cheerful and smiling and well put together. That's what was so strange about that night. She was sobbing and very disheveled. It wasn't like her at all."

Will thought for a moment. It seemed the narrative was changing. Penny had made it seem like his mother had been chronically depressed since Will's birth, but that wasn't what he heard from Loretta or Father Hudson. Both women were close to her. Why would they have drastically different views?

"Is there anything else you can tell me, Loretta? I didn't know how my mother died until a few days ago. Now, for my own sanity, I'm just trying to understand what happened to her."

"I'm so sorry, Will, I didn't know that. I know your father was never the same after he lost your mother. It wasn't until just a few years ago that he seemed to come back to himself a little, but even then, he was a changed man. I know he had a lot of regrets about his relationship with you. He talked a lot about it in his final days."

"When Penny told me my mother suffered from postpartum depression, I thought maybe he blamed me for my mother's death, and that's why he was always so distant. Do you think that's true?" Will asked.

"No, I don't. I think the truth of the matter is that you look just like your mother. You always have. If you ask me, I think that was probably too much for him to bear."

JESS SAT at the bar and waited for Will to come downstairs. She hadn't meant to eavesdrop, but what she had heard cut to the very center of her soul. When she heard Will leaving Loretta's apartment, she was curious to find out what he had learned and decided to head upstairs to make sure he was okay. But she heard him on the phone when she got to the door.

He was talking to his agent, discussing a potential project, and planning to return to LA. She suddenly felt like a fool for letting her guard down. What was he doing? Had he just been playing with her? It seemed that it had only taken one catalyst to change his mind about staying in Apalachicola.

Once she'd heard the conversation, she'd quickly and quietly descended the stairs. Now, she was consumed with heartbreak and disappointment. How could he do this to her?

She wasn't sure what to do. Should she confront him and get it over with, or should she let him tell her on his own? Part of her needed to start moving on if he wasn't staying, but the rest of her dreaded the idea. She'd loved him for so long that she didn't know what life would be like without the hope that they would be together someday.

And now, what would she tell Kip? Will had let the boy get close to him, and now he was pulling away. She felt her anger rise thinking about her child and the disappointment he would feel after Will left. Will knew how broken up Kip was over Grant's death. How could he do this to him?

When she heard his footsteps on the stairs, she turned her back so she didn't have to look at him.

"If we aren't going to open today, I think I'm going to head home," she said. "I've got some paperwork I need to do for the shop."

"Okay," he said. "I just called the hotel, and the restaurant is open tonight. Can I take you to dinner later?"

"No," she said, not turning around. "I don't think I can. I have a lot to catch up on."

Will was quiet for a moment and long enough to make her turn to look at him.

"What's going on, Jess?" he said.

"What?" she asked. "What do you mean?"

"Come on, Jess. I can tell you're upset. What's happened?"

"Nothing," she said. "Nothing's happened."

He went quiet again, and she looked at him. She could see the worry on his face. She sighed and put her hands on her hips.

"Are you going back to LA, Will?" she said finally. "I accidentally heard you on the phone making plans."

He stared at her for a minute, then walked around the bar to her.

"Yes," he said as he approached her.

They were quiet again as Jess tried to tamp down the anger rising inside her.

"Why would you do this to us? Why would you get close to me and Kip then leave? If I had known..." she said, shaking her head as she turned to go.

"Jess, wait a minute," he said as he caught up to her.

"No, I'm not interested in your explanations," she said as she spun around to face him. "You should have never let me believe you cared about me, Will."

"I do care about you, Jess, and if you will just let me talk for a minute, we can get this whole situation straightened out."

"What's there to straighten out, Will, if you are going back to LA?"

"For a meeting, Jess. I'm going back for a meeting."

"What?" she said, her cheeks flushed with emotion.

"My agent Tony called me about a project. I told him I couldn't take it unless I could work from here. The client agreed as long as I was willing to go out there for the kick-off meeting. I'll only be gone a few days, Jess." he said as he put his hands on her shoulders.

She put her head down as he pulled her close to him. As he did, he heard the tears catch in her throat. It was a defining moment for them both, but especially for Will. It was the first time he had admitted out loud that he wasn't going back for good.

"I'm not leaving you," he whispered.

She slipped her arms around his waist, and they stood that way for a long time, each content to hold on to one another.

Finally, he untangled himself from her and drew back. The look in her eyes nearly imploded his soul. This woman loved him, and realizing it threatened to overtake him. He'd never known anyone like her, and he knew he could wait a lifetime and never find anyone as loyal to him as she was. He would be a fool ever to walk away from her again.

He bent to kiss her and lingered there, reluctant to let the moment end. Finally, he broke away and looked into her eyes.

"Now," he said, "about dinner."

CHAPTER TWENTY-SEVEN

The morning air was crisp and cold, and the skies were startlingly blue. It was a significant change from the warm tropical winds that had swept through Apalachicola just a few days before. As Jess zipped up her jacket and shoved her hands into her pockets, she stepped up her pace. She hadn't realized how chilly the weather had turned when she decided to walk to town.

She had Jimmy opening the tavern. She needed to turn some of her attention to her shop. Will had proved to be a huge distraction, and she needed to do some ordering and merchandise some of the new items that had come in. They were things she couldn't leave for Tammy to do.

He was leaving for LA in the morning, and she couldn't get the worry out of her head. Worry he might realize he missed his life there and not want to return. Or realize she wasn't as sophisticated as the women in California. She suspected that she and Kate were very different. What if seeing her again changed his mind about everything?

After dinner the evening before and he'd taken her home, they had spent a few minutes saying goodnight on her front porch. How he'd kissed her told her his attraction to her was more than physical. But was he in love with her? That she didn't know.

She unlocked the door and stepped inside. Tammy wasn't due to come in for an hour, so she got right to work unpacking the boxes of merchandise and finding the best places to put them in the store. She was in the very back of the store when she heard the front door open.

She cursed herself for not remembering to lock it behind her. She didn't need the distraction of a customer right then. She had just enough time to finish her work before the shop opened.

Setting down the box she'd been opening, she worked her way through the displays to the front of the store. She couldn't see who it was until she got close.

She felt her heart skip a beat when he stepped out from the little jewelry alcove. She immediately recognized him even though she hadn't seen him in years. He hadn't changed at all, and that was one of the things that alarmed her the most.

"Hello, Jess," he said in a quiet voice. "I'm here to see my boy."

She didn't say anything momentarily as she absorbed what was happening. Her senses were keen, though, even though she felt numb, and she could smell the alcohol on him. Seeing him brought back bad memories, and the reality that he was there nearly paralyzed her. But somewhere in her subconscious, she always knew he'd come back.

"He's in school, Wade," she said as she stepped backward.

"Well, go get him then," he said with a snicker. "I don't have all day to hang around here."

"I'll have to call the school and let them know I'm coming to get him," she said matter-of-factly as she walked quickly by him and grabbed her phone off the counter.

She knew what she was going to do and had to be ready for his eventual reaction. Wade wasn't stupid, and he was volatile.

When he figured it out, it wasn't going to be good. She dialed Will's number and prayed that he would answer.

"Hey," he said. "Where are you?"

"Hey," she said. "This is Jess Wilder, Kip's mom. His father is here and would like to see him, so we will head over to get him in a few minutes if that's okay." She paused for effect. "Oh, he's in morning assembly? Okay, we'll wait a little while before heading over then. I'm at my shop, so it will only take us a couple of minutes to get there." She paused again. "Okay, thanks so much," she said as she hung up.

Wade looked at her for a moment as he assessed the situation.

"That was too easy, Jess," he said with a sly smile. "What are you up to?"

"What are you talking about, Wade? You said you wanted to see him, so I'm trying to make that happen for you."

"I know you, Jess. You couldn't wait to get rid of me. Now you are just ready to hand the kid over? Who did you call?"

She didn't say anything as she narrowed her eyes at him.

"He doesn't know you, Wade, and he's doing just fine without you. Why do you want to do this now? All it's going to do is mess up his head."

"He's my kid, and I want to see him."

"And the last seven years, Wade? You didn't want to see him then?" she asked, the tension in her voice rising.

He didn't answer and instead sauntered toward her. When he got close to her, he reached out and grabbed her by the back of the neck.

"You always had a smart mouth, Jess. I should have taught you a lesson a long time ago," he said as he pulled her face close to his.

The anger washed over her in one giant wave, and without thinking, she spit in his face. Before she knew what was happening, he raised his hand and backhanded her across the mouth. The shock made her knees buckle and disoriented her as she slumped to the floor. He loomed over her, grabbing at her, and she put her hands up to her face to try to ward off any more blows.

She heard the bells on the shop door ring as it opened, and suddenly, it was as if all the air had been sucked out of the room. Wade released her as Will descended upon him, and she fell back to the floor, instinctively covering her head.

She heard the sounds of a scuffle, and someone go down with a loud grunt. When she crawled out from behind the counter, blood pouring from her split lip, she saw Wade face down on the floor and Will with his knee in the center of his back.

"I don't know who you think you are, but if you ever lay a hand on her again, I'll hunt you down wherever you are and snuff you out in your sleep," Will hissed in his ear. "You got that?"

Wade stayed quiet. Jess guessed the takedown had knocked the air out of his lungs.

"Call the police, Jess," Will said finally, without taking his eyes off the back of Wade's head.

With shaky hands, she dialed 911.

JESS WINCED AS WILL DABBED at her lip with ice wrapped in a clean cloth. The shame and embarrassment consumed her, and she found it hard to look at him.

"You could probably use a stitch or two," he said as he leaned back to examine it.

"It's okay," she said, putting her head down and averting his gaze. "I'm sorry you had to get involved in that. I panicked and didn't know who else to call."

"I'm glad you called me Jess. Now I know what he looks

like. If I see him again, I won't be so nice," he said, his expression serious. "Besides, if I hadn't gotten there when I did, I'm not sure that busted lip is all we would be dealing with right now."

"I'm worried when he bonds out, he's going to come after Kip. He would do it just to hurt me. He doesn't care about him at all," she said, her voice shaking.

Will thought for a moment.

"I don't think I'm comfortable going to California tomorrow with this going on. I need to stay here to make sure you and Kip are safe. I wouldn't put it past the bastard to show up again."

"You can't put everything on hold for us, Will. You have your career to think about, too," she said.

"I absolutely can, Jess, and I will. I don't need this project. If the client can't work with me on this, then so be it. I can walk away. Nothing is more important than this," he said as he put his hand on her chin to raise her face to meet his gaze. "Nothing is more important than this."

"I can't tell Kip what's happened," she said, her eyes filling with tears. "He would only be confused by it and be hurt."

Will nodded as he dabbed at her lip again.

"How will I explain this?" she said, pointing to her lip.

"We can tell him you walked into a door. Kids will believe anything," he said with a laugh.

She laughed, too. "You're right. He would believe anything you told him."

"Then that's what we'll tell him," Will said as he shrugged. "You were at the tavern, putting supplies away, and ran into the storeroom door. Keep it simple."

She was suddenly serious again. "How will we protect him, Will? How will we keep Wade away from him?"

Will thought for a moment as he looked at her. "I think it's better to meet the problem head-on rather than hiding from it. I think you should press charges and file for a restraining order."

Jess knew he was right. If Wade thought trouble was coming his way, he would run. He didn't like being held accountable.

"Come on," he said. "Let's go get Kip from school. You'll feel better when you see him."

∽

"I CAN'T DO IT, Tony. I've got something going on here that I need to take care of," Will said, his frustration growing.

"Will, this is an important project, and the client wants you. Can't you slip away for just a couple of days? It's just one meeting."

"I can do a meeting via teleconference. If the client won't agree to that, it's a no-go for me."

"He just wants to meet with you, Will. This project is a high-cost venture. He just needs a little reassurance that he's making the right decision."

"Tony, my work speaks for itself. As I said, if a teleconference won't work, then I'm out."

"Are you trying to suicide your career, Will? Because if you are, you're doing a damn good job!"

"I got to go, Tony," Will said. "Let me know what the client says."

Will quietly disconnected and stepped back into the restaurant. Kip and Jess were sitting at a little table in the corner where she was helping him color in a picture the waitress had given them.

"Everything okay?" she asked.

"Yes, I was just talking to my agent about the project."

"Are you sure you are doing the right thing, Will? I'm sure we will be fine for a few days if you need to go out there."

"I'm sure," he said. "I'd rather stay here, at least for the next week or so."

She nodded. They couldn't talk in much detail because of

Kip, but he could tell she was worried he might be making decisions he would regret later.

She had her head down next to Kip's as the two concentrated on coloring in their picture, but he could see her lip was still very swollen. The sight of it raised a wave of anger in him that he was unaccustomed to, and when he thought back on the chance he'd had to beat Wade to a pulp, he wished he'd taken it. The thought of him coming back and hurting her again was almost more than he could stand.

When he'd gotten her phone call that morning, he'd felt a panic that had changed him. He realized then he'd lived a detached life for over a decade, never really investing his emotions into anything. He'd carefully put the pieces of his life together and had taken almost no emotional chances. Being with Kate was safe, and so was his career. He'd kept himself in a box, never really feeling much, and now that he'd seen how artificial it all was, he couldn't unsee it. Jess was real, and her authenticity was now something he craved. He couldn't lose her now, and even the thought terrified him. He could never go back to the life he had before.

And then there was the boy. Looking at them together, side by side, he realized they were mirror images of each other. And now that he'd fallen in love with Jess, he realized he had also grown to love the boy. He needed them in his life. Through them, he'd healed parts of his soul he thought would be forever damaged. Fate had turned the tables on him.

Somewhere in his mind, he'd thought that if he had to walk away, he could. Thinking about it now was unimaginable. It was time to step up and make a bold move. Part of that meant dealing with Kate and talking with Connor. He didn't relish doing either of those things.

"Will look!" Kip said as he held up their picture.

"That's pretty good, Sport," Will said. "What kind of turtle is that?"

"It's a loggerhead. Mom and I saw their nests on St. George Island."

"Well, that's pretty cool," Will said. "Hey, you never told me how things went with your paper. Did you get a good grade on it?"

"I did," he said. "I got a B+."

"You got a B+? What? You got robbed. That was an A paper for sure," Will said, laughing.

Jess and Kip laughed, too, and when Kip went back to coloring, he turned to Jess.

"Did you pack a bag for the two of you?" he asked.

"Yes," she said. "We are all set for a couple of days, and Mom is up in Georgia visiting family, so no worries there."

"Does he know you are both staying with me?" Will said, nodding his head towards Kip.

"I thought it might be better to let that unfold naturally," she said. "It seems things are better for him when we do it that way."

CHAPTER TWENTY-EIGHT

T he morning delivery had been large, and Jess struggled to get the cases into the storeroom. The tavern had been bustling lately as some of her local marketing had started to kick in. Kendrick's Tavern was transitioning from the old established watering hole to a hip destination for young residents and tourists.

She'd dropped Kip off at school that morning and had felt the need to reiterate to the office that he was not to be released into anyone's care but hers or her mother's. Her worst fear was Wade showing up and smooth-talking the ladies into handing him over. Unfortunately, she'd had to give them more details than she wanted to.

Kip hadn't asked a lot of questions about staying with Will. It seemed the sleepover during the tropical storm now made staying there a little more normal for him. She feared the arrangement might be awkward for everyone, but instead, it had been a smooth couple of days. Will had made the boy breakfast the last couple of mornings, and she'd enjoyed listening to their funny and engaging conversations.

Where it all was going, she was still unsure. That he was

willing to give up the project in California to look after them said a lot, but she knew he still had strong ties out there. He had a career, a home, and a relationship he still needed to sort out. The thought of him going back there to do that made her uneasy.

She noticed that Will had not been staying in Grant's bedroom while they were there. Every night, they would put Kip to bed in the guest room, and after spending time together talking, she would crawl into bed with Kip, and Will would sleep on the couch. She suspected he was still working through his emotions about his father, and sleeping in the bed where he died was probably too much for him. But she knew the arrangement was unsustainable. Sooner or later, life was going to have to return to normal.

But what she noticed most was his preoccupation with the circumstances surrounding his mother's death. He hadn't gotten far in his quest to learn the truth, and she could tell the frustration was getting to him. In his gut, he knew that things weren't right, but she could tell he was running out of leads. She'd found him more than once studying the same tidal charts.

She'd been shocked to hear the details when he told her about his conversation with Loretta. In all the years since, she had never known any of it. The secrecy surrounding it was odd, and she realized it had always been spoken about in whispers and behind closed doors, and as the years went by, it was talked about less and less.

They'd shared intimate moments over the last few days and were growing closer to becoming lovers. That they hadn't was partly because they had her young son in their presence. But there were other reasons she was reluctant to take that step. She had to shield her heart until she knew precisely where they were going with their relationship. If she let that happen and things didn't work out, that would be just another painful memory she would have to learn to live with.

She finished her work and checked her watch. The tavern was due to open in about an hour, so she moved on to her other duties out front. Will had gone to meet with a contractor about one of his buildings, so she was alone downstairs.

She'd had to order more glassware since the tavern had gotten busier, and Loretta had helped get them all washed and ready for service. She carried the racks to the front to get them loaded onto the back bar and into the cabinets. When she was close to finishing, she heard a tap at the front door.

She looked up and saw a woman she didn't recognize peering through the glass. She thought about ignoring her, assuming she was there to try to sell her something, but the tapping was persistent. It seemed the woman had spotted her and was not giving up.

Jess went to the door and opened it a crack.

"I'm sorry," she said. "We aren't open yet. If you could come back in an hour…"

"I'm not a customer," the woman said, interrupting her. "I'm here to see Will Kendrick."

Suddenly, Jess recognized her as the blonde woman she'd seen in pictures with Will over the years. The realization that it was her left her speechless.

"Is he here?" the woman asked.

"No, he's gone out. Can I help you with something?"

"Will he be back soon? He doesn't know I'm here, and I'd like to surprise him."

"I'm not sure," Jess said as she opened the door. She was hedging, and she could tell the woman knew it.

"Well, I'd like to wait," she said, her tone impatient,

"That's fine," Jess said. "You're welcome to sit anywhere."

They were quiet momentarily as the woman slid onto one of the barstools and watched Jess doing her work.

"I'm Kate, by the way, from California. I'm sure you've heard Will speak of me."

"I'm Jess," she said but offered nothing more.

The woman drummed her fingernails on the bar top, and even though Jess had her back to her, she could feel her eyes on her. She didn't know how long Will would be gone, and the thought of Kate blindsiding him when he returned made her angry. She decided to text him to let him know she was there.

"If you'll excuse me for a moment, I need to go to the office to make a phone call. Just make yourself comfortable. I'm sure he'll be back soon," Jess said as she exited the front of the tavern.

Kate's here

What?

She's here at the tavern waiting for you

I'm on my way

When Jess returned to the front, Kate was still at the bar, scrolling on her cell phone. She went back to work but kept her eye on the door. She didn't want to miss the look on Will's face when he saw Kate. She knew she would be able to tell a lot about his thoughts by his expression.

He wasn't far, only a couple of blocks away, so she knew he'd walk in any minute. As she waited, her heart thumped in her chest. Whatever happened in the next few minutes would be important.

She saw him coming as he crossed the street in front of the tavern, and from the look on his face, he was angry. She had known that look since they were kids. When he was mad, his eyebrows knitted together in a way that no other emotion affected him. In her heart, she was glad to see it.

When the door opened, Kate spun around in her chair to see who it was. When she saw it was Will, she jumped up and quickly crossed the room to him.

"Hello, my love. Are you surprised to see me?"

Will glanced at Jess, who was trying to look busy behind the bar and working hard to show no emotion.

"What are you doing here, Kate?" he said, his expression serious.

"I just wanted to see you, Will. Is that so wrong? You haven't been home in weeks now."

When he didn't say anything, she kept going.

"I've just been chatting with your barmaid here while I waited. I'm sorry," she said as she turned towards Jess, "I've forgotten your name."

"Her name is Jess, Kate, and she's my partner."

"Oh," she said. "This is your *friend* you spoke about?"

Jess could see Will was getting angrier by the minute.

"We need to talk, Kate, but not here."

Jess decided she'd heard enough and turned to leave the room. From the back, she listened to the front door open and close. When she looked out, they were gone.

"WHAT'S GOING on with you, Will?" Kate said as she studied his profile. "You leave for what was supposed to be just a few days, and now it's been weeks. Why are you doing this?"

He had taken her down to the waterfront and found an empty bench where they could talk. He needed the fresh air and the sight of the bay to calm him. He hadn't been expecting to have this conversation right then and there, but as long as it was happening, he planned to finish it. He needed to end things.

"I can't go back to the life I was living in California, Kate," he said flatly.

"What was wrong with your life in California, Will? You have a stellar career, a beautiful home, great friends. You're the envy of everyone."

"And us, Kate? You didn't mention us."

"It goes without saying, doesn't it?" she said, her voice a little thin.

"Does it? We've been together for five years and never even talked about getting married. Don't you want to get married someday, Kate? Have children?"

"I'm not a big fan of marriage or children, but if that's what you want, I'll give it to you."

"I'm not asking you to, Kate," he said, looking at her for the first time since they sat down.

She went silent as the meaning of his words sank in. She tore her eyes away from his and looked out over the bay.

"Well, this is embarrassing. You're dumping me?" she said. "I came all the way out here to get dumped?"

"I'm sorry, Kate. I was planning to go out there this week to talk to you, but something came up here."

"So now I get to go back and tell all our friends while you hide here in this place?" she said as she waved her arms around. "You're throwing everything away, Will, for what?"

He didn't say anything and waited. He knew she would figure it out eventually.

"It's her, isn't it?" she said quietly.

He turned to look at her, and she looked away disgusted. "You're throwing everything away over some barmaid."

He felt the anger rise in him again. "She's no barmaid, Kate. She's one hell of a businesswoman. She's running two businesses and raising a child on her own. I know you're upset, but that's an unfair thing to say."

"She has a child? So this is where this idea of having children is coming from?"

"Being here has changed me, Kate. I'm a different person than I was when I got here," he said. "I'm sorry." He reached out and touched her cheek. "I didn't mean to hurt you."

Her expression softened, and she grabbed his hand.

They sat for a while, not saying anything.

"I can't get a flight out until tomorrow morning. Is there a decent hotel in this town?" she asked.

He had to smile—quintessential Kate.

"As a matter of fact, there is. Come on, let's get you a room, and I'll buy you lunch."

~

"WE JUST WANTED to let you know, Miss Wilder," the officer said. "He bonded out a few minutes ago."

Jess felt all the air go out of her lungs. "Okay," she said breathlessly, "thanks for letting me know."

With shaking hands, she hung up, called the school, and put them on alert. They assured her that he had not shown up and that they would be on the lookout for him. She called Jimmy and asked him to take over for her at the tavern. Then she tried to call Will. When he didn't answer, she called Conner.

She locked the tavern's front door and walked briskly to the end of the street, where she stopped and looked towards the bay before crossing to head towards Conners's office. When she did, she saw Will and Kate sitting on a bench down by the water, holding hands. She stopped and stared at them, and as much as she wanted to, she couldn't tear her eyes away.

Finally, she crossed over and hurried towards Market Street. Connor pulled to the curb, leaned over, and opened the door. She jumped in and pointed toward the side street, the quickest way to the school.

"When did he bond out, Jess," Connor asked.

"The officer on the phone said just a little while ago. I called the school, and they know not to release him to Wade, but I'm terrified he'll do something, Connor."

"Better safe than sorry," Connor said. "You're doing the right thing by going to get him."

"But then what? I can't go home. He knows where we live.

We can't stay at Will's anymore." She paused to look at Connor, but he kept his eyes on the road. "He's bound to come looking for me at the tavern. I'm just going to get out of town for a while."

"Any ideas on where you want to go? I've already filed for a restraining order, so it's just a matter of getting it before a judge. That won't take long, and he does have the pending charges. Maybe when he cools off and realizes the trouble he's in, he'll take off. He's never been one to stick around and face the music."

"You're right about that. Maybe I'll just take Kip up to Georgia to my aunt's place where Mama is. He can stay there indefinitely if need be, and I'll give it a few days and see what happens."

They were quiet for a moment as they thought about things.

"Where should I pull up?" he said as they approached the school.

"Just right there. I can run in that side door and get to the office." She hopped out of the car and ran up the steps. Just as the door closed behind her, she saw a motorcycle pull into the parking lot and cruise by the school's front entrance. She didn't need to look very hard to see it was Wade.

When she had Kip, she called Connor on his cell phone. He'd seen Wade, too, who had parked in front and sat waiting for school to be dismissed.

"I'll pull up to the south entrance. He won't be able to see you from there, and we can head out the back of the parking lot," he said.

"Okay, we are on our way there," she said as she changed direction. When they reached the door, she paused to look first, and Connor waived her down. She didn't waste any time hurrying down the steps.

"What's going on, Mom?" Kip said when they got in the car. "How come you got me out of school early?"

"We're going on a little trip, buddy, to see Aunt Dottie up in Georgia, where Nana is."

"Oh," Kip said. "Is Will going with us?"

Jess glanced at Connor. "No, honey, he's not."

She could tell Kip wanted to ask more questions, but he'd taken a hint from his mother's serious tone and gone quiet.

"If you could just take me to the house and stay with us while I pull some things together, I promise it won't take us very long," she said.

"It's no trouble, Jess. I'm glad to do it. Take your time. I'll wait with you and follow you to make sure you get out of town okay."

She hurried through the house, gathering things they would need over the next few days. When she was ready, she texted Jimmy and asked him to get ahold of a few of their part-timers for coverage at the tavern for the next couple of days. She took one last look around, then hurried down the front walk with Kip.

CHAPTER TWENTY-NINE

As Will started across Market Street, he took a deep breath, taking in the cool afternoon air. With it came the salty smell of the bay, and he smiled. This time, it brought good memories, and he suddenly had a flashback of him and Jess catching fiddler crabs on the shell-strewn marsh beaches along the bay.

His mind was clearer than it had been in a long time. When he thought about his life, he no longer saw a road of obstacles in front of him. Looking back, it should have been simpler to see, but he'd been too much inside of his thoughts.

The conversation with Kate hadn't been easy, but he was glad to have it behind him. He'd been honest with her, and it felt good to finally say some things that had been on his mind. As predicted, they swiftly settled the other matters once Kate overcame her pride. Luckily, due to their separate living arrangements, there wasn't much.

He had to admit it felt odd not to be entangled with Kate. They had been together a long time, and she was a brilliant player in the business. It had always felt good to have her in his corner. Now, with all the decisions he was making, it felt like the pieces of his career were falling away a little at a time. So be it.

Now and then, though, he had a panic run through him about the project he'd all but walked away from. He hadn't heard back from Tony, but he suspected a call from him was part of why Kate had come. Desperate to get the deal done, he was sure Tony had asked her to try to wield her influence and persuade Will to take the meeting in person. Will knew how the game was played. It was all pretentious posturing. He couldn't be more tired of it.

He was surprised to see Jimmy working the tavern when he got back. It was late afternoon, but the evening shift didn't usually start until six o'clock. When he didn't find Jess in the back, he headed upstairs to look for her. He began to get an uneasy feeling when he found the apartment empty. He checked his watch. It was well past the time that Kip usually got out of school.

"Hey, Jimmy," he said as he came back down the stairs. "Do you know where Jess is?"

"No," he said, "I don't. She called me earlier and asked me to cover for her. Then I got a text from her asking me to pull in some part-timers to help cover the next few days. Said she was going out of town."

Will felt the fear rush through him as he checked his phone. He saw he had missed a call from her hours before. Something was happening, and he felt he knew what it was.

He dialed her number, but it only rang, which added to his anxiety. Where was she? He sat down at the bar and tried to think where she might go if she was running. She wouldn't go home. He was sure of that.

The tavern door opened, and he was so deep in thought that he didn't notice when someone sat on the bar stool beside him.

"Will?" a voice said.

He looked up and saw Conner staring at him.

238

"Yes?" he said.

"He's out. Wade's out, and he's looking for Jess and Kip. He went to the school today and later parked outside her house. I'm still waiting for her protective order to be signed by the judge. We had to get her out of town."

"Where is she?" Will asked, relieved to hear she and Kip hadn't just vanished.

"She asked me not to tell you, Will. She's under a lot of stress right now. She doesn't need any more."

"What?" Will said. "She doesn't want me to know where she is?"

Connor paused and looked hard at him for a moment.

"Why don't you leave her be, Will? It seems you're always disappointing her."

"What? What are you talking about, Connor?"

He paused again as if thinking about what he wanted to say.

"You know, in the years I've loved her, I've always known her heart was somewhere else. I've asked the girl more than once to marry me, but she could never say yes. I often thought about it, trying to figure out who she was carrying a torch for. Then, when you came back to town, I figured it out. I've felt her slipping further and further away from me these past few weeks, and I realized it was you. It's always been you."

Connor paused as he signaled Jimmy to bring them a whiskey.

"She's loved you for as long as she can remember, Will. She's waited all these years for you to come home, and now that you're here, she knows this is her last chance. And you've kept her uncertain about whether you're staying or going all these weeks. It's not right, Will. She deserves more than that from you."

"Connor, I..."

As if he didn't hear him, he kept going. "So you made her a partner in the tavern to keep her close to you without any real commitment. You occupy all of her time, so she's distanced from anyone else, and when she needs you, really needs you, you are off with some other woman."

Will was stunned at what he was hearing. Was this how Jess saw things? Was this how things really were, and he couldn't see it?

"So why don't you just leave her be, Will? If you care about her at all, go back to California and let her get on with her life. I love this woman and am willing to give her the life she deserves, along with all my love and attention. Kip, too. I'll never leave her, and she'll always know she can depend on me to be there for her. Why do you think she called me today? Because she knew I would answer the phone. Please, do what you wish with the tavern and everything else, but let her have some peace, Will. Just leave her alone."

Will pushed the whiskey away and stood up.

"Say what you want, Connor, but that's not how things are. Those have not been my intentions. I see I can't trust that you'll get a message to her for me, so I'll do it on my own. Thank you for taking care of her and Kip today. I'll be forever grateful to you for that."

Will turned and headed for the stairs, his heart pounding at the thought of Jess having these ideas. Certainly, she knew better. By now, she had to know he was in love with her.

He had to contain himself and not slam his door when he reached the apartment, and once he was there alone, he felt like screaming. Had he blown it? Had he lost her? Was there any truth to what Conner said?

He had to admit that his feelings and actions had been all over the place the last few weeks. He'd been through an awakening after coming back to Apalachicola, and his perspective on everything had shifted. It had unsettled him and made him question even the most basic parts of his beliefs. He wasn't even sure who he was anymore.

He was still having a hard time reconciling what happened to his mother. He hit a brick wall everywhere he turned, which frustrated and disturbed him. He felt a force pushing him toward the truth, and he knew the shroud of secrecy could not keep the truth from him forever. He would not give up until he got to the bottom of it.

But had he been unfair to Jess, keeping her guessing about his intentions? If he had, it wasn't because he intended to keep her off balance. Realizing he wanted to stay in Apalachicola for good had been a journey for him. There had been no predetermined path, agenda, or preconceived ideas about what would happen between them.

To hear Connor say she had been in love with him for as long as she could remember rocked him to his core. They had been close as children, and he regretted moving on from that in high school. But to think she had waited all these years for him to come home was almost inconceivable to him. That she had never committed to Connor on the chance they might be together someday made him realize the depth of her love for him.

As much as Connor's words angered him, he began to see how things must have looked from his perspective. He'd been a gentleman when other men might have been inclined not to be. Watching the woman you love being taken from you was something no man worth his mettle would take sitting down. Connor had played it straight, and Will admired him for it. But it didn't make some of his assumptions fair.

The timing of his break with Kate hadn't been good, but he was not to blame for her showing up when she had. He hadn't asked her to come and would have rather handled it in LA. But once she was there, he'd tried to do the right thing by being honest with her and ensuring she was okay. Settling things between them meant no further overlap with his life there in Apalachicola. To think Jess thought he was "off with another woman" when she needed him made him want to punch a wall. Surely, she knew him better. Was he such an enigma that she didn't trust him at all? Was he responsible for that, or did the years she'd been waiting engrain that in her? He didn't know.

He felt lost and wanted to talk to her, but he didn't want to pressure her since she hadn't answered her phone earlier. Having Wade coming after her and Kip must have been terrifying, and she was probably still coming down from it all. Once he collected his emotions, he would send her a text. Not communicating with her at all was out of the question, even if she wasn't ready to respond.

~

JESS LAY AWAKE, listening to Kip's breathing as he slept beside her. It had been a long day for him, and she was glad he'd fallen asleep easily. Still, she worried about him having nightmares again since they were in an unfamiliar place. Anticipating that it might happen kept her awake.

She grabbed her phone off the nightstand and reread Will's message. As much as she wanted to, she hadn't responded. She needed some distance and space to figure things out. Since Will had come home to Apalachicola, she'd felt confused about things.

Every time she thought things were coming together for them, something happened to throw her into a state of doubt. Would it always be like this for them? After so many years, they still couldn't seem to come together. Could she live a life with a man she felt so insecure with?

Connor was such a rock and had handled everything that afternoon with a level-headed steadiness she had never appreciated more. She wouldn't have these doubts if they were together. He was too predictable, and she knew her life with him would be too. What he lacked in excitement and spontaneity, he made up for in certainty.

Maybe she should rethink things. Maybe now, after these past weeks with Will, she could finally get him out of her system and settle down. Connor was ready and able, and it would be easy to say yes to another proposal. She could make it happen by barely trying. Even though Kip was fascinated by Will, he might find more to attach himself to in Connor for the long haul. At least Connor would be a steady force in the boy's life. Would Will?

After seeing Will holding hands with Kate on the bench that day, something had shifted inside of her. If he was keeping a part of himself in LA, she would be a lot more careful with her heart and take a step back. While she realized it wasn't his fault that Kate had shown up unannounced, what happened after was entirely his responsibility. It had taken him hours to return her call, and she could only assume he'd been with her during that time. And where was Kate now? Probably still in Apalachicola. Were they having dinner together? Spending the night together? The thought made her furious and heartsick. No, she wouldn't make herself that vulnerable to him again. Things were too uncertain.

She'd been in wait-and-see mode for too long, letting things unfold on their own. Now, she felt the right thing to do was to force his hand. Either he loved her, or he didn't and wanted to make a life with her or not. She couldn't play around with her heart or Kip's, either.

His text had said Connor had let him know what was happening and that he was sorry he hadn't been there for her. He wanted to hear her voice to know she and Kip were okay, but he understood if she needed a little time to decompress. She shouldn't worry about the tavern, and he hoped things resolved quickly so she and Kip could come home. He didn't mention Kate.

She put the phone back on the nightstand, snuggled up to Kip, and tried to put Will Kendrick out of her mind. All that mattered now was protecting Kip and figuring out how they could return to living their everyday lives. She didn't know exactly how that would happen, but she couldn't think about it anymore. Right then, they were safe, and she was determined to keep it that way. Will or not, she wasn't returning to Apalach until she was sure Wade was no longer a threat to them.

CHAPTER THIRTY

When Will opened his eyes, he saw it was barely light outside. He'd spent a restless night thinking about Jess and worrying about her and Kip. When he checked his phone, he saw it was just a few minutes after six o'clock. He also noticed that Jess had not responded to his text.

He had to admit it angered him a bit. He felt he was being unfairly judged by the events of yesterday. The break from Kate was necessary, and she was already on her way back to LA. He felt he'd handled it gracefully and with as much care as possible. That Jess seemed to withdraw from him in the wake of it seemed utterly unjust.

He got up, made coffee, and spent time catching up on the news to distract himself. Knowing he wouldn't see her that day was depressing. Her and Kip's things were still in the apartment, and the sight of them caused angst to run through his soul. He saw a small bottle of her perfume in the bathroom and couldn't resist the urge to take in the scent. It was torture, but he couldn't help himself. He needed a tiny part of her.

He also needed to get out of the apartment and the tavern.

Being there was too hard without her. He had contacted and arranged a visit with one of the old timers in town, an unofficial expert on the river and the tides that affected it. He was curious to show him the tidal maps he'd found and run his theories by him.

He skipped breakfast, took a coffee with him instead, and exited via the back of the tavern. It was too early to meet with the old fellow, so he headed to the waterfront. It was a clear morning, and the sun reflecting off the bay was a spectacular array of shimmering blues. He found solace in the bay now that he hadn't in all the years he'd grown up there.

He hadn't been there very long when he heard footsteps behind him. Sawyer Hayes lowered his large frame onto the bench beside him but said nothing.

"We have to stop meeting like this," Will said without looking at him.

Sawyer chuckled but said nothing.

The two were quiet for a while, just watching the boats moving up and down the creek and into the mouth of the river. The brisk breeze off the water would have made it uncomfortable if Will hadn't slipped on a sweater at the last minute. He was glad for the cool air, though. It did a lot to clear his mind.

He was not in a good mood, and remembering his last conversation with Sawyer annoyed him. He decided to bring up the subject again.

"Sawyer, tell me what you know about my mother and how she died," Will said bluntly.

Sawyer was quiet for a moment, then took a deep breath.

"I think you know all there is to know, Will. It seems you're just having a hard time accepting it."

"Maybe I'm having a hard time because so much about it doesn't make sense. Why does everyone get so uncomfortable when I start asking questions?"

Sawyer went quiet again as he seemed to contemplate Will's question.

"It's a hard thing to remember. It was devastating for all of us."

That Sawyer had dodged him again raised his ire. Every time he asked a direct question, he got a similar response. Everyone seemed to be following the same party line.

"I'm not buying it, Sawyer. She deserved to be remembered, but everyone erased her like she never existed. If everyone loved her so much, why have they snuffed out every memory of her?"

Sawyer didn't answer him, and Will felt his anger rising further.

"I think you know more than you're saying. I think you all do. I'm not going to stop, Sawyer. I will get to the truth about what happened to my mother, with or without your help."

Sawyer remained silent, and Will could sit there no longer. He got up, walked a few paces, and turned back to look at him. When Sawyer never took his eyes off the water, Will walked away.

THE RIVERKEEPER LIVED on Sixth Street in an old house that had seen better days. Will tapped lightly on the screen door and waited. After a few minutes, he heard shuffling footsteps and the old gentleman appeared in the doorway. Without saying a word, he pushed the door open, motioned Will inside, and led him into a side room that used to be a sun porch.

A large wooden desk sat in the middle of the room, piled high with maps, charts, and what appeared to be newspaper articles and magazines. He motioned to a chair facing the desk and sat down after clearing a few things out of the way.

"Let me see what you have," the old man said as he extended his hands. Will handed him the maps, and when he rolled them out on the desk, Will walked him through his theory and the questions he had.

"Well, I agree with you," the man said as he leaned back and removed his glasses. "Something dropped off the bridge at that time would not have likely ended up in the place you have marked here. I would guess it would have ended up about here," his pencil pointing to another part of the map. "But it would depend on the size and the weight of it. What are we talking about?"

Will hesitated, not sure what to say.

"A body," he said finally.

The two looked at each other for a moment.

"You're Grant Kendrick's son?" he asked

"Yes."

"We are talking about your mother?"

"Yes."

The old man nodded silently and leaned forward, putting on his glasses again.

"I have to tell you it didn't make sense to me at the time. I wasn't living in Apalach. I lived across the bay in Eastpoint, but of course, I heard about it. I didn't know your mother, but I met your father a few years later."

He paused, removed his glasses, cleaned them on his shirt, and put them back on.

"Where her body was found, it would make more sense that the tides carried her out, not in," he said, looking at Will over his glasses.

"Meaning what?" Will asked.

"Meaning, if you ask my opinion, I would say she went into the water either up the Apalachicola River or, more likely, up Scipio Creek."

Will was silent as the implications sank in.

"You feel pretty certain about that?" Will asked.

"Yes," he answered. "I do."

He looked at Will for a moment, his expression serious.

"I don't know what happened to your mother, son," he said. "But I don't think she jumped off that bridge."

AFTER HIS VISIT with the riverkeeper, who he learned went by the name of Cyrus, he walked slowly back to the tavern. Will guessed him to be well into his nineties. Cyrus had spent the better part of a century studying the river and its tributaries. When it came to the ways of the water, Will was sure he knew what he was talking about.

The information confirmed what Will had known instinctively all along. The secrecy and the lies surrounding his mother's death were covering up something very dark. But what? Had she been taken? Murdered? What was it that everyone knew but him?

He needed a change of scenery, so instead of going into the tavern when he returned, he climbed into his father's truck, looking to get out of town. He had no particular destination in mind as he backed out of the gate and headed across town to the coastal highway. He didn't care where he ended up. He just needed to get away for a while.

The beautiful scenery from his driver's side window barely distracted him from his thoughts as he drove along. When he approached the turn-off to the cape, he decided to take it.

It had been a long time since he'd driven the road to the end of the peninsula. Cape San Blas was more inhabited now than he remembered it. Still, it was beautiful and pristine, its white sand beaches nearly blinding in the late morning sun. He drove as far as he could, and when the road ended, he parked the truck and got out. There was no one there, and he kicked off his shoes and rolled up his cuffs before trudging through the deep, white sugar sand to the water.

As far as he could see, there was nothing but the stunning turquoise water and white sand. It was an almost surreal scene as he noticed there was not a shred of evidence that other human beings had been there. There were no footprints in the sand, no discarded remnants of a picnic, just pure beauty that stretched for miles. It was precisely what he needed.

He didn't know what to do with the information he had. Confronting people seemed to get him nowhere. Small towns, it seemed, buried their secrets deep, and no one outside of the inner circle was allowed to know the truth.

But he couldn't just let it go. For the sake of his mother's memory, he needed to know. She deserved it. Whatever happened to her had taken her life and stolen her entire existence. He owed it to her to uncover the truth and reestablish her place in the history of this world.

He walked for the better part of an hour, taking in the peace and quiet and the sights and sounds of the gulf. Earlier, he'd felt unbelievably tense with everything closing in on him. At least now he felt like he could breathe.

He returned to the truck and drove the long road back to the coastal highway, but instead of turning right to head back towards Apalachicola, he turned left and traveled further west. He wasn't ready to give up the peace he'd found on the cape. Not yet.

When he got to Port St. Joe, he remembered the little seafood shack he'd visited before. It would be a good place for him to sit outside and think, and it had no memories attached to it. He ordered, then sat back, sipping a beer. Even though the day had warmed significantly, he enjoyed the steady, cool offshore breeze and the sun on his face. He may not be able to hang on to his mood forever, but he was determined to make it last as long as possible.

He still had not heard from Jess, and his worry about her and Kip was growing. Was she done with him? He didn't understand it. He thought she trusted him and his feelings for her more. He thought he had made it clear how he felt about her and the boy and that he intended to stay in Apalachicola. Were they really that fragile? If so, what chance did they have of making it in the long run?

His cell phone vibrated in his pocket, and he quickly retrieved it, hoping it was Jess. Instead, disappointment washed over him when he saw it was his agent, Tony. He contemplated ignoring the call but thought it better to get it over with. It would be one less stress on his plate.

"Hey Tony, what's up?" he said.

"Hey, Will, I've just gotten off the phone with the client. He's upped his offer to have you on the project and agreed to everything you've asked for. I've tried every way I know how to negotiate this meeting, but he's insistent. It's not that big of a deal, Will. It's a small ask for you to come to LA and meet with him, considering the size of the project and the money involved. Can't you just come out for a day or two? I'll arrange everything. Just get your ass on a plane, and I'll have you in and out of there in no time."

Will thought about what Tony was saying. If Jess was safe and sound somewhere, and Wade wasn't a threat at the moment, was it really necessary for him to be in Apalachicola for the next few days? And, if things were falling apart between them, did nuking his career make any sense now? If she was backing off, staying for good might be out of the question anyway. He couldn't imagine having her so close and not being with her. No, it would be unsustainable. He needed to hedge his bets. He was willing to give it all up for her, but if it wasn't enough, there was nothing more he could do.

"Okay, tell him I'll take the meeting," Will said.

"Great!" Tony said. Will could hear the relief in his voice. "When can you leave to get out here?"

"Right away, tonight if possible," Will said. "Make the arrangements and get back to me."

"I checked, and there is a decent airport near you. If I can get a charter there in the next few hours, can you make it?"

"Yes," Will said. "Make it happen."

He disconnected just as the waitress delivered his food. It felt good to have decided to take the meeting. It was one less thing that was in flux. By tomorrow morning, he'd be back in LA, and by the afternoon, he would be sweet-talking the client into feeling good about paying him an obscene amount of money to do what he could do in his sleep. The certainty of the situation felt good to him. LA was his town. There, he walked on water.

CHAPTER THIRTY-ONE

When Jess's cell phone rang at eight-thirty in the morning from a number in the Apalach area, she stared at it. She didn't recognize the number, but it was unlikely she wasn't connected somehow to the person calling. She was tempted to let it go to voicemail, but with everything going on, she thought she should answer it.

"Hello?" she answered tentatively.

"Miss Wilder?"

"Yes?"

"This is Sargent Greer from the Franklin County Sheriff's Office."

"Yes?" she said again.

"I was asked to call and give you some information."

"Okay," she said a little breathlessly. She had no idea why he was calling her.

"Wade Carter was killed in a motorcycle accident last night on the Apalachicola causeway. We're in the process of notifying his next of kin, and since he is your son's father, you're getting a call, too," he said. "I'm sorry. I know this is shocking news, and I regret delivering it over the phone, but we couldn't locate you."

"It's okay," she said, her voice shaking. "I understand."

They were both silent for a moment.

"Is there anything we can do for you, Miss Wilder? Anything at all?" he asked.

"No, but thank you for letting me know. I appreciate the call."

"If you have any questions or need more information, please don't hesitate to call me directly. This is my cell phone. I have it with me all the time."

"Okay, I will," she said, not knowing what else to say.

"Goodbye, then," he said as he disconnected.

She sat very still as the implications of the news sank in. Guilt washed over her as she realized that all she felt was relief. The news would be devastating to others but not to her. She'd felt the same way when Wade left town after Kip was born. Now, he was gone for good, and she was glad.

She wasn't sure when or what she would tell Kip. It would not be easy, but at least he wouldn't spend his whole life wondering about a dad somewhere out in the world. She would let him memorialize him in any way he wanted. She wouldn't tell him the awful things he'd done to her. If he wanted to create a hero in his mind, she'd let him.

Now, they could go home and get on with their lives with no worries hanging over their heads. She'd been putting off having the conversation with Will until they could do it in person. Watching his face, she would be better able to read his emotions. He would have his chance to explain things, but it might be over for them if she didn't like what she heard. She'd waited for him long enough. If he wasn't ready to commit to her and Kip, it was time to move on.

It was a beautiful morning, and she'd stepped outside to clear her mind, listen to the birds, and enjoy the cool air with her coffee. Kip was inside having breakfast with his Grandmother, and she was glad she'd been alone when she'd gotten the call. She probably would not have been able to hide the shock of the news from him.

She returned to the house and found her mother and Kip still at the kitchen table, conversing and laughing. She sat and poured herself some juice, and tried calming her mind. Knowing her daughter well, her mother could tell she wasn't herself.

"Mama," Jess said, "how long are you planning to stay here at Aunt Dottie's?"

"Oh, I don't know, maybe a day or two more, depending on you and Kip," she said, trying to sound casual and not raise attention from the boy.

"I think we are going to head back today," she said, giving her mother a look that told her there was more to the story.

"Kip, honey, run upstairs and get my glasses, please. They are next to my bed on the nightstand." her mother said.

"Okay," he said, getting up and running to the stairs.

When he was out of earshot, she turned quickly to her daughter.

"What's going on," she whispered.

"Wade is dead. Wrecked his motorcycle on the causeway," Jess whispered back.

"Oh, my," her mother said, glancing over her shoulder at the stairs. "What are you going to tell him?"

"I don't know yet," she said, "but I'm anxious to get him home and settled back in. He's missed too much school already."

"Well, if y'all are going, I'm going," she said. "What time do you want to leave?"

"Before noon if that works for you. I want to get home early enough for him to get back into his evening routine," Jess said.

"Okay," her mother said. "I'll be ready."

WILL PUT the key in the lock and hesitated. He hadn't been home in weeks, and it felt odd to be there. What was once his sanctuary now felt cold and sterile. Much like how it felt to be back in LA.

He'd gotten a decent amount of sleep on the flight over. He'd forgotten how nice it was to fly charter instead of commercial. No howling kids or security. Just reclining leather seats and peace and quiet.

Tony had scheduled an afternoon meeting with a dinner afterward. He would have rather turned it around and gone back that evening, but, with Jess out of town, he might as well stay, enjoy the dinner, and return in the morning. There was no rush.

He showered and checked his watch. He still had an hour before the car would pick him up. He decided to review the project notes Tony had sent him. He needed to get his head in the game before the meeting anyway and not let his thoughts be consumed entirely with Jess.

He still had not heard from her and had no idea what was going through her head. When he'd decided to give up the project to stay and ensure she and Kip were safe, he thought that had shown how he felt about her and his intentions. Connor's words had shaken his confidence, though, and with her going dark on him, he didn't know what to think. Figuring out what she was thinking would have to wait, though. He'd come all this way to do his job. Now that he was there, it was game on.

WILL SAT at the conference table and lightly tapped the end of his pen on the papers before him. He'd forgotten how much he despised these meetings. Meant to get everyone on the same page about the project, they only served as a stage for pretentious posturing and self-promotion. It was a complete waste of time, and he was ready to be done with it.

He'd done his part to show the client he had things well in hand. While he agreed with Tony that this was an important project, he'd worked on similar films in the past. He'd quickly fallen in sync with it and knew exactly how he would approach the work. When he'd presented his ideas, he could tell from the smiling and the nodding around the table that they were all impressed. He was on familiar turf and had to admit it felt good to be back at the top of the food chain.

Well into the meeting, he saw his phone light up. As discreetly as possible, he checked his messages. It was Jess.

> Wade is dead. Wrecked his bike on the
> Causeway last night. I'm headed back to
> Apalach. Can we talk later?

The news was shocking, and he took a minute to think about it. That Wade was gone and out of their lives was good news, though. Fate had a way of evening the score. He had gotten what he deserved.

Though it was not uncommon for people to use their phones in such meetings, there was a distinct protocol. Yes, they were all busy and had important matters at hand, but checking your phone meant lowering your status. If you were an admin or an underling, you were waiting for the world to hand you your orders. If you were an important player, the world waited on you.

Still, he wanted to respond to her. He'd waited three days to hear from her. There was no way he could excuse himself from the meeting for a few minutes. The subject at hand was too critical, and he didn't see a break coming in the next hour or so. He quickly typed a reply.

I'm in LA

Before he could finish the text to tell her he'd be back the next day, the attention of the meeting turned toward him, and he quickly turned his phone face down. He'd have to finish it later.

When the meeting broke an hour and a half later, and he was on his way to the car, he brought up his message to her and saw that it had inadvertently been sent when he'd laid his phone down. His heart sank when he saw her reply. *Never mind,* she'd said. He quickly dialed her number, but she didn't answer, so he typed a message.

> Sorry for the short reply. I was in a meeting. I'll be back tomorrow. Glad you and Kip are safe. Miss you.

It was the best he could do now if she wouldn't answer the phone. They were entirely out of sync, and he knew it. He turned to Tony when they got in the car.

"Have that charter ready to go," he said. "After dinner, I'm out of here."

JESS FELT like she couldn't breathe. Admitting that it was over between her and Will was harder than she imagined. Somehow, deep in her heart, she'd thought it would eventually work out. Yes, they had obstacles and difficult situations in their way, but she'd felt just a few days ago that they were going to make it.

After what transpired when Kate showed up and his detached text, she knew his heart was really in LA. She'd been kidding herself to think he would give up his entire life for her.

Now, it was just a matter of cleaning up the fallout. She was going to exercise her exit clause in the tavern partnership and try to put her life back together the way it was before he ever came back to town. She would no longer put her life on hold for a man she knew now she could never truly have.

The fact that he was in LA was the real kicker for her. She hadn't been out of his sight very long before he jumped at the chance to go back. Even if they could push past these latest setbacks, she would fight that forever. Even if he did stay and worked from Apalach, every time he went back, she would worry. Would he see Kate? Would he decide not to come home? Would the lure of the big city lights overtake him? It was too much uncertainty to live with.

Kip was in the back seat, head down, working on a drawing. She was glad he couldn't see her face. Even with her sunglasses on, he would have known something was wrong. She wiped away the tears as fast as she could, but it would have been evident to anyone who got a good look at her. Even though she thought she was strong, she couldn't make them stop.

She wasn't just grieving for her own heart. She was grieving for Kip's, too. He talked incessantly about Will, and she knew it wasn't just that they had gotten close and were kindred spirits. Will was a connection to Grant that the boy desperately needed. Grant had been the only father figure he'd ever known. He was also the first person close to him he had ever lost. Will would be the second.

As she got close to Apalach, the pain ratcheted up a notch. She knew she would face memories and longing that might never leave her. If it weren't for her mother, she would consider taking Kip and making a fresh start somewhere. No, she was destined always to be reminded of him, and the realization made her feel hopeless. Letting him go would take a long time if she ever could.

The drive home was slow going. With her mother following

her and construction on the back roads, their progress was slow. That was fine with her. The more time she had to process her feelings, the better. By the time she went into the tavern tomorrow, she had to have herself back together. She would have to be strong to get through this next season of her life.

CHAPTER THIRTY-TWO

T he plane touching down at Apalachicola Regional
jarred him awake. He must have been in a deep sleep
because he was slow to push the fatigue away. The jet
lag had already set in, and his circadian rhythm was off. It
would take a day or two to sort out.

He'd been dreaming of her, and the feel of her was still with
him. He hadn't heard from her again after he'd sent the last text
from LA yesterday afternoon. He had no idea what he was
heading into. Had he lost her? He thought maybe he had.

Connor's words still echoed in his mind. *It seems you're
always disappointing her.* He struggled with the idea that might be
true. She was always fixing things for him, even when they were
kids. Then, he had abandoned her for the better part of a decade
and a half. Now it seemed he couldn't convince her his feelings
for her were real. He couldn't blame her.

The sun was coming up, and the brightness seemed to pierce
right through his soul. He welcomed it, and as he turned onto
the coastal highway toward town, the contrast between there
and LA had never been more striking. He'd spent an hour and a
half in snarled traffic the night before getting to the airport.

Now, there wasn't a soul in sight as the quiet, calm bay reflected the reddish colors of the sky. It seemed a storm was coming to Apalach, and he had an eerie, foreboding feeling that it would be in more ways than one.

He pulled Grant's truck behind the tavern and sat for a moment. He wasn't sure he was ready to face it all. It was too early for Jess to be there, but just being in the tavern and the apartment would be enough to stir up his angst. If it was truly over for him and Jess, he realized then that he could never stay. He would have to return to LA for a while but knew he couldn't stay there either. It didn't suit him anymore. He would have to find a place that soothed his soul enough to let him forget.

The apartment seemed to have captured a moment in time. Kip's turtle drawing was hanging on the refrigerator, and Jess's jacket was draped over one of the kitchen chairs. In his whole existence, he'd never been able to attach himself to anyone. Not until they had come into his life. Now he realized being with them and taking care of them was everything. He would do everything he could to persuade her to let him.

JESS TEXTED Jimmy and asked if the tavern was covered for the day. She didn't think she was ready to face Will yet. Her emotions were too scattered, and she needed to gather her strength to get through what was coming.

She'd turned her phone off after she'd sent her last text. Whatever he had to say to her after that didn't matter and would only stir up more emotions she would have to deal with. Jimmy was capable of running things, so she wasn't worried about the tavern. If anything came up, he could handle it, or it could wait. What was most important now was getting Kip settled in at home and at school and focusing on her life ahead.

A life that didn't include pining away for a man who didn't want her.

When she turned her phone on, she saw his message and skimmed it, not letting any emotion sink in. He would be back in Apalach that day. Later that evening, she would head to the tavern to check on things. If he were there, she'd retrieve her and Kip's things from the apartment and end things with him. The sooner, the better.

Connor had been trying to reach her, and she knew she should call him and let him know she was back. After everything he'd done for her, it wasn't fair to keep him waiting. She'd done enough of that already.

"Hey," she said when he answered.

"Hey," he said. "Where are you?"

"I'm here in Apalach. We got back yesterday evening."

"Oh," he said. "Do you think it's okay? Wade hasn't shown up, has he?"

"I got a call from the sheriff's office yesterday. Wade is dead. He died two nights ago after he crashed his motorcycle on the causeway."

Connor was silent for a moment as the news sank in.

"Well, I can't say I'm surprised. He liked to live dangerously."

"Yes," Jess said, "he did."

They both went quiet again.

"Have you talked to Will?" he asked.

"Just a couple of texts," she said. "Why?"

"Just wondering. Can I see you?"

"I can't today. I've got some things I need to do. Then I'm going to the tavern later. Tomorrow?"

"Okay," he said and paused a moment. "Are you doing okay with everything, Jess? It's been a tough few days for you."

"I'm okay," she said. "I'll get through it all."

He wasn't sure exactly what she meant, but he sensed the

tides were changing. He only hoped they were changing in his favor.

She spent the rest of the day running errands and organizing her thoughts. Kip had a good day at school, and she was glad the incident with Wade had seemed to pass over him, leaving him unscathed. She would take her time figuring out what to tell him about his father. There was no rush. It had been a while since he'd asked about him anyway. What she would say to him about Will, she didn't know.

She passed by the rear of the tavern on her way to the post office and saw that Grant's truck was there. That meant Will was back. The realization sent a shiver and a streak of pain through her heart. It wasn't going to be easy to face him.

A little before ten in the evening, she kissed her sleeping son goodbye and headed out on foot. She stopped by the waterfront to listen to the water lapping at the docks, take in the fresh air, and collect her thoughts. The cool winds blowing in from the north for the last few days had shifted, and it was unseasonably warm in Apalach. She wasn't sure what the next few days would mean for her, but she knew that when the sun rose in the morning, it would be the beginning of her life without Will.

Jimmy was finishing up the closing when she came in through the back door.

"Everything go okay these past couple of days?" she asked him as she surveyed the place.

"Yep," he said. "Everything good with you?"

"Yes, it is now."

"Have you talked to Will? He was looking for you earlier," he said.

"No, but I will. Is he upstairs?"

"I think so," Jimmy said. "I haven't seen him leave."

She helped him with the last few closing tasks, and when they were finished, she quietly closed the door behind him and locked it. She paused momentarily and pressed her forehead to the cool glass of the door before turning and heading up the stairs.

HE'D SPENT a miserable day feeling jet-lagged and worrying about Jess. She still hadn't contacted him and didn't show up at the tavern that day. He wanted to see her and hopefully set things straight between them. More than once, he'd been tempted to call her, but his instincts told him not to. If she needed space, he would give it to her.

He heard the footsteps on the stairs and went to the door, expecting to see Jimmy or Loretta.

"Hey," she said when he opened the door.

"Hey," he said softly. He extended his hand to her, but she ignored it and walked by him into the apartment.

"I've just come to pick up our things," she said. "I hope I haven't come too late."

"No, of course not," he said as he watched her gather her things around the apartment. "Hey," he said, taking her bag from her. "Can we talk for a minute?"

She looked at him, her eyes studying his.

"Do we really have anything left to talk about, Will Kendrick?"

Her words stunned him. "Why would you say that?" he said.

"Because the truth of the matter, Will, is that you've still got one foot in your life in LA, and I don't see that changing."

"Why? Because I went back to take a meeting? You leave town without telling me where you are going, and then Connor tells me you don't want me to know where you are. And you are mad at me for spending ten hours on a plane to spend six hours in LA and get back here as fast as I could."

He turned his back on her so she wouldn't see the anger

brewing inside him. He didn't want to be mad at her, but what she was saying was unreasonable.

"No, because when Kip and I were in danger and needed you, you were holding hands on a bench with your California girlfriend and couldn't be bothered to return my call for hours. Then, the minute I leave to take my son somewhere safe, you hop on a plane to LA. You're never going to be able to be happy and satisfied here, are you, Will?"

He opened his mouth to speak, but nothing came out. What she had said was so different from how he saw the situation that he could hardly comprehend it. When she saw him at a loss for words, she turned and headed for the door.

"Wait, Jess," he said, catching her by the arm. "I'm sorry I wasn't there for you and Kip. I didn't mean to be out of touch. Ending things with Kate was..."

He started to say hard, but that wasn't the truth. It was more an untangling of their lives built together over several years.

"...complicated," he said finally. "We were together a long time, Jess. It took more than a simple conversation."

"Look, Will, I can't spend my whole life worrying that I'll never be enough for you, that being here won't be enough for you. And I won't put Kip through it. I'm sorry," she said as she wrestled her arm away from him. He felt helpless as he watched her go.

"I love you, Jess," he said when she got to the door. "Please, give me a chance."

She stopped, and he heard her sigh deeply.

"I've spent my whole life giving you a chance, Will."

As the words landed on his heart, he closed his eyes and tried to squeeze away the pain. When he opened them, she was gone.

CHAPTER THIRTY-THREE

The next few hours, he distracted himself by packing up his belongings and trying to organize things to make it easier for whoever would move everything out of the apartment. He wouldn't let his mind go to all the implications of her words until he sat down to write his instructions to Connor. In the hours since she'd left, he'd sorted out the details of his affairs instead.

He would relinquish his share of the tavern to Jess along with the building. She loved it as his father had, and he couldn't bear the thought of anyone else owning it. She could do with it what she wished, but at least it would not pass from his hands to a stranger. The rest of the buildings were to be sold except the building that housed Jess's shop. That would go into a trust for Kip, with Jess as the trustee. The rental income from the tenants upstairs would be escrowed each month to pay the taxes, insurance, and upkeep. The excess funds would be deposited into an investment account to pass to him along with the building when he turned twenty-five. If he couldn't be around to care for the boy, at least he could do something for him.

He also asked Connor to arrange storage and maintenance

for his father's truck until Kip turned sixteen. He could handle that however he wanted, and Will would fund it. He only needed the details on where to send the money. Everything else of his father's would be donated except the few things Will had packed into boxes to ship to California. That included his father's bible and his classic novels. He needed something to remember him by.

Near daybreak, he felt ready, and as he turned to go, his eyes landed on the door to his father's bedroom. He hadn't been in there since he'd arrived in Apalachicola, but now that he was leaving for good, he needed to.

He had resigned himself to the fact that he would probably never learn what happened to his mother. It made him sad to think he had somehow let her down. Everyone deserved a legacy, and hers had been stolen from her. But he would remember her, even though everyone else seemed to want to forget.

He slowly turned the knob and tentatively pushed the door open, expecting a musty smell to overtake him. Surprisingly, the room seemed clean and fresh even after being shut up for months. He suspected that was Loretta's doing.

Stepping inside, he slowly walked around the room, tracing the tops of the furniture with his fingertips. When he reached the window, he stopped and gazed down at the street. It was barely light out, but he could see enough to realize the longing he would feel in his heart when he left this place.

His eyes traveled around the room and landed on his father's nightstand. Leaning against the lamp was an envelope, and as he got closer, he saw it was addressed to him. He recognized his father's writing, even though he could tell he'd been frail when he wrote it. It simply said, *William.*

Carefully opening it, he unfolded the pages inside. When he did, a gold coin and a St. Christopher medal slipped out and landed in his lap. He picked up the coin and turned it over in his hand. He had no idea why they were there or what they meant.

As he looked through the pages, glancing at the words, he instinctively knew the answers to a thousand questions lay within. What he didn't know was if he was ready for them.

Flipping on the light next to the bed, he began reading.

Dear William,

My life is coming to a close, and I have some regrets. Not seeing the man you've become is one of the biggest, but there are other things I need to tell you about. I could have taken this all to my grave, but there are things you should know, even though I realize your life will look differently to you once you do.

Your mother was the light of my life, and I guess you could say, my obsession. From the moment I met her, she consumed me. I would have done anything for her; in fact, I did, as you will read about in these pages.

I murdered your grandfather because he spent years abusing your mother and grandmother and other children. He was a violent, evil man who would have eventually killed her if I'd let him live. For some odd reason, I saved his St. Christopher medal. Do with it what you want.

I was never able to get over it, though, and to this day, I shudder when I think about it. He *deserved it, and if I had to do it again, I would, but it has haunted me since. I dumped his body in the bay. No one will ever find him.*

The thing that is most on my mind is telling you about the circumstances surrounding your mother's death. I never told you anything because I didn't want to lie to you. The truth was terrible enough, but making you believe she had taken her own life was something I was not willing to do, though others were. It was what we all agreed on the night she died, but I could never say it to you even though it was whispered about around you for years. I couldn't tell you the truth, but I wouldn't tell you a lie that might tarnish any memory you had of her. So, I told you nothing...

THE WORDS PLAYED in Will's head like a movie script, and as he read, he could see the events unfolding in his mind's eye. As his father revealed the truth, he could not read fast enough, and as he stumbled through the confession, it was both terrifying and heartbreaking.

Grant Kendrick was not his father. Conceived in a fit of lust and a momentary lapse in judgment, he had been brought into existence as the son of another man. Years of abuse had conditioned his mother to go along or be harmed. Faced with the situation, she had retreated and had neither the emotional fortitude nor the strength to stop him. Getting no resistance from her, the man had assumed she wasn't objecting.

But it wasn't until Will saw the man's name written in the letter that the magnitude of everything sunk in. Sawyer Hayes hadn't known he was Will's father until the fateful night his mother died. Faced with the truth, he had cried and begged for Grant's forgiveness. Grant, in a fit of rage, had tried to kill him with his bare hands.

Penny had brought Anna to the docks after she'd shown up sobbing and begging her to tell her where Sawyer was. Grant had already been there, and she'd told him Sawyer was working on his boat.

Anna Kendrick died after being accidentally pushed off the dock trying to break up the skirmish between the two men. When she went over, she hit her head on a concrete piling and immediately went under. Though Grant dove in after her, in the darkness and with the current, he couldn't find her. He dove for over an hour before being pulled, shivering and exhausted from the creek.

When they couldn't find Anna, Penny, in a blind panic, had run to the bridge to look for her, and Will realized she was the woman with long hair the passerby had seen. It was all starting to make sense. It was coming together.

When it was obvious that Anna was dead and nothing could be done to save her, they realized someone should alert the authorities. Grant called his attorney, Mason West. Penny, being a devout Christian, had asked for Father Hudson.

As the five of them sat and discussed what would come, Mason West decided what would be said. What good would come from telling the truth? Would baby Will lose another parent to a justice system that so often failed to get it right? No, it was better this way. They would say Anna Kendrick, consumed with postpartum depression, threw herself off the Apalachicola Bridge, and no one would ever question it. As long as they all stuck to the story, the truth would never come to light.

...I'm sorry, Will, that I couldn't be a better

father to you. I loved you like I loved your mother. It didn't matter that you weren't mine. As long as you were hers, it was enough for me. But I was a broken man after I lost her, and you were a constant reminder of how I failed her, how I lost her. I should have done better by you.

It is my hope that you will find a woman to love like I loved your mother. The love of a good woman is life's greatest blessing. If you do, don't ever let her go. There is no substitute for it – not wealth or fame or any other earthly pursuit. It's the only thing that matters in the end.

The enclosed gold coin was given to your mother for safekeeping in case you ever needed it. I'm sure you don't, but perhaps you know a boy you could pass it on to. You have made me proud, son, and you have made your mark on the world.

All my love,
Dad

Will sat, trying to let the magnitude of what he had just learned sink in. His father was right. He would never look at his life the same way again. Coming home had shattered his world and turned it upside down. But as the pieces fell back into place, his life seemed to make more sense.

He carefully folded the letter and put it in his pocket along with the gold coin and the medal. Quietly, he left the apartment and closed the door behind him. Leaving the tavern, he walked to the end of the street and looked towards the bay. A beautiful orange glow was on the horizon as the sun rose, and the sky was tinged with shades of blue and purple. As if fate were toying with him, he didn't think he had ever seen a more beautiful sunrise.

He walked toward it, and when he got to the waterfront, he stood and watched as the sky slowly brightened. The sun on his face was warm, and he was reminded of the summer days he'd spent in Apalach with Jess as a child and their day at the beach with Kip. They were memories he cherished, and he realized his father was right. Her love for him was priceless and irreplaceable.

Reaching into his pocket, he pulled out the letter and the St. Christopher's medal. After turning the medal over in his hand, the gold shimmering in the sunlight, he tossed it into the river. All that remained of the events of three decades ago was the letter, and after staring at it momentarily, he began ripping it into pieces. Just then, a gusty warm breeze picked up, and he let the pieces go. He watched as they fluttered in the wind and then disappeared into the watery depths of the river. When they were completely gone, he turned and walked away. There was only one thing left to do.

EPILOGUE

W
ill stepped out of the limo and onto the red carpet
as the persistent flashes of the paparazzi nearly
blinded him. He ignored the requests of the photog-
raphers to stop for a photo and the questions shouted at
him. He'd long since stopped caring about his image or what
might be printed on Page Six. He was only there because he had
to be. Otherwise, he wouldn't have even watched it on TV.

He made his way up the walk, shaking hands and smiling.
When you were perceived as important, everyone wanted to
touch you and steal a little of your soul. Celebrity was fleeting
in Hollywood, and when you were in the limelight, one never
knew how long it would last. Most wished it would last forever.
Will couldn't wait for the light to go out.

The film project had been a blockbuster success, and he was
proud of his work. Everyone said it was his best work, and his
talents had taken on a new level. In many ways, he agreed. The
time after he'd gone home to Apalachicola had changed him.
Pain had a way of opening up your soul as no other emotion
could. His writing now reflected a depth his talent had never
been able to capture.

Inside, he did the obligatory mingling and pressing of palms, and as he made his way to his seat, he checked his watch. It would be a grueling four hours, and even with the possibility of being recognized by the Academy, he wasn't sure how he would make it through.

He hadn't lived in California for quite some time, and whenever he had to return, it appealed to him less and less. It seemed the more time he spent away, the fakeness and the shallowness of the place became more glaring. He was no longer dazzled by the California landscape and the beautiful people. Those he had once thought were important now seemed small and superficial.

He was sure everyone thought his detachment was intriguing and eccentric, and he could only smile when he read the occasional reporter's version of him and his life. He wasn't famous where he lived, and nobody wanted to own a piece of him. It was an ordinary existence absent of high rises and big city lights. Whenever he left, he couldn't wait to go back.

Finally, the lights dimmed, and everyone settled. The room went quiet, and he could hear the low rumble of the orchestra as it began its opening score. As if right on cue, his cell phone vibrated in the breast pocket of his tuxedo. When he looked at it, he smiled.

Good luck, the message read. *We believe in you. Come home soon - I love you, Jess.*